Its Every Man for Himself

And God For His Own

SEAN P GAUGHAN

SECOND EDITION

All characters and events in this publication, other than those clearly in the public domain, are fictitious and any resemblance to real persons, living or dead, is purely coincidental.

GREEN CAT BOOKS

www.green-cat.co/books

DEDICATION

FOR CAROLE

CONTENTS

PART ONE

1

It was the day after they had pulled Pat Clancy's body from the river. He had been missing for three days. They had found him more than a mile downstream of the town bridge.

His wife Rose, now his widow, his son Thomas, who had lived apart from them in recent months, and his daughter Mary, were seated around their kitchen table, along with the priest.

Rose, never a strong woman, and for long wretched and morose, had aged ten years since Pat had vanished. Her lank, unwashed hair was covered by the faded, black rag of a headscarf she had donned quickly upon the priest's arrival. The little sleep she had taken in that time had been in an armchair, fully clothed. She was emaciated and dishevelled, looking like a bundle of dry sticks half-covered with a sack.

Father Kennedy, middle-aged, of serious, indeed, haughty disposition, was in charge of things. His fat red cheeks flanked an aquiline nose, like panniers on the back of an ass. Consoling the bereaved was part of his stock in trade, and he was good at it. His sonorous voice was assuring to some at times like these. He persuaded the family to join him in prayer for the soul of the departed and intoned calming platitudes about a man of whom he knew very little. He spoke with great certainty about the unknowable, his conviction authoritative and compelling.

Throughout this eulogy Rose remained seated at the table. She had stood briefly and shakily to receive the priest, then quickly resumed her seat. Her hands had remained joined as if at prayer throughout the priest's visit, elbows resting on the table, head bowed. She had spoken hardly a word, so enveloped was she in her misery.

Father Kennedy stood up. 'I'll bless you now before I leave.'

Mary, suffused with sorrow, was immediately on her knees, head bowed, hands together in the attitude of a supplicant.

Thomas, on his feet now in anticipation of the priest's departure, bowed his head and loosely interlaced his fingers across his body. He noted the irony of the blessing but suffered it for the sake of decorum. As the priest made the sign of the cross he cringed inwardly. It was like watching a shaman practising his black arts. He half-expected him to pull a cockerel out of the shadows and slit its throat and sprinkle them with its blood.

Thomas noted that the priest's hands were scrubbed clean white. There was not a trace of the tobacco that stained heavily the fingers of every other priest he had met or known. Nor was there the usual reek of sweat and tobacco that permeated their garments. Father Kennedy sucked peppermints incessantly to disguise the brandy on his breath. He was a fastidious man. Sterile, almost.

As the priest made for the door Rose said suddenly, 'Tell me Father, why do you think he would have walked all that way down the river-bank at that time of night?'

The priest gauged his reply. He did not want to intensify the woman's pain by adding detail to a tragic event, but she obviously needed his opinion.

'I doubt he had walked far Rose. It's a big, deep river with powerful currents. It could easily sweep someone that far down in the time he'd been missing.'

'It's a great pity that he'd gone for a drink. It must have made him unsteady on his feet. But he liked a drink'.

'And he was entitled to a drink,' said the priest, who himself liked a lot more than was good for him. 'Any hardworking man is entitled to a drink at the end of his day's labours. He was a good, hardworking man, Rose, a great member of our community. He's with Our Lord now, I'm sure, for the soul of such a man would hardly touch down in purgatory.

'I'll be leaving you now, but I'll call in again tomorrow. You know where I am if you need me. Some ladies of the Church will be calling in on you later today.'

Rose remained seated whilst Thomas and Mary escorted Father Kennedy to his car, parked on the dirt road against the railway line. Their last words were drowned out by the London connection braking for Banebridge Station. The priest ducked quickly inside his car as a plume of grey-black acrid smoke swept over them. Two Skewbald mares backed away from the hissing, smoke belching monster as far as their tethers would allow. There were gypsies' horses all over the scrubby grassland that bordered the track and a couple of dozen gaudy caravans, most of them displaying wire and wicker cages holding songbirds which sang outside their open windows.

Thomas and Mary went back inside, into the darkened kitchen where Rose still sat exactly as they had left her. The half-drawn curtains throughout the house increased the sense of gloom and despondency that prevailed. The stump of a candle flickered eerily in front of an icon of the Sacred Heart of Jesus, adding to the funereal atmosphere. The air was stale, oppressive. Three cups of cold tea remained on the table. The only empty cup was that of the priest.

'I'll make us another drink.' said Mary, flattening out the embers of the fire on which to stand the ancient blackened kettle.

Rose said nothing. Her head was still downcast, her face scarcely visible in the gloom. Thomas and Mary joined her around the table. They all sat silently, enshrouded in the tenebrous atmosphere.

'He's a nice man, Father Kennedy.' said Mary in an effort to break the morbid silence. The silence re-occupied the room.

Then Thomas spoke. 'Mother, what made you mention the drink? He mightn't have had any.'

Rose lifted her head and stared straight at him. There was a savage look on her face. She lowered it again towards the oilcloth-covered table. She was breathing deeply, fermenting the verbal onslaught she was about to deliver. Finally, she looked up at him, her face as dark as the rag that framed it, contorted with fury. Spittle formed on her lips that moved without sound. She hadn't yet found the vitriol with which she was about to scar him. She was full of the bitterness, the frustration, the sorrow of someone who has made every conceivable attempt to achieve a long-desired end and every effort has come to nought. She was now in the grip of a desperate recklessness that assails only a person who has lost so much that they cannot see what else there is to lose. Then the words came; controlled; measured; vehement. Spat in Thomas' face like the venom of a cobra.

'So it isn't obvious to you then?'

'No,' said Thomas, taken aback by this sudden rage, fearing that his mother was undergoing some sort of mental breakdown. 'No. It isn't.'

'It wouldn't be. Not to a person like you. An utterly selfish person. A person so wrapped up in himself he can feel for no one but himself. Someone who has no concern for his family and no gratitude for what they have done for him.'

There was a long pause. Thomas and his sister just stared at each other. Open-mouthed, they were too aghast to find words. They both knew, only too well, that their mother had the zeal of the convert who has found the faith that suits them and who would like to see that system of belief established by edict as a universal creed, but what they were about to witness was beyond their comprehension.

Rose continued. 'Let me tell you something about yourself, because it is clear that you cannot see what a rotten, self-centred good-for-nothing you are.'

Mary found words. 'Mother, what are you saying?'

Thomas said nothing. He knew this potent brew had been a long time in the making, and was sure there was more to come. Rose continued, breathing regularly now, intending to complete the denunciation of her son in every detail.

'We put you to a good school and the nuns and priests worked hard on you. They trained you for the choir and for serving on the altar. They thought you good enough for the priesthood and took you out of classes several times a week, teaching you on your own. Who else ever got that, tell me?' Without waiting for a reply Rose ploughed on. 'Private lessons in Latin and theology. Voice training for the choir. And when you were old enough they got you into the seminary.'

Thomas could not see where any of this diatribe was leading. It had obviously been forming in her mind for some time and now she was unstoppable. 'But then, after a couple of years, after all their efforts, you turned your back on them and said you didn't think you could be a priest.'

Thomas' mind was trying to form words of defence but his mother was speaking quicker than he could think, scything him down like corn before the reaper. He was severely impeded by the knowledge that she was at least partially right in much of what she asserted, but he couldn't see the point of it all, especially at this particular time. Rose forced him to listen.

'Even then, they didn't give up on you. You were offered a chance to train as a teacher. You thought you might manage that. Only God knows why you thought it. And, all the time, your poor father, working himself half to death to keep you, and the rest of us going without. But of course, you didn't qualify. You failed your exams and then left the college saying you weren't cut out for it. And then you turned your back, not only on every single person who had helped you but on God himself. You abandoned the faith entirely. You are an utter disgrace. A disgrace to yourself, to your family and a disgrace in the eyes of God.'

Here Rose paused, drawing several deep breaths. The silence was ominous, threatening. Thomas had time to speak now but he felt defeated. His mother had assailed him with so much brutal invective that he needed time to consider what to make of it. Then, in a surprisingly strong voice that belied her feeble state Rose struck him with a thunderbolt.

'So, is it any wonder that your father committed suicide?'

Thomas was appalled by this last blow. It tore at his heart and arrested his thought processes completely. He searched vainly for a defence, weakly finding words to deny the possibility. Mary, equally horrified, supported him.

Their mother would not hear them, she was so steadfastly sure of herself. She continued in the same vein:

'Now his soul cannot ever enter the gates of heaven. And you have the nerve to ask me why I mentioned the drink to Father Kennedy? Can you not see why? Is the obvious beyond your recognition?'

Rose waited.

Thomas said weakly, 'I'm sorry Mam, I just don't follow you.'

'It was because I did not want the ultimate disgrace of your father not being buried in consecrated ground. Isn't it a terrible thing when all a woman can hope for at the end of her days is a decent Catholic burial for her husband?'

Thomas was not unused to criticism, often trenchant criticism, from both of his parents, but particularly from his mother. He had moved out of the parental home a while ago because of it; there was too much tension at times. Perhaps he had been the cause of it. But this was cruel destructive calumny, the workings of a deranged mind. Could shock and grief turn someone so? His mother had always had a condemnatory nature and latterly she'd become withdrawn, distant in some degree from all of them. But was she losing her mind? He had asked himself this on more than one occasion. Or was there some truth in what she said? Did she know something he did not know? Now was not the time for considerations such as these. It was time to go.

Thomas stood up to leave. Mary remained seated, eyes staring fixedly as if trying to focus on some occurrence or other that might give substance to her mother's rant. She, like Thomas, had an inkling that their mother's tirade might not be entirely without foundation. However, if their father had ended his own life, she wasn't altogether sure that Thomas would have been the cause of it.

As he reached for the door-handle he turned and spoke quietly to his mother. 'This isn't the time, mother, for this kind of talk.'

'No. It's not. That time is long past.'

Rose was amazingly calm now. Her self-control was frightening to both her offspring. Until Pat's body had been found she had been almost demented, screaming, crying, praying. Walking around the room kissing a palm-leaf cross. Then, after the awful discovery, she had been for several hours as distraught as anyone might have expected her to be. After that she had become silent. Locked into herself. Apparently deep in thought.

'You're very distressed Mam,' said Mary. 'We all are. It's better not to say what we might regret.'

'I'll go now,' said Thomas. 'We'll talk again tomorrow.'

'Yes. Leave. And don't return. You've never been anything but trouble, so it's only trouble that is leaving. We'll be better off without you.'

'But Mother, we've been through this before. I cannot make myself believe. You left your faith because you couldn't believe in it and became a Catholic.'

'I did not. I had no faith. I found the true faith. The protestant faith is a travesty. History tells you that it broke away from the true faith. Go now. I've had enough of you.'

Thomas looked at his mother. Initial disbelief of her accusation now crumbling under the sickening thought that she must have reason for making it, filled him with a sense of despair. He needed to question her, ask her from what roots this unholy judgement had grown. Demand even, what were her foundations for such a damming opinion. He knew that he had, many times, behaved very poorly in his parent's eyes. He wanted to address this, find some way to make amends, however belatedly. But surely what she was saying now, what she appeared fervently to believe, could not be true.

His mother's gaze was both unnerving and unwavering. Her resolve following such a tragic event astonished him.

'Leave, will you, just go.'

Thomas departed, closing the door behind him. He had taken only a couple of steps when it opened again and Mary rushed out. She stood before him, tears in her eyes, looking as shocked and dismayed as he was. She put her hands on his shoulders, trying silently to communicate some sense of support for him.

'Mam's not well, Tom. I don't know where she got this idea from. I'm sure there's nothing in it. Try not to take it too badly. She'll come round. Give her time.' As they parted they both doubted Mary's words.

Thomas walked with the air of the prodigal spurned, making his way along the dirt road that edged the gypsy encampment, heading eventually for his rented room in town.

As he walked, the few gypsies around the place moved uneasily away from the road and around to the backs of their vans, avoiding contact with him. They had all heard about his father's death and most were, in varying degrees, sympathetic. Pat Clancy did not have an enemy amongst them and one or two he'd regarded as friends. But they did not know how *gorgios* dealt with their grief, or quite what to say to him. Time enough later on to offer him their condolences. They assumed that for now the man was best left to himself. Give him time for the worst of the shock to dissipate.

2

Mary Clancy, until now, had lived her life with an easy-going carelessness. Not much was expected of her except for a little help around the house and a portion of her meagre wages earned at the brewery.

Most of what she did accorded with everyone else's wishes and what didn't, she kept to herself.

She was always cheerful, outgoing – a bit too outgoing as far as relationships with the opposite sex were concerned, but that was the way her God had made her. The spirit was always willing and the flesh more so. She set great store by an expression frequently used by her father 'Ah, sure you can only be yourself.' Not that Pat had a lot of knowledge as to what exactly Mary's 'self' was. But in any case, about that particular facet of her personality, she was always very discreet.

Mary now felt enormous sorrow for Tom, as well as the vast sense of grief and loss at the death of their father. And also the merest touch of guilt. She knew that their mother would not relent and would never again accept him as her son.

Rose had, in a quiet way, rejected her own family when she married Pat Clancy. She kept in touch with them only by sending cards at Christmas. She never visited. There had been only one sibling to whom she had been deeply attached, an older brother who had often protected her from their overbearing father. But he had been killed in the War. Rose had never recovered from what she saw as the injustice of that. She said he'd been killed by the politicians, a class of people whom she forever after held in contempt.

Rose had never really talked about this estrangement that left Thomas and Mary effectively without aunts and uncles on their mother's side. She would simply say, if asked about them, 'they're a rough lot', or, once, when in a bad mood, she described them as 'a bunch of heathens.' It was as if Rose wanted to forget her past.

Thomas would now become part of that past. Mary knew that. It was part of her mother's nature. She had accepted some time ago that her mother was a condemnatory person who saw everything in simple, clear-cut terms. She knew that there would be no chance of reconciliation, despite Thomas' wish for it.

Nevertheless, Mary marvelled at the inner strength of this frail-looking woman who was able to reject her own son at a time like this, when she was now all the family Rose possessed. Rose could hardly draw on any support from Pat's family, although she liked them and was well regarded by them. They were scattered all over the world, in pursuit of their own fortunes. His parents were both dead, having succumbed to tuberculosis caused by drinking the milk of their own cow.

Rose knew many of the congregation from the Church, but she had never gone out of her way to integrate with them. She had also remained slightly aloof from the neighbours in the adjacent houses, and the gypsies round and about she saw as a separate race.

Mary alone would have to, and would most willingly, support her mother for the rest of her life.

Despite her mother's difficult ways Mary loved her. Rose needed Mary now more than ever. Mary would meet that need unfailingly. She would have to stay in at night, but she would manage somehow without the money the bargemen gave her.

*****

The death of her father devastated Mary. She had loved him deeply, loved his easy-going ways, his ability to get on with people. He was always one to make the best of a bad job and then try to improve its circumstances. She loved her brother as much and needed him more than ever before, but that was not so easy now that he was banished from the house. She had to somehow control her intense grief, conceal it as best she could and remain strong for her mother's sake. She felt sure that Rose would succumb to a depressive torpor from which she might never recover. She would now have to alter her own ways and apply herself to managing everything for both of them.

Mary was also seriously troubled by what her mother had said to Tom regarding the death and its strange circumstances. Could it really have been suicide? She herself had not for one moment thought of that possibility and had been amazed that the idea had so quickly lodged in her mother's mind.

Mary assumed that Pat must have fallen into the river accidentally, although he was not a careless man. And he might have had a drink or two. He was not what anyone might call a drinking man, but every now and then he liked a couple of pints. Occasionally, when, by chance, he had met a friend he had not seen for some time, he might go into a pub with him and have a few more than he was used to and return home garrulous and merry and just a tiny bit wobbly.

But if her mother was right, if he had cause to end his life, which still she doubted, why need it be because her brother had turned against their religion?

Mary was only too well aware of the huge disappointment this had caused their father, and it had followed closely on Tom's failure to qualify as a teacher, another bitter blow to him.

For a while Pat had been angry with Tom, and then just very sad. But as far as she could tell he had never become bitter or reproachful, as had their mother.

Whereas Rose was censorious, quick to condemn and reluctant to forgive, Pat had a more accepting nature. He could usually put up with whatever reality was thrust upon him if he saw no likelihood of changing it, and then get on with life.

He was often inclined to say, 'You never know, things might improve.' This difference in outlook was, in Mary's opinion, the cause of a long-established rift between her parents, something her father had always tried to minimise, to ameliorate, never making any retort to his wife's frequent barbed observations about the world and its inhabitants.

But just supposing something truly awful – she could not imagine what – had occurred, which combined with Tom's rejection of the faith his family held sacrosanct, could that have pushed him into a state of despair? After all the sacrifices that had been made for Tom, all the allowances made for his errant ways, could his rejection of all that they believed in and therefore the rejection of their community, their way of life, could this have proved too much for a father to bear?

Mary wondered what else might have occurred that would have added sorrow to a troubled mind. She herself was not beyond reproach. Could she have been part of whatever might have led to such an act of despair? Was it just possible that she and her brother together, but in their different ways, might have made a strong, resolute man feel that he had failed completely and, for all his efforts, had reared a couple of ne'er-do-wells?

She doubted that. For one reason, her parents had never reproached her, and as for her brother, well, he had been a source of consternation to their parents for as long as she could remember. They were inured to it. But her mother was no fool. Narrow in outlook she might be, bigoted even. But what she had claimed could not be lightly dismissed. She must have her reasons, thought Mary.

Unlike her brother, Mary had no doubts about her religious faith. It was an integral part of her life, something she never questioned. Not that she was given to questioning. A part of the way in which she lived her life did not accord with what the Church decreed, but somehow, without being excessively troubled by that fact, she contrived to separate her existence into contradictory yet manageable parts.

She was more often in church than just on Sundays and the obligatory holy days of the year, and she enjoyed being there. Mary loved her faith. Its rituals enthralled her. This of course ensured a harmonious relationship with her parents. They did not question where she was when not at home or at work, because for much of that time she was in church. But not always.

Mary attended the evening benediction service at least once a week, often more than that. She loved the mystery of it all. The aromatic incense from the censer swung mesmerizingly by the priest lingered in her nostrils like Arabian perfume.

She always endeavoured to be in Church early so that she could be in the front pews, close to the altar rail, in order to be near to the priest as he entered. She made the Stations of the Cross during Lent and fasted accordingly. She had long since preserved the integrity of her immortal soul by attending mass and receiving Holy Communion on the first Friday of nine consecutive months.

She said prayers morning and night and sometimes in the middle of the day that had the indulgences pertaining to their recital annotated in the margins of the missal. It was good to gain indulgences, a reassurance that one's soul would endure a shorter time in purgatory for the sins that one would inevitably commit during one's short journey through temporal life.

Mary was a good catholic: she believed wholeheartedly in the faith.

***

Mary had until now been saving whatever money she could from the little she earned legitimately and from the small 'gifts' she received elsewhere. She needed to save as she had ideas of eventually moving to London. She heard of hostesses in swanky London nightclubs earning a lot of money. But you needed a bit to start with.

Before she left school she had found that men were attracted to her and that for small favours that she didn't mind doing at all, in fact, which she found quite exciting, they would give her small amounts of money.

She had inherited her father's height, his handsome, finely chiselled features and his black hair. There was nothing of her mother's gingery mousiness about her.

At fourteen, although willowy, she had well defined breasts. She would often linger at the riverside after school, or during the holidays, watching the big barges passing through the locks. The bargemen would often shout compliments to her, ask her to catch the rope they threw at her, and tell her to wind it round a bollard.

Then they would jump from the barge to the wharf and secure it, all the time talking to her as if she were an adult. She rose to this, enjoying the role and pretending she understood the double-entendres they used, flirting with them shamelessly.

Sometimes the same men would pass through again in the space of a week or two and she would recognise them and they her.

She often wondered what the boats were like inside. One day she had the opportunity to find out.

A bargee was mooring up for the night. It was too late to press on. It was the middle of summer and the river was low. He had been stuck on a sandbank above the town, beyond where the tide reached, for most of the afternoon. Eventually another vessel had managed to pull him clear. He was going no further today.

Mary had spoken to him several times before. He was handsome, he seemed nice. He was older than herself by perhaps ten years or so.
'What's it like inside?' she called to him. 'I've never been on a barge.'
'Come and have a look.' he replied.

He was on his own, the older man in charge of the vessel having just departed towards the toilet block to clean up. Both were in a filthy state. Mary stepped on board and was shown the small wheelhouse.
'I'll show you below.' said the man, skipping lightly down open steps to the grain-filled hull.

She walked down after him. She knew he was looking up at her so she avoided his gaze. But she didn't mind. It was nice. There was nothing else to see down there. Only the cargo. This time it was grain, but it could be timber, steel, fuel-oil, just about anything.
'Shall we go back up?' said the man.

Mary thought he would lead the way, as he'd led the way down. But he didn't. So she climbed back up the ladder. She knew he was looking up at her. She knew he could see a lot. She paused for a moment, feet on different steps, and half-turned and smiled at him. He was nice.

She stepped off the barge and he followed. The man in charge was making his way back, so the younger man set off towards the washbasins.
'I'll be cleaner the next time you see me', he told her. 'We've had a filthy day today. If you want I'll take you down to the next lock when we're coming through again. It's only about a mile to walk back.'
'I'd like that.' said Mary.
'Depends who I'm with though,' reflected the man. 'We're not supposed to take passengers. I'll tell you when it's O.K.'

A fortnight later, the same man came through the lock again. This time he was with another man about his own age. Again the barge was carrying grain, this time in sacks, hundreds of them.

'Want a lift to the next lock?' he asked. 'My pal's O.K. about it'.

Mary was hoping he'd ask. She went aboard. It took only a few minutes to clear the lock, then away downstream.

'I've bought a new bike on my travels,' said the man, who now introduced himself as David. 'Want to see it? It's down below.'

Again he led the way. Mary didn't think to question why the bicycle was below the deck and right at the front of the hull, from where it would have to be hauled out awkwardly when the final destination was reached. She had to clamber over mountains of grain sacks to get to it. Then, when they reached the bike she had to slide down off the top sacks to David who had already jumped down to assist her. It was an all-revealing moment as her skirt momentarily caught between sacks. David smiled approvingly at her, so she didn't mind.

Occasional trips between locks became more frequent. It was possible often to ride down on one barge then back on another going upstream. It just depended on how well you knew the bargemen.

Mary got to know them well. Very well. Small notes were offered for small favours. Sometimes larger amounts were offered for larger favours, but Mary would not take that risk.

Everything was hurried. The distance between locks took only a few minutes to cover, despite the man at the wheel holding back against the current if they were travelling downstream. Mary didn't mind hurrying. It reduced the chances of her being put under pressure to take greater risks. The little they paid her for a bit of fun was all right. Mary didn't mind.

The barges did not move at night. They moored up at the locks. The bargees often left them unattended and went to the nearby pubs. Some stayed on board.

Flashily dressed women in heavy make-up might stroll slowly along the waterfront after dark. They would invariably hold an unlighted cigarette between their fingers. If a face appeared at the wheelhouse door it might quickly be followed by the offer of a light and then a brief conversation might ensue.

These women usually lived in the slums beside the river, close enough for bargees to follow them home, walking discreetly twenty paces behind. A few, like Mary, after furtively glancing around, might go on board, depending on the cargo. Those carrying reeking fuel oil or steel were avoided. The grain barges were all right, so long as the men on them were reasonable. Most of the women were doing now for a little extra money what they had found necessitous a few years earlier.

Mary was saving hard. The money she earned at the brewery was barely enough to live on. By the end of the week, every penny was spent. The barge work was quick and easy. She could earn as much in an hour at night as she could in a long dreary day at the brewery.

Mary found most of the men she met were safe to deal with. Some were really nice, well-intentioned. Just making the best of the night away from home. They were considerate and not overly demanding. As she got to know them better she found she could relax with them. They were often just as glad of female companionship for half an hour or so as they were of anything else. The few who were less pleasant she avoided when they next passed through. She had become adept at making quick assessments of people and at dealing with awkward ones.

Mary never dwelt on her relations with men. She was open and friendly towards most of them. She flirted with many. She liked the attention of men. It told her that she was attractive. All activity with them, with any man anywhere, was, as far as she was concerned, superficial. She never had, never wanted, a deep or lasting relationship. Each meeting was a brief episode, uncommitted to by either side. A little money changed hands, so nothing was stolen. Mary would no doubt have justified it to herself, if ever she felt the need to, by saying that she was as her God had made her. By nature generous of spirit, munificent even, warmly disposed towards the rest of humanity. She related as easily to her own sex and was well liked by most.

She was never perceived as likely to lead a man away from his marriage or his present relationship. She would not have wanted to do that. She dispensed her good-natured warmth to one and all and ignored the rare criticism of being sometimes a little too forward. Always amiable, there was no room for discord in her make-up.

3

As he blundered on down the lane, eyes downcast, lost in a haze of tears and confusion, Thomas struggled to make sense of his mother's accusations. Mary's last words to him, suggesting Rose was unwell, if correct, would offer some sort of antidote to the poison-tipped arrows with which she had pierced him. Time then might heal the wounds. But that kind of infirmity would presage its own sorrows. He did not wish to contemplate such a future. He had, in the recent past, forced himself to question what might it be that at times so disfigured his mother's thoughts. He had found no answers then; nor could he now.

Rose had completely overwhelmed him by the suddenness and the ferocity of her attack, but her dismissal of him seemed coldly calculated, rational almost, clearly thought out. They were hardly the words of someone deranged; more the sentiments of a fanatic.

The relationship between Thomas and his mother had for long been strained and the fiasco that had ended his time at the seminary had stretched them to breaking point. But he knew, or thought he knew, that his father had not condemned him for that, although it had torn his mother apart.

That rift, and it had not occurred to him before, must have had a serious emotional effect upon his father. Why had he not seen that? Perhaps he was every bit as selfish as his mother had claimed.

The training to be a teacher was a different issue. His father had been deeply hurt when he failed his teaching practice, although his mother appeared less concerned. Perhaps by then she was becoming resigned to her son turning out to be a failure and hardly cared anymore. Her wish to see him garbed as a priest had been everything to her; there was no acceptable substitute.

The final cut that had crippled both his parents had been delivered by Thomas only months ago when he told them that he was finished with the Church. He had found his own separate living accommodation shortly before making this cataclysmic announcement, knowing that from then on he would struggle to maintain any worthwhile relationship with them.

He recognised that he had never considered himself excessively self-indulgent. He used to think that self-indulgence consisted of taking too much, helping yourself to whatever you wanted. Now he questioned was it not also about giving nothing? He was guilty of both of these faults. All he had done so far in his life was to turn things down, to walk away from what he didn't like. To find fault with everything. He was undoubtedly a malcontent. In that much, at least, his mother's invective in her bitter denunciation of him had some foundation.

His father, an itinerant Irish labourer in a foreign land that was often hostile to him had achieved more. He had rubbed along with people without giving ground to them, had raised a family, settled in a community to which he had made commitments. He had even owned his own house. And now he was dead, and worse still, according to his widow, Thomas was the cause of that death. Maybe, just maybe, she could be right. If her belief was going to destroy the rest of her life, then he had much to answer for. He had to admit to himself that he was not an outstanding example of what a son should be.

Too late now to repair the past. From now on he would have to stop hurting people.

***

Thomas reached the towpath and headed for the lock basin. He was intending to make a dangerous short cut into the town by walking across the narrow gangway atop the lock gates and then through the maze of dark alleyways that led through the yards and workshops. It was a route he used often when the weather was dry. It was potentially lethal when the boards were wet, or in winter, when glazed with ice. The lockmaster, whom he knew well, contrived to look the other way.

But today there was a barge and a tug in the lock and the lock was full, so the gates might open at any time. He decided to continue along to the towpath until he reached the bridge road, then over the bridge into town. It was not much further that way.

He was so enervated by the events of the past few days, by lack of sleep and the tension in his mother's house and her rejection of him that every step was an effort. He had been walking in a mental haze for the last few minutes, trying to unravel his scrambled thoughts. Then the noise and bustle of riverine industry jolted him back to reality, grating obtrusively on his jaded nerves.

Passing the dry dock he heard in advance of the warning sign the crackle and hiss of steel plate being welded to the side of a dredger. He did not need to read the warning to avert his gaze from the welding arc. He'd once paid the price for failing to obey when he was a schoolboy and had spent the next couple of days wearing bandages over his eyes. Then he'd had to entrust his guidance to others, whose sighted assurance made scant allowance for his own faltering steps over precarious ground.

Then on, on past the banging and hammering of a couple of small boatyards where hulls were under construction. Coming up next was the tannery where a swarm of flies buzzed incessantly around a stack of stinking hides piled high on the bed of a wagon. The stench of the chemicals used in the tanning process nauseated him as much as the sight of the bloody hides themselves.

Standing back from the river and apart from the other closely clustered buildings was one of the town's two slaughterhouses. Thomas kept as far away from this as its proximity to the river would allow. Today, as on every other warm day, the doors would be open and the sight and sound of animals being killed and dismembered could, all too easily, be seen and heard. The smell of fear and blood and excrement reached his nostrils and the long, intense squeal of a pig made him shudder.

Trudging glumly on he focused his gaze on the towpath itself. Whilst the huge barges and their tugs always moored to the massive bollards by the water's edge, smaller craft often anchored against the wharves by running ropes or chains right across the path, tight to its surface, to iron stakes driven into the nearest bit of penetrable ground. Thomas had, more than once, when lost in his thoughts and gazing skyward, caught his toes under such cables and gone sprawling on his face.

Quite suddenly he was aware that a shadow had enveloped him and he looked up. A small crane had hoisted a load of timber from a barge and it was turning slowly in the air high above his head. He could not decide instantly whether to rush forward or to back away. He was momentarily trapped within the shadowy circle of his own uncertainty, before the crane driver expertly planted his load on the ground to the side of the towpath, whilst laughing at his dilemma and shouting ribald insults at him from the cab window.

Before leaving the riverside, Thomas passed the yard of Lud Henty, a man of indeterminate age, possibly mid-way in years between himself and his father. Henty was feared and hated in equal measure by all who had the misfortune to fall foul of his vicious temper, although neither Pat nor Thomas had ever been troubled by him.

They had never taken much notice of Henty, except on one occasion when Pat had spotted an oil drum in his yard that he'd thought might make a decent rain-water barrel. He'd taken Thomas round there to give him a lift should Henty part with it for a couple of shillings. Henty had demanded too much. Pat had said 'you must be dreaming, I wouldn't give you half that price. But good luck to you if you think you can get it, although I doubt you will.' As they were walking away Henty asked Pat how much he would pay, and, surprisingly, accepted his offer. Afterwards Pat had said to Thomas, 'There's a Henty in every walk of life; you just have to deal with them.' Pat always knew how to deal with people.

Thomas left the towpath and climbed the ramp up to the huge stone bridge that would take him over the river and into the town. The river was wide here. It took nine cavernous arches to span it. His legs seemed leaden as he forced himself up the steady incline. On reaching the centre of the bridge he paused, resting his elbows on the balustraded sill. He looked upstream where the river narrowed into the locks, towards the house where he had lived since his schooldays until a few months ago. He could just discern the roof-line and chimney from which a thin wisp of smoke was still rising. A train passed by it obliterating it entirely in a pall of smoke. Thomas wondered when, or if, he would visit the house again. He surveyed the insalubrious scene before him. He was now looking down from the height of the bridge into Henty's yard which he had passed a few minutes ago. Surrounded by high walls topped with broken bottles set in cement it was another wound on that forlorn landscape. High though they were, the walls were dwarfed by mountains of crushed and buckled metallic objects, mostly old vehicles awaiting disposal. Within the midst of this wasteland stood a caravan wherein Henty lived out his squalid existence. He kept his rusting livelihood as secure as bullion in the vaults of a bank.

He could see Henty working, his shock of white hair erupting from under a black cap identifying him immediately. Henty was an albino, supposedly of a Romany family who had settled locally a couple of generations ago. His unusual appearance belied any gypsy origins, but the men he called his brothers were swarthy roughnecks who blended a Romany vocabulary with the local dialect.

Henty was levering the door off the cab of an ex-army lorry. He was using an iron bar as long as himself, forcing it into the metal. The derelict truck with its smashed windscreen and shattered headlights, its exposed steel ribs that had once been skinned with a canvas roof, looked like a stricken eyeless beast. The scene appeared to Thomas like that of a stone-age savage spearing some huge pre-historic animal.

Although he was not inclined to criticise others, he had an intense dislike of Henty. Even now, when suffused with guilt about his own shortcomings, he could feel resentment at Henty's very existence.

Henty was notorious for his innate tendency to violence. Thomas had witnessed on several occasions Henty goading a man into a fight he did not want so that he could then beat him mercilessly. He would accept no submission; he sought to crush anyone who opposed him. He had always been like that. As a young boy he had attracted the cruel nickname 'Snowy', which he hated. He would fly into a rage and attack anyone who called him by that name, even grown men. Having beaten them he would find a corner to hide in and cry bitter tears like a rejected child.

Whilst Henty's notoriety was possibly exaggerated, there was no doubt that he was a dangerous man. It was alleged that he had once picked a fight with a uniformed guardsman in a tavern yard. He'd found that he had overreached himself, the soldier being much taller and stronger than he. So Henty, it was said, stabbed him in the neck with a broken bottle, killing the man. Charged with this capital offence Henty had claimed self-defence against the bigger man, arguing that the bottle had broken accidentally in the melee and that the soldier was going for it anyway.

The pub landlord was too afraid of him to tell the court that in fact Henty had snatched the bottle from a customer's table several feet away, broken it against the wall then jumped upon a bar stool to reach the soldier's neck. The jury, uneasy about sending a young man to the gallows, gave him the benefit of its considerable doubt.

Against Henty also lay the accusation that he had pushed a man, well known for his drunkenness, off a low-walled stone bridge into the weir-pool below. Apparently Henty had waited in the shadows in anticipation of the man's return from a nearby riverside tavern. The case was impossible to prove. It was well established that the drowned man had left the tavern in an inebriated state. However, he had traversed the same route home countless times in a similar condition without mishap. It was interesting, to those who knew, that the dead man had thrashed Henty in a fight the previous day.

Thomas wondered how could such a man live with himself, how could he tolerate the abject existence of a social pariah?

He also wondered if he could live with himself now that it was seemingly possible that he might be the cause of a man's death, a man whom he loved and admired. In the last few days his world had become a confusing place, and in the last couple of hours it had fallen apart. Was he in danger of becoming an outcast if his mother's accusations became known to others?

Thomas stared down into the depths forty feet below him. He wondered how long it might take for a man to drown. The thought sickened him.

The malevolent dun-coloured river slunk sullenly beneath him dragging its sinister secrets along its greasy bed. Its dark inscrutable surface slicked with the iridescent sheen of diesel was pocked with the flotsam and jetsam of all the wharves and factories that fouled its banks.

A dead cat drifted downstream. It was momentarily lifted by the dying wake of a barge heading for the locks. Its head and tail were briefly and separately animated, giving the weird appearance of it having suddenly regained life. It startled him.

For a split second it seemed that there was a life to be saved somehow, but the grim reality of death immediately reasserted itself. The inexorable nexus of life and death overwhelmed his senses. His whole body shook and his legs buckled. Only his arms hooked over the bridge wall kept him upright. His stomach convulsed and he retched violently over the side of the bridge, adding minutely to the ordure and detritus, the filth of existence that drained beneath his feet. He spat, breathed deeply and pulled himself together, then lurched uncertainly towards the town.

Thomas reached the external iron stairway to the room he rented above the rope-makers shop. This was now his home. He paused before ascending, still reeling from the crushing blow his mother had dealt him. He toiled miserably up the awkward steps, rust flaking off the handrail into his palms.

He turned his key in the lock and ducked under the low doorframe. The gantry and pulley-wheel projecting over the door indicated the original use of the building. It had not been designed as a dwelling.

The large rectangular low-ceilinged room was not well appointed. At one end was a long, shallow stone sink with a cold-water tap high above it. Hot water was served by an old gas boiler mounted on the wall. A small, ancient hip bath of good quality, salvaged long ago from a nearby hotel that was being refurbished, stood near the sink. By means of a swivelling chrome-plated pipe, the water heater could be used to fill either vessel.

At the opposite end of the room a corner had been boarded off. It enclosed a W.C. In the middle of the room stood Thomas' bed. A large scrubbed-pine table and two worm-eaten chairs, plus a half-decent comfortable armchair completed the furnishings. His few clothes hung on a row of stout metal hooks that ran along one wall.

The floor, of wide elm boards, was bare except for two old rugs, one adjacent to the bath, the other against the bed.

An old gas cooker met Thomas' basic culinary needs and lent some assistance to the ancient gas fire, although even in combination they struggled to raise the temperature to an acceptable level in winter.

The room had a small window at each end and although the light was not good it was fairly consistent throughout the day. The one naked light bulb, which he had still not got around to shading, was as much as he wanted right now, as he found the price of electricity demanded frugal usage.

He collapsed onto the bed. Time to reflect. But he could not think. The events of the past few days had bewildered him.

His father's sudden disappearance augured a tragedy; he was never the sort of man who would intentionally lose contact with his family. The discovery of his body in the river raised more questions than it answered. Pat Clancy was not a careless man and he knew the river and its dangers only too well. He couldn't swim, so he never took chances with it if he didn't have to.

Thomas knew also that his father was not a heavy drinker. In any case the only pub that stood right on the waterfront was a dubious tavern that his father disliked, so it was doubtful if unsteadiness through drink had played any part in the tragedy.

And now, as if to add to the mystery, to the sense of loss and bewilderment that surrounded him, he was ravaged by this explosion of anger and bitterness with which his mother had just condemned him in her hateful sermon.

It was the sense of finality that broke him. Although Thomas doubted the truth of what she had said, he did not doubt for one moment that she believed completely in her own words and would never forgive him. He was still of an age that made him disinclined to question his parents' pronouncements, deferring, at least in some small measure, to their acquired wisdom.

He gazed around the room, absorbing the elements of his little world. He saw a rented roof over his head. A few belongings that wouldn't make even a decent fire and, in cash terms, were next to worthless. Not much for a tolerably well-educated man to point to as a list of achievements.

But it was not his material possessions – or lack of them – that seriously troubled him. What he did not possess but needed most was himself. A sense of self. He wanted to know who he was, what he stood for, what he wanted from life. He needed to know what he believed in. He had until now stated only what he did not believe in, and he hadn't expressed that with any stamp of certainty. He lacked a goal, something to strive for. Something that would give meaning to his meandering, directionless existence. If he had that much at least, it might give him some sort of substance to hold him up against the iniquities of the world.

Thomas began to examine his conscience, to try to analyse how and why he had alienated himself from his parents. Why, if what his mother had said was true, he had caused such heartbreak. He was not seeking to exonerate himself or to deny the truth if that could be established. He needed to reach an understanding with himself as to how far one can or should go in questioning the beliefs of one's own society; in dissecting the basis of an established order.

Perhaps it was acceptable to criticise or reject something if one could offer evidence of a better way. Gratuitous iconoclasm was perhaps nothing more than irrational negativity combined with vanity, the destruction of something without a hope or a notion of how or what to replace it with. If this was so then he had to admit *mea culpa.*

Thomas recalled that his father had by no means been condemnatory about his leaving the seminary. In fact his mother had admonished Pat in front of him for the forbearance he had shown regarding what she saw as a monstrous change of vocational direction by his errant son.

He remembered clearly his father saying to him, 'If you cannot cope with it then better to say so now.' But he could not deny to himself that his father had added, with a trace of anger and perhaps a little bitterness, 'It would have been better still if you had thought more about it earlier. You've spent two years of your life there.'

But there was no mention, from his father at least, of the support, financial and otherwise, that he'd been given. Pat had been one for moving forward, not for looking back. He had seemed prepared to accept that his son would now have to make a fresh start in life.

Thomas knew that his mother's remarks about his early schooling were irrefutable. He had been given preferential treatment by the nuns, blatantly so, something that, at the time, he found onerous and embarrassing.

They thought they had detected a special talent in him. What they had seen was someone who was malleable, or so they thought. Someone who could be moulded by them and whose family would rejoice with them in admiring the finished product they had cast.

That was his own fault, Thomas thought. He had always a tendency to go along with the suggestions of others, especially those of his superiors, for a quiet life, then protest when it was almost too late. Rather like walking too far down a road that you thought might be taking you in the wrong direction, then, having travelled so far, you wonder if you should follow it to the end rather than face the long trek back to the beginning.

Such decisions he had always found difficult. So it was with the seminary. He was bright enough; he had no trouble with its academic demands. He loved learning and had, somewhat naively, imagined that studying there would be an uplifting experience, full of intellectual challenge. So he had entered with high hopes of achieving some form of enlightenment that he felt he had failed to grasp so far.

He had, perhaps without realising it, been swept along to some degree by the prestige that training for the priesthood conferred upon him in the eyes of his community. It had brought immense joy to his mother, lifting her up out of her dull existence and apparently weakening the grip of the unexplained despondency that had been relentlessly descending upon her over the last few years. It had also seemed to find favour with his father, although he was by no means as delighted with his son's choice of vocation as was his wife. But Pat had said no more than, 'Think it over carefully Tom. It can be a hard life.'

The nuns who taught him were ecstatic. This was the greatest achievement they could have wished on any pupil and, although they prided themselves on the influence they had had on his decision, they were genuinely excited for him too. They firmly believed that all the priestly class, of whatever rank, towered over the rest of humanity. There was no knowing how far up this ladder of success a young man like Thomas might climb.

But Thomas had doubts. He could doubt almost anything, but these particular doubts he had pushed to the deepest recesses of his mind. He ought to have extricated these niggling fears from their dark burrows and given them a voice. But he hadn't. And now, when faith and hope began to falter and he was forced to make the turn in that particular road, it had brought considerable anguish to many.

He knew that his mother's assertion that he had been helped by the Church into a teaching college a year after his departure from the seminary was incorrect, but it made little or no difference to the broad substance of what she had stated.

The only help he had received in that direction was a reference from the one nun with whom he had remained in contact by the occasional letter after he had left school. She had, no doubt, helped him gain entry to the course he applied for, but it was not a catholic college that he had entered. Such establishments would have had no time for the likes of him.

They were well accustomed to taking in novices who had left seminaries, and were generally glad to receive them. These were mostly young men from good backgrounds who were seriously committed to their new studies and they usually did well. They would not have changed course for the same reason Thomas had. They had no doubts about the truth of their faith. On the contrary; they were solid in their belief, but doubted themselves, doubted if they were good enough to become priests, so became teachers instead and promulgated the faith in that way.

He knew that he would find no welcome in their halls, nor did he wish to. So it was, to the great dismay of his mother, that he applied to a non-catholic college that readily accepted him as a trainee teacher.

He had narrowly missed the deadline for that year's intake so he spent the intervening months working with his father at a job Pat had found for him on a construction site, such work now being Pat's usual mode of employment.

Thomas loved the physicality of the work, once the initial pains and strains of hard labour had diminished. His strength and fitness developed quickly. He was as tall as his father and the heavy work was developing his physique. He now had the wide shoulders of Pat, although not yet the massive biceps. He was slim at waist and hip whereas Pat was starting to thicken.

Pat was still in good shape though and did not look his age. With the same black hair, naturally wavy, at a distance they would easily have passed for brothers rather than father and son. Within a couple of months Thomas felt he was fit enough to jump over the moon, while Pat was beginning to find the work hard. He was glad that Thomas had been accepted by the college. He did not want him doing this sort of work for the rest of his life.

Once again Pat had got his errant son back on track. If he could keep him there for a couple of years he would have a good career ahead of him. Thomas was also saving hard and living frugally, so between them they would manage for a while.

When the new academic year began Thomas enrolled eagerly, full of enthusiasm.

He enjoyed his time in training. He had no difficulty in meeting the academic requirements and related well to students and lecturers alike. Being a little older than most of the first-year students he found he was accorded some respect by those who had entered straight from high school. Something he thought unwarranted, but nonetheless pleasurable.

His problems arose when placed with a school for teaching practice. Although his lesson plans were essentially profound, meticulously constructed and enthusiastically endorsed by his lecturers, he failed to adhere to them. He allowed the children's thoughts to roam, as did his own, encouraging them to pursue every possible avenue that the subject might contain. The result was that no lesson was completed; the lesson plan was not fulfilled.

Whilst the pupils undoubtedly enjoyed these imaginative excursions and loved to have Thomas standing or sitting amongst them helping to resolve a problem that had developed out of all proportion to the original point of inquiry, his supervisors were less impressed. He failed his teaching practice.

He could have tried again, but for a mixture of reasons, decided not to.

4

The inquest concluded that Pat Clancy's death was by accidental drowning. There was not the faintest suggestion of suicide or foul play.

Rose was greatly relieved by the verdict, although she did not for one moment believe that it was the correct one. She still held her wastrel son responsible for his father's death. But the judgement at least made possible a requiem mass and burial in hallowed ground.

The two local newspaper reports stated little but suggested a lot. Oddly enough they too did not hint at suicide but concentrated upon emphasising the mystery surrounding Pat's death.

They were wide of the mark in describing him as an 'Itinerant Irishman' and as an 'Irish gypsy', the latter, no doubt because of the proximity of his house to the gypsy encampment.

The row of houses in which it stood had not been completed when the war intervened, so an official address had not been conferred upon it. It was known locally as 'The Cut' because a short canal with that name ran close by, draining the surrounding wash-land into the main river. Every inhabitant of this oppressive neighbourhood was regarded by the townspeople as gypsies whatever their origins or way of life.

Pat and his family were well used to any newspaper report beginning with the nationality of the people involved, if they were less than English, as if that somehow explained the nature of the incident described.

Pat's body had sustained no more signs of injury than might have been expected after three days in a turbulent river that carried heavy traffic. Cursory police enquiries had revealed no neighbourhood discord. The gypsies, whilst not intending to be helpful had convinced the police that none of them disliked him, let alone wished him harm.

His catholic community described him in glowing terms. He had commanded great respect within it and all who were asked about him had spoken of warm and dependable friendship with him, someone who was as solid as a rock, quick to help, slow to condemn.

Deaths along the river were not uncommon. Presumed suicides were often the given cause, but boating accidents were not at all unusual. In summer time children bathing were sometimes caught in the currents. The tragic deaths of these young innocents were perhaps the cause of the greatest sorrow.

But the drowning of a cautious, capable man in the prime of his life, well-rooted in his community and devoid of enemies it seemed, took some explaining.

The news of Pat's demise travelled far. Whilst those who had known him well were united in praising his industrious, good-natured dependability, others were given to wild rumour.

Mystery always leads to speculation and speculation creates its own truth. It was suggested that he had been troubled by a ne'er-do-well son who had been thrown out of the priest-hood for some misdemeanour or other. And that his daughter had dubious inclinations. And that his widow, who was known to take her sorrow to the Church every day, might be grieving, or might just be salving her conscience. Such is the nature of hearsay and gossip; they tend to discolour the truth.

The inquest over, the funeral could now take place. Pat's three brothers who were working in England and Scotland attended, as did his two sisters who were nursing in London. The brother and sister living in America had both changed addresses recently, so contact with them, when made, was too late. They would probably have had difficulty in financing the journey anyway but they did send money for a headstone. Pat's brother in Australia had not been traceable for several years.

Thomas held his sister's hand for comfort throughout the ceremony and she linked arms with their mother. Rose remained grimly resolute throughout, never once losing her composure, although her grief was palpable.

On leaving the Church they realised that a few gypsies had stood inside the porch to hear the service, a mark of respect few *gorgios* earned from the travelling community. Despite the warmth of the day they wore dark overcoats to cover their rags. They escaped quickly before the rest of the mourners reached the doors.

A traditional wake was never suggested and, after a few hours at a nearby tavern where a little food was provided, the funeral party broke up. Not simply because people had distances to travel and jobs to return to; it was more to do with the deep sense of unease felt by most of the mourners about the circumstances of Pat's death. There was a sense of unfinished business, a feeling that there were questions requiring answers. 'Why?' and 'How?' formed in everyone's mind, if not on their lips. No one had any sense of confidence that an answer would emerge.

The estrangement between Thomas and his mother passed unnoticed, everyone being so enveloped in their own silent sadness, bewildered by the sudden and inexplicable death of this much loved, well-respected man.

5

Pat Clancy and his small family had lived for several years in their humble dwelling. He had never intended to settle permanently in this foreign land. He, and many like him, had responded to advertisements placed in Irish newspapers by English farmers and contractors needing labour. They had come, year after year, looking for seasonal work. In summer for potato picking and the grain harvest; in winter chopping sugar beet.

Between these seasons, if nothing else was available, they went home. There they brought in the turf for winter fuel, or re-thatched and repaired the old folks' crumbling cottages.

Pat saw no wrong, perhaps even a little justifiable vengeance, in making sporadic forays into the homeland of the invader, despite a commonly held view that he was stealing from England by sending money home. It kept the homestead going and gave him an acceptable standard of living for a few months of each year.

One day, when he had saved enough, he would turn his back on the insults and settle down 'back home'.

But that day never drew near. In fact it moved further away. Although the English were often hostile – in the minds of many, Ireland's political neutrality equalled colluding with Germany – there were plenty of people who were friendly towards him, and he and his kind rubbed along well enough with the majority.

Scorned by some they might be; often the butt of scurrilous slurs about their behaviour or their beliefs. Accused of stealing work that should remain the prerogative of Englishmen. But they were liked well enough by farmers and by the constructors of roads and aerodromes. Indeed, by any employer who needed men and women capable of sustained hard work and more than willing to do it.

As time went by they integrated, blended in, became assimilated, and found themselves spending longer in England than 'at home.'

As Pat's understanding of the ways of this foreign nation increased he had found himself becoming more critical of his own country. He began to feel that Ireland was imprisoned by more than its English dominated past.

Rome also had a part to play in its languid isolation. The intransigence of the priests and the power they held over the population concerned him. They seemed to revel in the control they could exert. Pat felt that they thought the country was theirs alone. They seemed to bask comfortably in its backwardness. He disliked seeing the priests living like lords when his parents could barely eat. Where they grazed two milking cows on the common land the local priest grazed twenty head of store cattle. How did he square that with his vow of poverty when he sent them to be sold at the market in Mullingar?

The dead hand of the Church limited freedom of thought and speech. Much information was banned, hidden from the populace. The government was not allowed to think for itself. It was, in Pat's eyes, well on the way to becoming a theocracy.

The economy never improved, nor would it for as long as the young people left at the first opportunity. There was no inward investment to deter their ceaseless migration. Soon the lordly priests would have no population left to dominate as the 'old folk' entered the mossy Churchyards for the last time.

England was perhaps a better place to settle, he felt, though at first he was reluctant to admit it, even to himself. England had tried to obliterate his culture, his language. Indeed, it hadn't cared if the people themselves were obliterated.

The more Pat dwelt on that the more he became inclined to pin the blame for it on a certain class of people – the big landowners, the aristocracy. The English labourers with whom he mingled and worked alongside were decent enough.

Although they had better living conditions than any labourer in Ireland they had little security. History told Pat that they too had been oppressed by the same class of people. He knew that less than fifty years ago they had no significant voting rights, little control over their own lives. No reason, then, to condemn a people of a country for the injustices caused by a minority of its inhabitants.

Since the war had ended the Irish, though still belittled, were no longer viewed as a threat. England was moving forward, Ireland was not. There was little point now in hoping to return. Pat knew he could never earn a living there. His offspring would go about unshod, like the rest, and would one day have to leave, as he had left, to make a life wherever they could.

For some reason Pat never understood, Rose would have jumped at the chance to live in Ireland. It was as if she wanted to escape from her own country. She had, Pat felt, a misplaced romantic view of Ireland; she had loved living there a couple of months at a time with his family when he was 'between work' in England. This was the only issue over which Pat had steadfastly opposed her.

Unfortunately Pat had never voiced to Rose his growing unease about the lamentable condition of the country he had once loved dearly. He could not find a way of explaining to her his criticisms of Ireland without appearing to be condemnatory of the faith they both followed.

He loved his faith and had always, overtly, demonstrated his strong commitment to it. Wherever they had lived he had always attended Sunday Mass, often cycling many miles to the nearest catholic church. Through his devout actions he had shaped Rose until she wanted to share his beliefs. He had been delighted when she, of her own volition, converted.

Now, as he began to realise that a check on clerical power might one day be necessary in some parts of the world in the interests of democracy, Rose prayed increasingly for theocracy. She was fast becoming a zealot. Pat somehow felt he was the cause of this. He had no idea of how to close the rift that was developing between them.

Over the years Pat had worked around much of eastern England, mostly on farms, occasionally mending roads when farm work was briefly unavailable.

But it was the flat, fertile farmlands that held him. What he saw as featureless prairies soon became interesting to him. The wonderful fertility of the region appealed most of all. Neither the sucking bog-lands, nor the salt-laden Atlantic storms that scoured the life out of the land on Galway's cliff-top fields, existed here.

There was no need to search for a pocket of land between bog and mountain just about good enough to plant a meagre crop of potatoes that might succumb to disease anyway. Or to put in a few sad rows of cabbages, or a few carrots which, when pulled, would be forked or as twisted as corkscrews. Here was abundant, lush growth, acres and acres of it, level as a lake, for as far as the eye could see.

Pat loved this land under the great endless skies, where rain, it seemed, fell in just sufficient quantities to grow the crop, instead of pinning you down in the bothy for days on end. He tended it as if it were his own, even though the work was seasonal and eventually had to be searched for by moving from farm to farm, village to village.

That had not been difficult when he was single. A train ride with his bicycle in the guards van would put him in the vicinity of a place of work; an hour or two on the bike would do the rest. A suitcase of clothes would be delivered later by a carrier, when lodgings had been established. Accommodation could always be found, as struggling spinsters and widows were glad of a pound or two if they could get it. Pat had even slept in a barn for a night now and then whilst a farmer made enquiries about local lodgings.

Pat was very much at one with nature, loving the sights and sounds of the fen-dwelling creatures as much as he loved the land itself. In his homeland he was used to seeing mostly shoreline birds as much of the hinterland was mist-hidden mountain or treacherous peat bog, both largely denuded of trees.

Now he would often catch sight of a heron at daybreak rising majestically from a reed-hidden waterway, or in spring, hear the haunting cow-like boom of the bittern. He loved the song of the lark as it ascended vertically to a tremendous height before disappearing from view. The sight of huge flocks of lapwings with their light bleating calls as they followed the plough delighted him. Even in the black depths of winter when the January snow dusted the jagged frozen clods Pat was out on the fields before daybreak. It was then that he would catch sight of the ghostly owls swooping silently, picking rodents from between the rows of beet.

Pat envied their freedom, the freedom of all the birds, but he was starting to realise his own liberty was greater now than ever before. Moving from place to place suited him. He'd always have a few pounds in his pocket and enough to buy a postal order at the end of the month to ease his parents' poverty.

Mostly the locals were friendly enough in the villages where he lodged. Occasionally a publican might refuse him service but such discrimination was becoming rare.

The village dances were occasions that he enjoyed most. They were free and easy, men and women mingling without embarrassment or awkwardness. In Ireland the priests maintained strict segregation of the sexes at the end of each dance. It had always seemed strange to him that men and women, many of whom were older than the priests, sat in separate rows each side of a dancehall and hardly dare speak to each other when they came together on the dance floor.

It was at a dance that Pat had got to know Rose. He had met her in a potato field a couple of days before, when she had declined his invitation to accompany him to a dance at the village hall. She knew that he'd taken a friend of hers to a dance at another village hall, and another friend to another dance before that. Rose had no intention of becoming just another date.

But there she was, sitting all alone. Pat approached her and smiled warmly.

'So you decided to come, Rose? I'm glad to see you. Are you with anyone?'

Pat could see that she was not.

'No,' she said. 'Not until now. That is, if you want to join me.'

'I'd be pleased to; can I get you a drink?'

'I wouldn't mind a glass of lemonade.'

Pat walked over to the bar and bought it, and a beer for himself. The barman served him sullenly, and as he placed the glasses on the counter he asked 'And is that all you want? Paddy, emphasising the last word.

'That'll do for now John,' said Pat. He smiled to himself as anger flickered momentarily across the man's face. He re-joined Rose.

'I'll not be staying long Pat,' she said.

'Have you someone waiting for you? he asked.

'I lodge with an old aunt. She won't go to bed until I come in. Not that she'll sleep then; the noise from this place will keep us both awake for a while.'

Pat learned that Rose did not, as he had thought, originate from this village, but from another several miles away. On leaving school at the age of fourteen she had gone into service at the big manor house there, but for reasons she did not want to go into she had left abruptly. Now she eked out a living at a nearby farm where she said she was well treated.

'Will you dance?' asked Pat

'I'd like to.' she said.

They danced. They seemed to get on all right.

'It's about time I was going.' she said, so Pat walked with her to her aunt's cottage on the other side of the village green. He left her after she'd agreed to see him again.

Pat didn't know what attracted him to Rose. She was quite a bit older than most of the single girls. That had something to do with it. He found the young girls brash and silly. Rose was serious. She had the nervousness of a hare, the same colouring and the big startled eyes.

Yet he quickly found that her looks were deceptive. She would round on someone with the ferocity of a wildcat if they made a statement which she found offensive, particularly so if it was a man. Pat had smiled to himself on several occasions when Rose had berated someone for something he thought trivial, such as using coarse language or making an unwarranted derogatory remark. He noticed too that she had a tendency to stand up for the vulnerable. A mentally impaired youth in the village often attracted ridicule, but not when Rose was around.

It was obvious to Pat that Rose's defensiveness stemmed from a sense of insecurity, but the fact that she could find the courage to defend others impressed him. She was like a cat with kittens; she might be terrified of the dog that threatened them but she'd fight it to the death. Rose could do with a little protection herself, Pat thought, and then she might make a good mother to someone's children. His, perhaps. Eventually they married.

Freedom of movement was not quite so easy now. Instead of homely lodgings, Pat needed to find a home. Some farms had cottages to rent, but usually only for the benefit of permanent workers. Farmers needed the itinerant labourers only for seasonal work. They mostly employed a stockman the whole year through and he got the cottage if he needed it.

Pat now had to take work where he could find it and whatever accommodation he could find, wherever it was, often several miles away. Cycling between villages before and after a day's hard labour was an arduous task. Rose picked up cleaning work in the big houses if she could find it, and sometimes a bit of potato picking.

Life became more difficult. Eventually there were children to add to Pat's responsibilities and Rose could no longer work. Pat had always wanted children of his own. His parents' cottage had been filled with the noise they made, the clatter and bustle, the slap of bare feet on the flagged floor, the squawks of indignation when one child grabbed another's piece of bread. Then the spontaneous laughter of the rest of them as his mother boxed the ears of the offender.

Being the oldest child, Pat had memories of the births of several siblings. Old doctor Kelly, who enjoyed a working retirement, would arrive at least a couple of hours before the event, having been sent for by Pat's father, who would then have to find some way of making recompense in kind.

Kelly would plant himself in the only armchair, a kettle boiling at his feet as he warmed them against the turf fire. He would supply himself with copious amounts of tea during the early stages of labour and, if he'd remembered to bring it with him, he would read his newspaper. When the delivery occurred everyone gathered round the bed to rejoice at the arrival of the new mouth that would help them starve.

So Pat was a happy man when Tom was born, the first of many he hoped. But it was several years before Rose bore the daughter she'd always wanted. Rose liked children but the means of creating them held no appeal.

Perhaps it was as well that there were no more as moving around the countryside, living in rented hovels, often without electricity, once even without running water, was a primitive existence.

When work was scarce Pat took his family to Ireland where they all squeezed into his parent's cottage. The cost of travel was offset by the savings on rent for the hovels in which they dwelt. His parents were glad to house them, pleased with the help Pat gave them in their declining years. Cows needed to be milked, turf cut and stacked, the cottage roof re-thatched.

But it could not go on. Kids needed to stay in one place; needed an education. Pat did not want them schooled in Ireland. Learning Gaelic was not in their interests, he felt. He was not denying them knowledge of their Irish heritage. They had spent so much time there, on and off, that when they returned to England they always had the faintest trace of an Irish accent. They liked it over there. But to keep them there would be to blight their lives.

England was now, in Pat's eyes the better place to live but he knew that if he were to give his family any chance of improving their lot he had to move them away from the far-from-anywhere fenlands that he loved. The vast green and golden acres encompassing half-asleep little towns and drowsy hamlets that sometimes seemed no more than tribal settlements held no possibility of permanent work.

He had to move them into a city, or at least a sizeable town, somewhere with a railway, bus services, arterial roads. Somewhere with industry, a place that was growing, not stagnating. There he might find a regular job.

He felt he had a few years of physical labour left in him, so he might get into some kind of construction work for a while; then, maybe a factory job. That thought appalled him, he so loved the labours of the field. That was the work he had always known; it was second nature to him. A factory would be a prison. But that could be held off for a few years yet.

Pat's mind travelled over the areas he had worked in and the towns within them. He remembered a farmer for whom he had done seasonal work a few years ago. The man had a place towards the midlands, only a few miles outside of a large town, a promising town whose environs Pat had enjoyed. He'd made a few friends there at the time.

The farmer, Peter Wilkinson, had a son, also named Peter, who lived in a decent house just beyond the edge of the town. He also owned a couple of near-derelict cottages that stood close to the house. Pat had once lodged in one of them, during the sugar-beet season and had travelled with the son each day in a battered old van to his father's farm. He'd got on very well with both of the men. Pat knew that then the cottages sometimes stood empty for a while, although perhaps not now.

Any kind of habitable property was hard to come by. But it was worth looking into. If he could rent one for a while it might enable him to find work within the town, construction work perhaps, or any regular labouring job. Then perhaps he could rent a better place.

It was a move he would have to make sooner or later. Farming was becoming highly mechanised. There would soon be no place for him on a farm. There would surely be more possibilities if he lived near a town.

***

Pat found things had changed. The old man had died and the young Peter Wilkinson had inherited the farm and had recently moved his family into it, intending to sell his own house near the town. But the war had thwarted his plans.

A German bomber, probably aiming to destroy the railway or demolish the town bridge over the river, or maybe succumbing to some humane impulse, had apparently missed his mark and the bomb had fallen on the pasture land across the line from the dwellings. The two ancient hovels had dropped in a rat-infested heap. They had taken the brunt of the blast and had, to some extent, protected the better house. Although its windows and a door were blown out and half the slates lifted off the roof, it was basically still sound.

The house was at the end of a terrace of six more and the closest to the railway and furthest from the river. It was the first of a planned development that was interrupted by the first war and afterwards abandoned altogether.

Around this incongruous row of dwellings, in the few mean acres squeezed between the line and the river, a gypsy encampment had sprung up and grown over time. More than half of the travellers were quite nomadic, but many had a reasonably settled existence there. They left for only a month or two at a time to do seasonal work elsewhere, then returned.

The area was all marginal land, fit for little, wash-land that flooded badly every winter. In summer the gypsy children played around the vans. They were wary, aloof, suspicious of anyone who was not one of their own.

In the autumn they picked blackberries from the brambles that grew on the railway embankment, smearing their clothes and their faces as they gorged greedily on the abundant fruit.

Their dogs, lurchers and mongrel terriers, accompanied them at all times, quick to pick up the unwary rabbit that strayed too far from the warrens beneath the line. These they sold for a shilling, when they had enough for their own pots, to anyone who would buy.

The whole area was littered with all manner of debris, much of it washed up in the winter floods and left there after the gypsies had combed through it for anything that might be useful. Much had been added to it by the gypsies themselves.

The lonely row of houses looked even more derelict than the gypsy vans. Those at least were all well painted. The doors and windows of the houses were bereft of paint and the brickwork was grimy, blackened by the smoke from the trains. Some had no curtains and where they did exist were faded and frayed with age. The bleak impoverishment of the war-torn century showed itself almost everywhere.

Because of the condition of the house and its proximity to the encampment and to the railway – one could almost have touched the passing trains with a broom-handle – Wilkinson doubted if he could ever find a buyer. At least not until he had spent a lot of money restoring it. Even in these straitened times, when almost any habitation was in great demand, it was something of a liability. He wanted to be rid of it. The few pounds he might get for it could be put into new stock.

The price he was hoping for was not beyond Pat's means. He had the skills to carry out the repairs if he could beg a little help from friends. It was a risk, but a risk that was worth taking, he thought. It had to be taken. Currently, Pat was becoming like a gypsy himself, moving from one hovel to another, now often having to search for work rather than walking straight into a job as used to be the case.

Pat agreed to buy the house. Despite its obvious drawbacks it appealed strongly to him, especially as the farmer had agreed to him having also the land on which the two bombed cottages had stood. That would provide enough ground on which to grow all the vegetables needed for a family, keep a few hens, and maybe even a pig or two.

Although the river, when it flooded, jeopardised some of the caravans and the first house at the other end of the row, the water, even during the worst of the floods, had never reached the one Pat was intending to buy.

But there was another problem, and a serious one at that. Pat had never paid income tax. Drifting in and out of the country over the years like a nomad, being paid in pound notes at the end of the week, he had hardly ever considered it. And if he had considered it he still wouldn't have paid it.

But that had put him on the wrong side of the law. He knew that he was at risk of being charged with tax evasion now that he was living in England permanently. To officialdom he had not, in earlier years, existed. With the boy now registered at school and the girl soon to start, this discrepancy would surely be noticed by the authorities. And owning a house might take some explaining.

It was Rose who raised the question, much to Pat's surprise. The possibility of settling down in a house of their own thrilled her. The best she had ever hoped for was to be able to keep some kind of a roof over their heads, but she was getting sick of the squalor and the constant moving about. The thought of a place of their own near a town strongly appealed and she didn't want to say anything that might make Pat change his mind. But the problem had to be raised.

'Do you think the income tax people might take an interest in us if you buy that place?' asked Rose.

'That's a good question. I've been asking myself the same thing. I think they might.'

'Matt Cafferky was locked up for not having paid any tax,' said Rose. 'I would hate that to happen to you.'

'Paddy Whelan too,' said Pat. 'A month ago.'

'I didn't know,' said Rose, 'You never said.'

'I didn't want to worry you.'

'His poor wife. How will she manage?'

'They've got a couple of big lads who've just started work. They're holding things together. They're getting by anyhow.'

There was a long silence whilst they both pondered the problem. It was Rose who spoke first.

'It has to be faced sooner or later Pat, although I don't know how. If you're never going to live in Ireland again you've got to get a tax code somehow and make things official.'

'I can't go back home,' said Pat. 'I wouldn't want to. It would be impossible to make a living there. And it won't get any better. We'd be living like pigs if we went back there.'

'We're living like pigs anyway for much of the time.' said Rose.

Pat was stung by what he took for a reproof. 'I know we are Rose. I know. But this could be a chance of something better. If we had our own house and I could find regular work and pay tax we could pull ourselves round. It has to be done Rose. We can't go on living like this. It's worth the risk. It's the best chance we're ever going to get. And if the Revenue find out that I've never paid income tax they'll have to lock me up. It's not a hanging offence.'

'How will you go about it?' asked Rose.

'I'll go and talk to Peter Wilkinson. He might have some ideas. After all, he wants to be rid of the house. He'll hardly put obstacles in my way.'

'Can he be trusted?'

'I do trust him Rose. He's a nice man. He's always treated me very fairly when I've worked for him and his father. They were both very decent with me.'

Wilkinson had an accountant and a solicitor and he paid for Pat to see both of them. Some explanation to satisfy the authorities was concocted – Pat never quite knew what – and his domicile was legalised. Pat soon found himself to be a man of property, albeit a near derelict property.

He fastened tarpaulins over the damaged roof and boarded up the windows. It had been a dry summer, so rain damage to the interior of the house was minimal.

The harvest over, Pat and three friends occupied the place leaving Rose, Mary and Thomas where they were for a few more weeks. Building materials were in short supply, but much of the damage was made good fairly quickly using reclaimed timber and slates. Pat began a useful relationship with the gypsies by getting them to look out for salvage and paying them a fair price for their trouble. He never paid them what they asked for but always more than he knew they would accept. That way he established himself as a fair-minded man, but nobody's fool.

Pat and his friends slept on the floor, cooked whatever food they could buy on the open fire, and drank copious amounts of tea to keep themselves going. Such hardship was not new to them. They had all known much worse in the past. All had been involved in building or extending their families cottages back home. They had the skills and tenacity between them to restore a dwelling to something vaguely habitable with just a few tools and a lot of effort.

Within weeks the family were together again in no greater discomfort than before, with hope of considerable improvement, and with no rent to pay. Pat found work on building sites and every spare penny went towards refurbishment. Soon the house became comfortable, homely. A place where a family could live at ease.

Despite dire warnings from many about the iniquities of gypsies, Pat never expected serious problems between them and his family, and didn't get many. Whilst they were aloof and detached from him, they were not hostile. Perhaps that had something to do with the fact that he was Irish, for several of them were too. Until recently signs could be seen on some tavern doors saying, 'No gypsies' and, less frequently, 'No Irish'. These were rare now, but memories lingered. Possibly this made some of them feel a slight degree of empathy with him.

Pat knew also that the accusations frequently lodged against the travellers, that they were thieves, tax evaders and fist-fighters, were not peculiar to any one social group. In any case, these offences, when true, scarcely amounted to large scale civil disobedience. When put into perspective they were a social nuisance, but little more than that. So he was not in a hurry to pass judgement on them, nor to let pass unjust slurs from others, who made them without wider consideration.

Pat had been occasionally challenged to a fistfight by travellers, not out of malice but as a test of his manly prowess. He always declined. The last thing he wanted was to be labelled a street fighter.

When he was younger he had the makings of an outstanding boxer, but in his own country the people could not afford to pay to see him fight and he'd no intentions of getting knocked about for nothing. A professional trainer had offered to set him up in America and Pat had seriously considered it. But then he decided not to go, it was too far away from his parents who might need his support with the passing of time.

Once, a traveller new to the camp, who came with the reputation of a fighting man, challenged him. Pat declined. The man called him a coward. Pat said, 'Think what you like,' and turned aside.

The tinker spat on the ground then threw a contemptuous punch at him. The blow never found its mark. He didn't even see the return punch that knocked him cold. Five minutes later he was still unconscious and two other men carried him off on a gate like a pig on a bier. After that, cowardice was never mentioned to Pat Clancy.

Pat was not a condemnatory person. 'We are all fallible creatures,' was a favourite saying of his. The only thing that he, and his son detested about the travelling community, was their predilection for trapping songbirds. Both Pat and Thomas hated this cruel trade.

They were caught with bird-lime, a concoction made by boiling crushed mistletoe and applying it to the stems of tall grasses. A scattering of crumbs and seeds attracted the birds and when they perched on the stems they were held fast. The larger birds pulled themselves free, but the tiny linnets and warblers seldom escaped. They then spent the rest of their lives in small wicker cages where they sang their tiny hearts out, the purity of their song undefiled by the cruelty of their capture. Neither Pat nor his son ever became inured to this facet of gypsy life.

Despite that, Pat would always lend them a helping hand if he could, although they were a very self-sufficient race and asked for little. But on more than one occasion they were glad of his willingness and strength.

The first winter he was there the river broke its banks as usual but his own house remained dry, being as far from the river as one could get before being blocked by the railway line. Pat made space on his garden for a couple of vans that were perilously close to the river. He pulled and pushed with the best of them, shoving slabs and boards beneath spinning wheels to aid traction. He finished the day by being generally well regarded, or at least, not disliked, by most of the travellers.

But it was an act of great courage and formidable strength during the following winter that created a decent and enduring relationship with the inhabitants of the camp. The flooding was worse that year than anyone could remember. All the vans had closed up together against the railway embankment as far away from the river as it was possible to be. There were two vans that had arrived at the site late the previous day and were dangerously close to the water.

Pat had told them to get up on his land, but they were delayed by others that had to be moved first. When room had been made, Pat, along with several established site dwellers, was helping to drag the newcomers out of the mud into which they were becoming entrenched. The relentless rain had hammered down all day and was now turning to snow. The whole place was turning into a quagmire.

Pat was right on the edge of the bank with a baulk of timber, trying to lever a bogged down wheel out of the mud. Suddenly, from twenty yards upstream there came cries of horror, then a cacophony of hysterical screams. Part of the riverbank had collapsed and a gypsy woman was in the water. She was coming down fast but had not yet gone under. Although only a few feet out no-one dared to brave the torrent to help her.

Pat had the reflexes of a cat. A couple of yards upstream in front of him a huge willow tree grew out of the bank, its roots and lower trunk in the torrent. A massive outward curving bough hung far out over the raging river, no more than four feet clear of the surface. Pat took two strides forward and launched himself out diagonally in a desperate dive. He knew the bough was too thick to grasp so he let his outstretched arms fly over it and took the impact with his chest. A lesser man would have been knocked backwards into the river but Pat hooked the backs of his big arms against the branch and hung on.

Immediately the woman was between his trailing feet and she clung to his ankles with a grip that might have proved the end of both of them. Pat was almost pulled off by the force of the current and her weight, but he clung there, took a breath and little by little inched his way back towards the bank. A traveller threw a rope at the woman but the current whipped it away instantly. In any case she was not going to lose the grip she had, the only connection with life itself.

Pat looked down over the bough into the foam and realised that his frame was so stretched out by the strain that the woman's face was almost beneath the water. He had to get his body further over the bough or both of them would die.

With a supreme effort of will and physical strength he hauled himself higher until he was draped over the bough, staring down into the frothing water beneath him. The woman's face was clear of the water now, but he was precariously balanced. If she lost her grip he'd dive head first to his death. She hung on, and Pat inched them both nearer and nearer to the bank.

Five gypsies, with barely a word between them, had formed a human chain, the innermost one holding onto the back of a van, the man at the far end leaning far out over the foam with total trust in his friends, reaching his hand out to the woman. Eventually she was within his grasp and he grabbed her and pulled. She let go of Pat, whose legs, relieved of the strain, lifted abruptly. For a second he was almost gone, but he regained his balance and moved himself in to safety.

The sobbing woman was taken away to recover from her ordeal. Pat was thanked and congratulated on his strength and courage by the men. After that incident he was always well regarded by that community.

6

Neither Pat nor Rose had been fully aware of the real reason for Thomas leaving the seminary. His mother did not consider any reason good enough. She felt ashamed of her son. He had failed in what to her was the most privileged calling a man might have the opportunity to follow. He had shattered her hopes completely.

Pat had understood the loneliness of the priesthood. The fact that you might be sent anywhere in the world to work, even if you didn't have the language of the people in that country. That was isolation indeed. You had to manage without meaningful friendships outside of the brotherliness of the priesthood itself.

Then there was the celibacy, something that Pat himself had endured for longer than he cared to remember. Was it any wonder that many of the priests that he'd known were given to the consumption of too much tobacco and alcohol and even days at the races to help them cope with their considerable responsibilities?

Pat had been deeply concerned about his son's future from quite an early age. When he had looked back on it, he recognised that Thomas had always been given to a somewhat disorderly life style.

He and Rose had always to try and keep him on track as it were. Thomas was a scatter-brained boy, dreamy, forgetful. He would work hard at something he liked, some new diversion he'd discovered. Then he would lose interest.

The nuns had squared him up many a time with a good belting, and Pat was pleased they had. He could not bring himself to physically chastise his son and he didn't want Rose to do so. He avoided bringing discord into the home. Although, if he'd witnessed the purple-faced passion of the nuns when they violated their young charges, leaving both victim and oppressor tearful and gasping for breath, he might have preferred to administer the required correction himself.

Thomas had been consistently good at art. He could draw and paint anything. But that was, in his father's opinion, a dead end. Nobody could support himself with that talent. He also had Pat's skill with woodwork and had benefitted from much patient and knowledgeable instruction from his father. Between them they had built several structures.

Thomas could also carve figures out of wood, something Pat could not do. He could not seem to see the potential form concealed within a piece of timber as Thomas could. Pat was generous in his praise whenever he created some minor work of art in this way, seemingly without much effort.

He had once thought Thomas might become a carpenter or joiner. They were useful trades and he'd encouraged him in that direction.

However, the school had detected an academic inclination in him. He was outstanding at English. He loved literature. He read and wrote poetry. He grasped Latin readily. There seemed to be the makings of a teacher in him, the nuns had said.

Pat had warmed to the thought of that. He had always admired teachers. He had listened to them avidly in his home village. Many of them could play an instrument and would do so in the pubs of an evening. Pat would listen, entranced. And afterwards he would talk with them. They seemed to know so much, he loved to listen to them. He was prepared to expose his ignorance to them and have them correct him. He felt that even the tiniest nugget of information was worth having.

So if Tom could pursue that profession then he would be delighted. No point in working with your hands thought Pat, if you could earn a living using your brain.

Unfortunately, about a year before Thomas was due to leave school, a group of priests from abroad visited and spent most of the day talking to the pupils in front of their teachers. They were stressing the need for more priests. Apparently the intake at seminaries throughout Europe was declining.

They ate in the refectory where Thomas and a couple of other outstanding pupils were asked to wait upon them. They engaged him in warm conversation asking him about his career intentions, talking to him as if he were an adult.

They were well-travelled men of the world, it seemed to him. They mentioned all the countries they had worked in. One, a Portuguese man, had spent several years in Brazil. That afternoon he showed a cine film of the Amazonian jungle. Another had worked in the prairie towns of the U.S.A. and described them in fascinating detail. A third had lived in Africa.

Thomas had never before imagined that priests could lead such exciting lives. With the naivety of any schoolboy, he was beguiled with the thought of international adventuring, but lacked the maturity to be able to consider the wider implications.

The next day the nuns told him how much he had impressed their visitors. From then on subtle pressure was placed upon him and he was edged towards the seminary.

***

Thomas had enjoyed his first months in the seminary. The buildings were quite grand, set in spacious grounds with well-tended gardens and greenhouses. One could easily find quiet places, outdoors or in, to study in private. The camaraderie, too, seemed at first exceptional, much stronger than he had expected. The seminarians were mostly on first name terms with the priests who instructed them, or if not entirely so, only the title 'Father' prefixed the Christian name.

This informality was possibly brought about by the number of older men who were studying for the priesthood, many of whom were older than their lecturers. Thomas had not expected to find so many older men, but it pleased him considerably. He liked their company, respected their knowledge of the world.

Whilst a few were entrenched bigots, he found most were reasonable in their assertions, more circumspect than many of his own age. These men had endured the horror of war, had witnessed the capacity of the human race to devise ways of attempting to destroy itself. Some of them had found, in its aftermath, that trying to establish any normality in civilian life was beyond them. Existence had become pointless after years of unbearable destruction and the breakdown of civil respect. So they had placed their faith in a Faith and this was now their chief means of guidance.

This pleased Thomas, because, until now, he had felt that an opposing viewpoint prevailed. He had heard so many people say that never again would they listen to the advocates of religion, believers in an omnipotent deity that would not intercede to stop the world tearing itself apart. If such a God existed, then who was the devil?

He still preferred the argument that if humans committed evil it was because they had the free will to ignore God's teachings. He enjoyed the company of these interesting, experienced men and the discussions he had with them. Their devoutness gave him hope and his own doubts remained submerged.

After a year or so his doubts returned. He had been naïve in imagining that studying at the seminary would be a feast of intellectual challenges. He had assumed that all the seminarians would be thirsting for knowledge and that an abundance of academics would be helping them to search for it.

Unfortunately this was not always the case. Subtle indoctrination prevailed. A great deal of reading material was proscribed by the Vatican. Even some novels that he had read and thought to be excellent, he found, much to his surprise, to be on the very considerable list of forbidden books. Several films were also banned. Certain intellectual challenges were disallowed.

Thomas learned that an eminent continental theologian had recently been excommunicated for questioning the logic of a basic tenet of the faith. Worse still, he found by scouring the libraries that much of what he was encouraged to take on trust as fundamental and ancient doctrine had been introduced in relatively recent times by various popes. Therefore, there may have been legitimate grounds for questioning this. But you were never told that might be so. It was as if the mountain of doctrine was forever growing, becoming more detailed, all encompassing, cutting off any avenue of free thought. Much was being added over time, it seemed, with little being taken away.

Thomas' doubts started to become fears. It was not that he was afraid to try to make a fresh start in life outside of the seminary should that become necessary, although he knew that would be awkward, to say the least.

His main fear was that he might lose his faith if he found too many flaws in it. How could one live, how could one even contemplate starting life over again if one believed in nothing? If there is no truth, then what is there to live for? he asked himself.

The problem with doubt is its insistence. It will not be silenced. Like a cancer it has a life of its own and cannot easily be extinguished. One doubt can lead to another. Dripping water can wear away a rock. A crack in a dam can lead to a catastrophe. An edifice can collapse if its foundations are undermined.

Thomas did not want to find any more fault lines in his Catholicism. Or in Christianity. Or any religion. Oh God, what was he thinking? This was getting close to heresy. It could break him. What made him think like this? What made him think at all? Why could he not just accept?

It wasn't long before he found himself worrying about the notion of transubstantiation during the sacrifice of the Mass. The bread and wine were not mere symbols of the body and blood of Christ but were actually those elements. This was the miracle that occurred during every mass. Could that be relied upon as scientific fact? He felt that it could not. Such things could only be symbolic.

But did it really matter? Symbolism was a perfectly valid device. It was evident in every pageant throughout history. But pageant is specious, an empty show. The Mass surely was more, much more than that. It meant a great deal to him.

He wondered if the insistence of the reality of the body and blood was begun in earlier times to impress upon the minds of an uneducated congregation the huge magnitude of Christ sacrificing his mortal body as an act of atonement for the sins of the world. If so, it was a deceit he felt uncomfortable with.

Then the notion of the three entities of the Godhead began to trouble him: The Father, The Son, The Holy Ghost. How could you understand this trinity? The Son was a man from Galilee, or thereabouts. A human being born of another human being but begotten by a spiritual entity.

Of the historicity of Jesus the man, Thomas had no doubt, although the details were somewhat sketchy. The anthropomorphised vision of a mystical creator of universes fathering such a son without human contact bewildered him.

And what sort of creator was this? The effects of creation were all around him, manifest, beyond doubt. But they were just that - effects. What of the cause? The cause – God, supposedly – was without cause. The catechism said so. 'Was, is, and always will be', it said of the cause.

That in itself seemed difficult to grasp. Thomas explained it to himself: there had been a cause of everything that existed now, or ever had existed. It was unknowable, but its effects were everywhere. That cause was called 'God'. Was it necessary to know more?

The doctrine and dogma were perhaps just attempts to define the unknowable. Just a normal human trait to try to make sense of something, he had reassured himself. He had not lost faith. He believed in that great power that could not be understood. The doctrinal side of things he would leave to the enlightened elite. Perhaps, one day, he himself would find enlightenment. Until then he would get on with life in the seminary as before.

For all Thomas' questioning, there had been things happening around him that he tried not to see, did not want to question, certain behaviours that troubled him but about which he asked no questions.

Some men, a small number, seemed to have enrolled at the seminary for the wrong reasons. They seemed not to be particularly devout, nor keen to study, yet they had an obvious liking for the paraphernalia of ritual. They were very interested in the different vestments the priests wore, in incense and the censer. They blessed themselves ostentatiously, splashing holy water everywhere. They usually loved to sing hymns and to chant the responses during Mass. Many of them had excellent voices. They tended to be showy people who were quick to display their knowledge of Latin or even Greek in any conversation. Their main reasons for being at the seminary appeared to be because they wanted to meet other men. Some of them had a predilection for the youngest, boyish-looking males in their first year of study. These youngsters could be easily intimidated by their older peers.

This attraction of one man to another for more than friendship was new to Thomas and alien to his own feelings. He did not know if he disapproved personally of homosexual love. It was definitely illegal and disapproved of or condemned by all faiths. He felt that it was totally contrary to the teachings of his faith, although such a taboo subject was never talked about explicitly.

The Jesuits were generally quick to notice such behaviour and to stamp on it. Not much was ever made of it. The most egregious offenders simply left quickly and silently. However, not all of that persuasion were made to leave.

Over time, Thomas realised that one or two of the most senior lecturers, devout men of considerable learning and of significant influence, were displaying these traits.

That in itself was not what troubled him. What dismayed him considerably was the effect they were having on some of the youngest, most naïve seminarians. The older lecturers seemed to be using their positions of authority to intimidate some who were scarcely more than boys, boys who were away from home for the first time in their lives perhaps, unsupported by families, desperately seeking friendship.

These youngsters would emerge from lengthy one-to-one tutorials, sometimes with tears in their eyes, unable or unwilling to talk to anyone, sometimes for days on end. They would remain sullen and aloof and would fall behind in their studies, requiring further input from the same priests in order to progress.

Although Thomas felt that he approved of deep and enduring male friendships and was starting to see that perhaps they could become very close and progress to another level, he knew what was occurring here was not love but simply lust, used in a bullying, intimidatory way.

It would have been the same it if were of a heterosexual nature. It was the abuse of power, getting one's own way without regard for the feelings of the subordinate person. It was wrong. He asked himself would it also be wrong to bully the mind of another. Was that the same as an assault on the body? He did not know the answer.

Thomas never had to rebuff any unwanted attention from any lecturer. These priests always related to him in a considerate and helpful way. Lacking hard evidence for his suspicions he persevered in his studies, despite his misgivings, although the fear of uncovering corruption haunted him.

He found himself making mental comparisons between the rules of the Church and the civil laws of a Nation State. The fact that State laws were frequently broken, he felt, did not obviate the need for them, or necessarily mean they were wrong.

So too with the rules of the Church. If some of its members violated these rules, that did not invalidate them. The laws of a community of citizens, if developed along democratic lines, ought, he felt, to be observed for the greater good, but should always be open to question.

If a law existed that was felt by the majority to be unjust then a procedure for changing it should exist. The laws of totalitarian states had proved, and were still proving, to be horrific and were totally unjust in their outcomes. There was good reason to question the ability of the human race to govern itself.

A theocracy was different. It had rules that superseded all man-made laws. It was not intended to be democratic. It was above the devising and tinkering of mere mortals. They were flawed, therefore democratic rule was likely to be flawed. So Civil law was, therefore, subordinate to God's law. The instructions of a theocracy were divine, independent of their subjects will. Beyond question or doubt.

Yet doubt was what this comparison raised in Thomas' mind. These divine laws were communicated down through the ages by men to other men ad infinitum. Disseminated by the enlightened elite to the masses. He could not avoid asking himself just how enlightened were the 'elite'.

He began spending the little spare time he had in public libraries, the seminary library lacking much of what he now wished to read.

He knew of the Borgias, those renaissance popes who marked a dark era in the history of the Church. Whilst the Church had never denied their activities, equally, it had never gone out of its way to publicise them.

Thomas wanted to know more. He found more: a sickening history of depravity and murderous power struggles. These popes, this family, had once been part of the enlightened elite, formulating doctrine and dogma to which the unenlightened should genuflect. He extended his studies. He found later popes, some much later, who were also lacking in moral standards.

So the seeds of corruption that he sensed within the confines of his own place of study must exist at all levels within the organisation of which he was training to become a part.

The blow was shattering. What was he left with? A great sense of emptiness overwhelmed him. He had the feeling that the possibility of a huge lie, a lie almost as big as the world now threatened his very existence.

Thomas was now asking if myth, conjecture, superstition, were the equal of rational, logical, deductive thought. Was much of his faith simply the product of doctrine and dogma inculcated throughout his life? He wanted to believe, needed to, but how could he go on believing?

Apart from a belief in an incomprehensible creator of the world around him he felt like a man lost in a huge dark forest. Whichever way he turned might be the wrong way. The only way out of a forest is to walk in a straight line. But to maintain any direction now seemed a hopeless task. From now on it would be all too easy to wander around in circles.

Like an explorer who has lost both map and compass, and who feels now that he may also be losing his mind, Thomas sought help to steady his nerves.

He dare not broach his doubts to his lecturers. This might lead to an immediate expulsion from the seminary when he could not think what his next move ought to be. He decided to share, tentatively, some of his doubts with seminarians he called his friends. He was as much saddened by their responses to his questions as they were by what was being asked of them.

In answer to his doubts about Papal infallibility they rounded on him fiercely. The Pope, they said, was infallible only when speaking on matters of faith or morals *ex cathedra*, from his seat of authority, as it were. Thomas asked how they knew which historic pronouncements had been made thus, and which might not have been. It was clear that they had no answer. More troubling, it was equally clear they needed none.

On the subject of established miracles that had led to sainthood they had no doubt. These events had occurred by the power of God. Only catastrophes such as war were man-made. How about natural disasters? These might have happened as God's retribution for man's evil they said. Thomas wanted to know how mere mortals could discern which events were man-made, which by the hand of the Almighty. They were appalled by the question. There was no necessity for it.

He felt that it was unfair to intrude so far into the faith of his friends. He had been exploring his thoughts and fears aloud only to clarify them, not to elicit support. He did not want to infect anyone's mind with the anguish that was now eating into his own. He was sure of nothing. His friends' faith seemed imperturbable. Perhaps they had a better understanding of theology than he did. He hoped so. He did not raise the issue with them again.

It soon became evident that these people had relayed his doubts to others. One of the older men who had been at the seminary for two years longer than Thomas contacted him.

Paul Hudson was a man for whom Thomas had the greatest regard. He was a serious and compassionate man. Although people said that he hadn't the greatest intellect and apparently struggled with a lot of the theory involved in the training, Thomas had always regarded him as a wise man. He generally kept himself aloof from the other seminarians and studied almost constantly, yet would always help anyone in any way that he could if he sensed that they wanted his opinions.

He had warmly extended the hand of friendship to Thomas when he first enrolled at the seminary. During those first months they had talked quite often. Paul was a good listener rather than a talker. He never said much about himself, yet, at the same time, he did not appear secretive, although, at the end of a conversation no one felt they knew any more about the man than they did at the beginning.

It was said that he'd had a bad time of it during the War, although in what way it was not clear. Apparently he had relinquished a promising career in business management to enlist in the army. He didn't have to, as the firm he worked for was connected to the manufacture of armaments.

It was said too that there had once been a woman in his life. No-one really knew. But by general consensus Paul Hudson was a kind-hearted, thoroughly decent, first rate chap, but one who liked to spend a lot of time studying on his own. Because of this, Thomas did not have the heart to burden him with his troubles.

He was therefore more than surprised when Paul asked him to have a drink with him at the nearby village pub. Especially as he had never heard of Paul going near a pub; he rarely left the seminary.

Moderate drinking was not discouraged by the clergy, and those who attracted attention by immoderate consumption of alcohol were soon reprimanded and brought into line. Every Friday and Saturday night there were a few seminarians in the pub mixing with the locals. They were well liked.

Thomas was glad of Paul's company as they walked the country mile down to the village. After the exchange of general pleasantries and enquiries about how each was getting on with his studies Paul soon came to the point. It was obvious to him that Thomas was treading water desperately, a long way out from the shore. Paul, in his usual caring way, wanted to throw him a lifeline if he could. But he hadn't expected to encounter such serious doubt on so many issues.

'This could be the ruination of you Tom. Everything you are saying you have hinted at before, but now it seems to have a terrible grip on you'.

'It has,' replied Thomas wearily, 'I cannot see a way forward.'

'Most of us have doubts at times. Any thinking man does. But we press on. We have to. As priests, that we are hoping to become, we must press on.'

'I can't go on,' stated Thomas.

Paul was dismayed by the level of defeat implicit in Thomas' voice; he had not expected to find such a dejected tone. He tried to rally him.

'The Church needs robust men, resolute in their faith,' continued Paul. 'Those who vacillate would hardly give succour to parishioners struggling with their own torments, and God knows, there are enough of them. The world is only just starting to pull itself back together after being turned upside down. People don't know where they are, who they are; they've lost all direction.'

'How do we know which way to point them? I certainly don't. I'm one of them.'

The depth of Thomas' despair was palpable; Paul felt himself being caught in its pull.

'It's a sad world you inhabit Tom. You are in a lonely place I feel. I couldn't live there.'

'Yes. It is. That much has dawned on me. And it frightens me. But there is no other place for me. I am extremely wary of absolutes. I feel all conventions, rules, ideologies, are devised by us, humankind, and we are all fallible. So I am sceptical of everything.'

'So I see Tom, so I see.'

By now they had reached the pub. The conversation ended whilst they ordered drinks. Luckily there was no-one in whom they knew, so they were able to resume their conversation.

'I really don't think you can help me Paul. I wish you could, but you can't.'

Paul was beginning to see that as a strong possibility, but he knew that he himself must not weaken.

'You could help yourself if you had a mind to,' said Paul. 'Can you not accept Pascall's Wager? If you bet on there being no God and live your life accordingly, then you are condemning yourself to everlasting darkness if it turns out there is. And that, I feel, is how it will turn out for you. Why not believe God exists and live according to that belief? Live according to the scriptures; spread that gospel and die safe in the knowledge that if He is there then your soul will find its way to Him.'

Thomas thought deeply. He liked Paul immensely and knew that he was trying his best to help him out of his inner turmoil. He therefore had no wish to reject his counselling out of hand. But it was no good. It was clear to him now that he must soon leave the seminary.

'Do you suppose many here take Pascall's Wager?' asked Thomas.

'Some of us – some do, sometimes. Just to help them through the dark days. It's hard not to falter now and then.'

Thomas took this to mean that Paul struggled sometimes. He did not want to push his friend any further, but neither did he wish to equivocate. 'That sounds a little like the Romans secretly worshiping their old Gods after it was decreed that Christianity was the official religion.' Paul didn't answer. Thomas broke the silence. 'The God you envisage Paul, indeed the God I think Pascall had in mind, would be an omniscient God above all else, would he not?'

'He would be; of course. God knows and sees everything.' There was a note of slight irritation in Paul's voice.

'Then he would know from the start if a man was simply hedging his bets, so to speak, by going through the motions of practising a religion that maybe he didn't believe in. In fact, surely He would know before the man was born what he would do, what he would think, throughout his life. This God could not be deceived surely?'

Paul said, 'I'm not sure I'm following you Tom.' He looked slightly disconcerted.

Thomas did not like the way this was going. Paul was a friend. He did not want this to turn into an argument about points of theology.

'I appreciate your concern Paul. I know it's well meant. I've always appreciated your guidance; you know that. I'm sorry things have turned out like this.'

Ignoring Thomas' conciliatory tone and barely concealing his frustration, Paul continued. 'And which signposts might you look for if you think the Church cannot be your guide?'

'I'm not sure,' replied Thomas. 'In fact I simply have no idea. It's not so much about finding a direction as learning to recognise the false signposts. That is something I don't find easy to do.'

'So you've decided that the teachings of many great thinkers throughout the ages are not enough for you?'

'Yes, I suppose that about sums it up.'

'So what do you believe in Tom?'

'I don't know what I believe. I just don't know.'

'You've much to learn Tom, and spurning the teachings of those who have studied these things for lifetimes is hardly the way to go about it. You've very much to learn.'

'I know I have Paul. I think, though, that I have made a start.'

'I don't see how you can have made a start Tom, if you believe in nothing. Surely, if that really is the situation you find yourself in then you can have only an aimless existence. I don't see how you can strive for anything. You cannot have any goals. Nothing could be achieved because you could not recognise an achievement.'

'I think I could, Paul. Whilst I don't feel that I believe anymore – in anything, I mean – I most certainly think. I have to. We all do. We have to make choices. All decisions are based on that. I could not cross the road unless I chose to. And I would only do that if I had decided I wanted to be on the other side. That does not mean I *believe* that the other side is better, or even that it is safe to cross. It's just that I'd make the decision *thinking* that it might be better on the other side. That's not believing. I think things are, or are not, with what I might call varying degrees of rational probability. I think some things are probably true, others, I feel, are highly unlikely. Some things I find practically impossible to accept as being in any way credible. So I veer towards what I think is probable, without actually believing it to be so.'

'So you're looking for tangible proof of God's existence before you are inclined to think he exists?'

'Yes, I suppose so,' replied Thomas in a dejected tone. 'A belief in a God is not something that should be too readily assumed. Too much hangs on it. World order possibly. Or perhaps worldwide division. So I suppose, on something so important, I am asking for something approaching proof. And it's not to be found, it seems.'

Paul was now wishing that he had not allowed himself to be drawn into this. A friendship was in jeopardy. He was beginning to see Thomas as obdurate, unreasonable, whereas he had always seen him as a most reasonable man. His anger was mounting, though he tried to suppress it. It was time to lower the tension, tempers were becoming frayed.

'Have another drink Tom; let me get you one.'

Paul walked over to the bar and ordered two more halves. The landlord did not look quite so friendly now as when he had first served them.

As he took Paul's money he said, 'Do you think you could keep your voices down a bit? You're attracting attention to yourselves.'

'Sorry,' said Paul. 'I guess we were getting a bit carried away with ourselves.'

He took the drinks back to the table. In a quieter voice now he asked, 'What is the matter with you Tom? What is this obsession with materialism? Much of what we do and say and think is not based on material fact. We are not machines. We have emotions.'

'I know,' said Thomas.

Missing the irony, Paul ploughed on. 'Can you not enjoy the warmth of a summer breeze, or delight in the sound of snow crackling crisply under foot on a winter walk? Are you blind to the beauty of a rainbow, or a baby's smile? Are you deaf to birdsong at dawn as the world awakens? Do you receive no sensation from the scent of a rose? If these things leave you unmoved then you must be a machine. And machines are not in touch with their maker.'

Paul's anger subsided after this outburst of emotion. He looked slightly embarrassed. For a few moments they both sat in silence. Thomas was moved by the images Paul had brought to mind and by his obvious feelings for what he had described.

'Yes, I can and do appreciate all of those things ...'

'Then can you not voice your unequivocal thanks to the God that created them?' Paul cried, his exasperation mounting again.

Customers in the pub were now looking across at them.

'I was about to say that any man with his five senses intact, and enough of an intellect to grasp what they were telling him, would probably appreciate those things. They are self-evident and are evidence of some creative force that I don't pretend to understand.'

'All right,' said Paul, 'the world itself, let alone the rest of the universe, is all the evidence a reasonable man might ask for as proof of the existence of God. But that's not enough for you?' Paul's rising frustration was outpacing his logic. 'Let me ask you this. If you want to insist on material proof of the existence of God, give me your material proof that he does not exist.'

Thomas was astounded at Paul's error. He knew him to be more intelligent than this. His anger had momentarily obscured his intellect. He did not want this argument to continue. He had not wanted it in the first place. But if you held an opinion then it would put you into positions where you had to defend it.

'You know that I could not do that Paul. No one could find material proof for the non-existence of anything. It defies logic.'

Paul knew that, even before Thomas had finished speaking. He had just been carried away by his emotions. There was no point in going any further. The man was a lost cause. He thought they would part for good today. He was sad, but something had changed between them. No need for recrimination though.

A long pause, a few sips apiece from the near-empty glasses. Then Paul spoke, softly now, almost forlornly: 'And what will you do for a moral compass Tom? I'm sure you'll always want to behave in an ethical way, a decent way.'

'All I can say to that is that I shall try, to the best of my ability, never to unnecessarily hurt another human being. I hope, and it may prove to be a forlorn hope, that that will suffice.'

'So, sometimes it might be necessary to hurt someone. Is that what you are saying?'

'Maybe,' said Thomas, 'but only for my own physical self-preservation. And then only as a last resort. I would never, I hope, hurt anyone for the sake of an ideology.'

There was a long silence as Paul dwelt on this. 'I hope that works for you Tom, although I think you are deceiving yourself. I fear you've over simplified things a great deal.'

'I'm a simple man Paul.'

'So was Our Lord,' Paul said this under his breath, almost to himself, with a faraway look in his eyes.

He looked and sounded like a child who has grown too old to believe in fairy tales but who is still enraptured by their magical qualities. A child who still enjoys escaping, at least momentarily, the hard realities of life and would love to lose himself in the cocoon of myth and make-believe forever.

Thomas picked up on Paul's last remark. 'Maybe he was *simply* a man. Albeit, perhaps, a very wise man.'

Paul's response was steely, resolute, a hint of anger returning to his voice. He'd been badly rattled. 'No. He was not simply a man. His wisdom was heavenly wisdom. How else could a simple man who spent His life around the shores of Galilee know as much about the world as He did? How could He, unless He was an integral part of the Trinity, carry with Him through His thoughts, words and deeds such vast numbers of believers throughout the world? Don't tell me He was simply a man Thomas.'

'If you look nearer to our own times Paul, Karl Marx managed to capture the imaginations of huge numbers. Many believe in his philosophy, if you could call it that.'

'And look where that's leading to. The next World War possibly. For heaven's sake Tom, don't tell me you're going down that atheistic road. It's the path of the devil.'

A man at a nearby table who seemed to be quietly involved in a serious discussion with his tearful wife said angrily, 'Can't you two find something else to talk about?'

Paul glowered savagely back at him. Thomas offered an apologetic, conciliatory smile.

In a much lowered voice he said, 'No Paul. Be assured that I am not going down that road. Most definitely not. I told you, I don't have a belief. I was just making the point that people can quickly become carried away by belief, any ideology can become self-perpetuating. And if it insists that it has the monopoly on truth, then it's dangerous. I'm sorry Paul. I chose a bad example there in Marx. He was another prophet with another truth. I have never found his work convincing.'

Paul scowled at the word "prophet" but said nothing.

Thomas continued. 'That's all I'm trying to say, Paul. From Zoroaster to Jesus, from Mohammed to – well, to Marx- these are just men with their own truths. Truths which their followers foist upon us, sometimes in the most barbaric ways.'

Paul controlled his frustration, channelling it into one last attempt to make him see sense – his sense.

'If we would all cleave to the one truth, the world might be a better place, Tom.'

'And which truth is that, Paul?'

'You know what my answer has to be to that, Tom.'

Thomas looked at him for several seconds before he spoke 'I do Paul. I envy your certainty.'

There was no more to say. They were both drained by the intensity of their discussion. They were not sure of each other, did not know if a lasting relationship could be sustained. They were somehow different now.

'I think it's time we were going.' said Paul.

They put their empty glasses on the bar, bade farewell to the publican, who scarcely acknowledged their departure and left. They were too locked up in their own thoughts to notice the glances of the other customers.

Not much was said on the way back. As they parted in the grounds of the seminary Thomas shook Paul's hand.

'Thanks for talking to me Paul. I'll soon be out of your way. I hope my faithlessness, vacillation, call it what you will, does not end our friendship.'

'I hope not,' Paul replied. 'I hope not.'

Two days later Thomas was summoned to the study of Father O'Mahoney, a lecturer with whom he had had very little previous contact. O'Mahoney was a short, stocky, bull-necked man, truculent and confrontational. No-one addressed him by his Christian name, it was always Father O'Mahoney. He demanded that people should recognise his position of seniority and basked in the respect this conferred upon him.

Thomas had to stand in the corridor outside his office as there was someone else in with him. It was as if he was back at school, waiting outside the head nun's office for a caning. He had a sense of foreboding. He was sure something was wrong.

After a couple of minutes the other man left and shortly afterwards Thomas was called in.

'Right Clancy, sit down and tell me what you know of Paul Hudson's whereabouts.'

'I'm sorry Father I … I'm not sure what you mean. I last saw him Wednesday evening. I've not seen him since then.'

'Nor has anyone else. I know you were with him on Wednesday. You were seen in the pub together. On Thursday he was missing his lectures. This morning a letter was received from him, bearing no address I might add, saying that he was unable to continue with his studies. I want to know where he has gone.'

'I honestly wouldn't know. I can't believe he would leave the seminary.'

'Well, it would seem that he has. I believe that the two of you were arguing in the pub. What was that about? Come clean about it. You were overheard.'

'We were not so much arguing as, well, he was trying to help me through some difficulties I've been having. Trying to talk me through some problems.'

'Don't beat about the bush, Clancy. What problems was he trying to help you with?'

'Some doubts that I've been struggling to overcome. I'm no longer sure that I'm cut out for the priesthood.'

'Now isn't that the understatement of the year?'

'Paul is very strong in his faith. He wanted to help me.'

'He would. He's like that. So he thought he might get you to recognise your errors and return to your senses? He was fooling himself. We were a bit slow to pick up on you Clancy. You're a devious one. I don't think it's doubts you have. Quite the opposite. You seem to think that everyone is out of line except yourself. You know better than everyone else. You're rebellious. We know you've been unsettling other seminarians lately. They have been talking about you. We should have had you out a while ago. You're a misfit. So, Paul Hudson thought he could save you. And now you've ruined him. That poor man has spent the last four years getting his life back together. He was not so very far away from being ordained. He would have made a good priest. He might still, if we can track him down. So you won't help us?'

'I can't. I don't know much about him. I don't even know where he came from originally. He never said much about himself.'

'He came from London, and it's likely that is where he's gone back to. But I doubt very much if you give a damn where he's gone to or what happens to him. You've not got much in common with him. He's a very decent person.'

'Of course I care about him. I wish I could help him. I liked the man very much.'

'You can help me Clancy. And everyone else here. You can get yourself off these premises in the next twenty-four hours. And I'll give you a piece of advice. You're always looking for material proof. I suggest your vocation lies within the legal profession. They're always pulling factual evidence apart. Mostly to obscure the truth rather than to reveal it. I think that's the place for you. You are not a man of God.'

PART TWO

7

A mid-May Sunday morning. Early, the town not yet on its feet. The cobbles of the ancient market square glistening after the soft rain of the night. Until yesterday, the weather had been fine and dry for a couple of weeks and still held the promise of later sunshine.

Thomas was already up and about. He paced the flagstones surrounding the square waiting for a newsagent to open for business. He looked disinterestedly into the shop windows with the distracted gaze of someone killing time.

The many enamelled metal signs hanging over shop fronts that advertised both the useful and the ridiculous drew a sardonic smile. The creed of Capitalism was both comically cunning but also ruthless in its powers of deception.

One billboard advertised a shoe polish with a "shine two feet deep". Harmless enough. Several encouraged women to doubt their natural level of attractiveness and instead to depend upon the dubious beauty treatments they offered. A tobacco firm told you "For your throat's sake smoke . . . ." Deception was the way of the world it seemed.

His quadrilateral perambulations brought him again to the window of Johnny Breasley's rope shop, above which he rented the storeroom as his austere living accommodation. His eye was caught by an insignificant example of his own handiwork displayed near the front of the window. It was the form of a draught horse, about a foot high, carved out of a block of pine. Painted brown with cream fetlocks, it had a cream coloured mane made from soft cotton rope. It was harnessed to the sidewall of the window by two short lengths of Breasley's rope.

Johnny had asked Thomas a month ago if he could make him a model horse to advertise the strength of his rope, and he'd finished the job yesterday morning. Yesterday being Saturday, Thomas was surprised that John had found the time to install the creature amongst his coils of rope, balls of twine, hammocks, sacks and other items derived from hemp, sisal and manila which cluttered up his window in an untidy jumble.

He had enjoyed fulfilling this small commission of Breasley's. It had not been difficult and he had been able to fit it in between the other jobs he did for various shopkeepers throughout the town. He had asked next to nothing in cash for doing the job, but Johnny was well-pleased and insisted on paying him more than he wanted.

A more creative example of his talent was displayed across the shop front above the window: a striking hand-painted sign showing the proprietor's name and listing some of the goods he supplied. This had been a more skilful job that Thomas had spent a lot of time on to perfect and it had commanded a worthwhile price. More usefully, it had attracted the attention of several other traders and Breasley had been glad to tell them who had done it for him. This brought him quite a bit more work.

By doing work such as this Thomas had earned a precarious living since leaving the college and his parent's home. He had acquired many craft skills from his father and could draw and paint for as long as he could remember. He was well able to make small display units and shop signs. Renting a room from Johnny Breasley, who was well known and well-liked by just about every trader in town, had put many of these little jobs his way. He was now becoming well enough known to find work for three, four or occasionally five days a week, which was just about enough to support his frugal bachelor existence.

Breasley was now far more than just his landlord. Thomas liked him a lot, respected his judgement and often sought his advice. Despite a considerable age difference the two had become firm friends within weeks of his renting the room.

He considered himself very lucky to have obtained this abode. Accommodation was still in very short supply despite extensive re-building programmes. Things had improved a lot since the end of the war, but many people were sharing homes with relatives or living in intolerable slums.

He had had the good fortune to have been passing the rope shop just as Breasley was placing a handwritten card in his window advertising living space above. Thomas had entered the shop and agreed immediately on the few shillings rent, paid for two weeks in advance, and shook hands on the deal. Even before he had left the shop someone else had entered to enquire about the room, such was the demand for accommodation.

John Breasley had only recently vacated the place himself. His older brother had died, leaving him their late father's cottage round by the slaughterhouse. For the first time in his life he was now living in relative comfort.

This morning Thomas was far from at his ease. In a couple of hours he was to meet a strikingly attractive young woman, a few years older than himself, and later, her parents. He had agreed to this because she had asked him to. He was intrigued by her; in awe of her beauty, mesmerised by her commanding presence. He found her charming and fascinating and couldn't say no to a meeting whose purpose he was unsure of.

Elaine Langdon was the daughter of Charles Langdon, the owner of by

58

far the largest and most prestigious store in town. He had met her many times in Breasley's shop, ten or twenty minutes before closing time each day.

Ostensibly she called in to see if Johnny had anything for the post as she was always on her way to the post office with an armful of business mail. They were clearly very good friends. As Thomas also dropped in on Breasley at the end of the day if he was free, the three of them chatted together.

After a while Elaine changed her routine. She called a few minutes earlier, picked up the mail and went straight to the post office, then returned to the shop and conversed for longer, often well after closing time.

Breasley was never in a hurry to leave his shop. Having lived in it for many years until quite recently, it was still like home to him. Elaine was not in a hurry either; her father would be a long while in closing his store.

Elaine was open and friendly towards Thomas. She seemed to him to be a very genuine, benign person, but he was acutely aware that she was rich, educated and of a social class that he distrusted. But he had to admit to himself that he found her alluring.

Johnny had told him that she had studied at a school of art. 'I think it was called 'The Slade',' he had said, without realising the significance of that.

Thomas was greatly impressed and curious to know more. He had a great love of modern art and wanted to find out what sort of art Elaine created, but their conversations never quite swung in that direction.

After knowing Elaine on this extremely casual basis for several months, they had met by chance one evening in the cloakroom of a city theatre. Elaine had gone with a female friend to see Rattigan's "The Winslow Boy". On discovering that Thomas intended to travel home by train she had offered him a lift. She introduced him to her friend and they set off to find the car.

They all chatted about the production, although Thomas felt that he was intruding on their evening out and wished that he had caught the train. Sitting in the back of the car he felt completely out of the conversation, rather like being in a taxi-cab.

However, his isolation was short lived. Elaine's friend lived on the outskirts of the City and was shortly dropped off outside her home. Elaine invited him to join her in the front of the car where he soon began to relax.

They discussed the play at length. Thomas was familiar with it. He had not only seen it once before but he'd also read it a couple of times. It had made quite an impression on him. Elaine thought it an outstanding production, although it was her first encounter with Rattigan. Thomas agreed that it was, but not, it seemed to her, wholeheartedly.

'I'm not sure that it isn't rather dated now,' said Thomas. 'I wonder how well it resonated with a modern audience?'

'It's a modern play,' said Elaine. 'Its premier was in 1946 wasn't it, or thereabouts anyway? It's not yet a decade old. I know that it's set before the first war, but Rattigan clearly felt that the values he expresses are timeless. Or perhaps you don't think they are?'

There was a slight edge to Elaine's voice in this last sentence; a hint of suspicion.

'You mean the boy being wrongly accused and his father wanting to clear his name at any cost, even if it ruined the family financially? Right the wrong as it were?'

'Yes, exactly. Wouldn't you want to do the same?'

Thomas knew that he would give anything to be able to refute a false accusation. He wished he had not started this. He did not want Elaine to know his history.

'Yes, of course I would. I'm not quite sure what I am trying to say. It's just that when the world has twice been in turmoil in the last forty years I'm not sure which values prevail. I firmly endorse Rattigan's values. No-one should have to live under a cloud of suspicion. But I still question whether today's audience would understand why a man might jeopardise his health and wealth to clear the name of his fourteen year old son who's accused of stealing a five shilling postal order.'

'I think you've missed the point Tom, if you don't mind my saying so. Not only would the boy's future have been blighted by the accusation, at least according to the social conventions of the time, but also the honour of the family would be denigrated. They would have become social pariahs.'

Elaine was right. He had viewed the play only from his own perspective that he had thought was that of the boy Ronnie Winslow. But Ronnie was part of a family. The honour of the family mattered equally to all of them. He, Thomas, was no longer in that enviable position, was no longer part of a family. Worse still, he could never clear his name.

'You're quite right Elaine. It's an obvious point and I missed it completely. I'm too blinkered I suppose. Yes, it would be a wonderful feeling, to be able to clear your name. I wish it were always possible.'

'It means standing your ground, fighting for the truth, like Arthur Winslow.'

'If the truth is there to be found.' said Thomas, half to himself.

'How do you mean?' asked Elaine.

'I'll try to explain what I mean some other time,' he said. 'I'm not sure I could right now.'

Elaine tried to glance at him. He was sounding troubled. But in the darkness of the car she could discern nothing. She quickly changed the subject.

They talked now about art and literature. Elaine was pleasantly surprised to find Thomas was better educated and perhaps more talented that his humble occupation and storeroom lodgings had hitherto suggested. By the time they parted they were quite at ease with one another.

Elaine resumed her late-afternoon calls on John Breasley. Her demeanour was exactly as before; warm, considerate, light-hearted, no mention of the theatre or the lift home for Thomas. Nothing, it appeared, had changed.

Then, only days ago, Elaine had mentioned that her father needed help with display work at the store. It would probably mean working late into the evenings, but would last only for a month or so.

Thomas had said he would be interested although such work would be new to him. He would like to discuss it with her father to see if it might be within his capability. He was very much bemused when, a little later, Elaine had invited him to lunch with her parents at their home.

He knew Charles Langdon and his wife – he didn't know her name – by sight. They were well known throughout the town. He had met her father very briefly once when buying something from their store for his father's birthday. He recalled Charles' rich, cultured voice.

He felt that he cared for neither of Elaine's parents, but then checked himself, feeling that he should not pass judgement with so little knowledge. But he saw no reason to socialise with them when they simply needed a worker for a short while. Anyway, he had agreed to it and was now waiting like a lamb for the slaughter-man. He hoped it would be less of an ordeal that he expected.

Thomas bought a newspaper and climbed the steps to his room. He made himself a drink and sat down to read. The room was no more comfortable than when he had first taken it. He'd at last shaded the light bulb and had built himself a wardrobe from some reclaimed planks, so his few clothes were no longer on show. His books, still in boxes, stood on the floor. Not that it mattered, no one came.

One end of the room now housed a workbench with a plane and a few chisels lying on top of it. He'd put a large shelf along one wall where a few tins of paint and some brushes stood. The hooks, on which he had previously hung his clothes, now held a couple of saws. If anything it was even less like a home than when he'd first acquired it. But he liked it. Liked the peacefulness of it. Especially on a Sunday morning.

He stood up and walked over to the window, from where he had a good view over the whole of the market square. He began to muse idly on the human traffic that now was beginning to stir and move across the centre of the town. Some people, casually attired, were simply out to buy scandalous, fabricated news, along with some tobacco, and would then no doubt spend the rest of the day at home. To them the purpose of the Sabbath was to take a well-earned rest from work.

Others, more smartly dressed, were doubtless making their way to some church or other. There were plenty to choose from. The Anglicans held their position in the centre of town. The redoubts of the Catholics and the Methodists were only a little further out. The more esoteric faiths, Christadelphians, Pentecostalists, Baptists and others, had their refuges scattered around the back streets of the town, some of them very poorly situated. Each group was upholding a belief and being upheld by it.

Thomas was almost envious of their certainty. Life must be easier for believers, he felt, unless one could live comfortably in the absence of faith, something that he struggled to do.

He imagined them travelling to their spiritual destinations in boats of various kinds, certainty afloat on an uncertain sea. He envisaged the mainstream faiths settled comfortably in luxury liners; smaller congregations in sturdy trawlers or tugs. A tiny few paddled perhaps in flimsy skiffs or coracles and he wondered if they would complete whatever journey they had embarked upon. As for himself, spiritual derelict that he was, he didn't have even a splintered spar to cling to. He would have to stay afloat as best he could.

In one corner of the square, looking damp and bedraggled stood a small group of young men and women of similar age to himself. The women wore trousers. They gathered here every Sunday to sing anti-war songs, handing out pacifist leaflets to anyone who came near. Not many were accepted. The war had ended barely a decade ago. It had supposedly put an end to war, but the "cold war" was gaining in intensity and fear was again in the air. But pacifism seemed not to appeal to many.

Thomas glanced at the clock. He had half an hour to put on a suit and his one good shirt. He had little choice of attire, but it hardly mattered, as he had no idea as to what would be acceptable. He donned the only suit he possessed, a soft lovat thorn-proof of high quality, bought cheaply from a second-hand goods shop. It fitted him well. He hoped it wouldn't look too informal. Another glance at the time, then away to the Church to meet Elaine.

***

The service was almost over and the organ burst into a crescendo which startled Thomas and then enraptured him. The voices of maybe three hundred people massed in song had an uncanny power. Although he had rejected religion the sound still affected him, reminding him instantly of the Latin mass he knew so well.

The responses flooded back into his brain; he wanted to chant them:

Kyrie Eleison, Christe Eleison, the words of the petition in the early part of the mass.

The sacrament raised aloft by the priest, the habits of the nuns, like the wings of great black hawks, contrasting eerily with their white-wimpled throats and scrubbed white faces.

Intellectually he had rejected all of this, this obscene sacrificial ritual, yet it still held his emotions prisoner, especially when he heard church music or plainsong. Guilt, death, resurrection, hell-fire, all these gripped him like the primitive superstitions of a pagan savage.

The organ stilled. The voices fell silent, at least to the listeners outside of the church, although Thomas knew that the last psalms were still being recited.

There was not so much difference he felt between the High Anglican service and the Mass that he was familiar with.

He moved now towards the main door in anticipation of meeting Elaine as she left the church. The great age-blackened oak doors opened and the congregation poured out onto the pavement and the street itself. Men in dark suits lifted trilbies to their heads. Ladies in swagger coats and decorous hats swirled and pirouetted on high-heeled shoes, exchanging greetings with acquaintances amongst the congregation.

They seemed to Thomas as if they were partners in some strange dance. He stood too far away to be able to hear what they were saying. The women moved around their men, fully six feet away from them, leaning backwards slightly on their heels, holding hats against the stiff May breeze as they smiled, nodded, spoke and then focussed on the next face to come into view.

The men, by contrast seemed almost rooted to the spot, anchors to their prancing wives, their faces cracking for a moment into guarded, formal smiles, accompanied by a brief tug to the front of their hats by way of acknowledging a lady's greeting. Then resuming their strict composure until the next response was required. They rationed their smiles like tiny glasses of an expensive liqueur, as if they were afraid of running out of them.

Elaine suddenly appeared from the midst of the crowd. She saw

Thomas immediately and waved and smiled, then glanced away again, clearly unable to quickly disentangle herself from the people around her. A few moments later she began to walk towards him, still turning around to speak to other friends and acquaintances.

He did not move towards her, afraid even to be introduced to anyone she knew. He supposed them to be out of his class. Elaine reached him in a few steps, the heels of her shoes rapping the pavement with a hard, staccato certitude.

'Good morning Thomas,' she smiled. A broad, genuine 'pleased to see you' smile. 'And how are you today?'

'I'm very pleased to see you,' he replied truthfully, but not too confidently, for he was still unsure how to reply to her spontaneous, assured questions and apprehensive as to how the day might develop.

'You're still joining us for lunch today I hope?'

'Of course, thank you very much.'

'Good. I'm so pleased. Daddy's car is parked on West Parade. He'll be with us in a minute. He's just talking to his accountant. Mummy is with him.'

Thomas hoped that his dismay did not show on his face.

'Oh, I thought you'd be alone. You said you would pick me up and I thought...'

'No, silly. We always attend church as a family. Mrs Buck has popped in to prepare lunch – we don't usually ask her to work at the weekend – and we'll help ourselves to it when we arrive home.'

He knew that the inevitable meeting with Elaine's parents was about to occur, only a little earlier than he had expected, but he would have liked to have had a few minutes alone with her before that.

He had to admit to himself that this imminent meeting was now troubling him a great deal. His nerves were distinctly on edge. He had heard that Charles Langdon carried great influence in the town, although he didn't know how that was. Langdon was said to be very wealthy and Thomas assumed that he would have little time for the likes of him, that he would scent his poverty as the gundog scents the cowering game and exposes it to the shooters. Why, he asked himself, had he put himself in this position? Especially as he disliked this class of people as much, he assumed, as they despised his.

Thomas had wished for a while that someone so lovely as Elaine did not belong to the monied class. But that was, in a way that he had not yet contemplated, part of the allure.

Her people did not live in the hugger-mugger fashion of his people. They did not have to conceal things from neighbours, whisper in their rooms or search for space for private moments. They did not have to endure the deprivation, the incarceration of the spirit, which living in cramped hovels inevitably brings. They had space and freedom, as well as security. Thomas, unconsciously, wished to know the background, the history of this beautiful woman.

He had known girls who were good looking. But Elaine had much more than looks. She had charm and poise. She was well educated and talented. Her varied perfumes always bewitched him. Her laughing eyes and sensual lips enthralled him. The jewellery she wore, so subtle and understated, fascinated him. Just to talk to her put him on a different plane. She was a prize indeed. And to think she had time for the likes of him…

'Hello Thomas, good morning, how do you do?'

He looked up, startled out of his momentary reverie. He accepted the proffered hand before he realised what was happening.

'Sorry to keep you waiting,' continued Charles Langdon. 'Had to have a quick word with my accountant. He was out of town all last week when I needed to see him. This is Delia my wife.'

'How nice to meet you, Thomas.'

Delia's voice had the same easy confidence but not the same warmth. Thomas was surprised to find himself making that observation. He had assumed that anyone so well-to-do as Charles Langdon would also be a cold, abrupt sort of person. The contrast between him and his wife was immediately noticeable.

'Good morning, Mr and Mrs Langdon,' he replied, trying to keep his voice as steady as theirs. 'I'm very pleased to meet you.'

'Come along to the car. It's just around the corner on West Parade.'

With that, Charles Langdon and his wife linked arms and proceeded at a brisk pace in that direction. Thomas and Elaine followed a couple of paces behind with Charles half turning his head and throwing the odd sentence of conversation back at them.

Thomas could easily discern the origins of Elaine's looks. Her mother was still a handsome woman. Her red hair was fading a little now, in contrast to Elaine's, and she was beginning to thicken in the waist, but she would still, very easily, catch a man's eye. Charles was distinguished in every way; tall and with a fine physique, he had a thick head of dark-brown hair and a powerful yet not domineering personality. He was clearly a man who was sure of himself.

The car was a Rover. Black and dignified, solid and powerful. He was surprised; it was the same car in which Elaine had brought him home after their chance meeting at the theatre. He had assumed then that it was her own. Despite the obvious quality of the car, he had expected her father to drive something more expensive. A Jaguar, perhaps, or even an

Armstrong Siddeley.

Delia Langdon and Elaine entered the rear seats leaving Thomas to join Charles in the front of the car. The engine purred into life and pulled smoothly away. He sank into the leather seats, remarking to himself that it was the best car he had ever been in. Not that he had been in many cars. A bicycle was his usual mode of transport for journeys beyond walking distance.

The car turned a few corners, then left the town via a wide road with tall lime trees on either side, their leafy canopy combining with the strengthening sunshine to throw dancing shadows on the car and its occupants.

It began to climb the only large hill that led out of the town, the engine never faltering, simply becoming more potent as Charles Langdon dropped down through the gears. They travelled north for a couple of miles, then west for another mile. Then Charles slowed right down and turned left off the road onto a private lane leading to his residence. This road was only slightly wider than the car but perfectly straight and well maintained for its half-mile length. It was bounded on both sides by lines of poplar trees, the fields behind them being laid to pasture. One field was empty, that on the other side of the lane held a small herd of Friesian dairy cattle and a lone red bullock. Thomas wondered if this one was to be butchered for the farmer himself.

The Langdon residence now stood directly in front of them. Built of red brick with quoins of golden stone, and widely overhanging eaves, it stood imposingly on an acre of lawn, a substantial, muscular house, but in no way ostentatious. It asserted itself over the landscape below, which was dotted here and there with decent but lesser dwellings.

The lane now split into two. Composed from now on of golden gravel it swept in symmetrical curves around the house. The outside of the curves were bounded by box hedges, the insides by wallflower beds and then roses. Clearly a full-time gardener was employed here.

The car crunched along the gravel, stopping at a point where a flagged footpath led from the drive to the front door. As they got out of the car the door swung widely open. Mrs Buck, a smiling motherly figure, stood there, welcoming them inside.

After a few words with Delia Langdon, no doubt about the state of the lunch, she was gone, away, Thomas presumed, to serve some scratch meal to her own family. For a moment he wondered where she might have to walk to, there being no dwellings in the vicinity. Then he remembered seeing a lone cottage soon after leaving the main road. Charles had said something to Delia about Mrs Buck's garden looking nice.

There was an air of unhurried calm in the Langdon residence. Coats were removed and put away at a leisurely pace. They all moved smoothly into the spacious, wood-panelled lounge where an agreeable pale sherry was served by Charles Langdon with a minimum of fuss. Mrs Buck had no doubt set the table. Lunch was obviously in the oven and tempting aromas emanated from the kitchen.

Thomas sank deeply into the armchair that Charles had decided for him. The sherries were consumed amid snatches of trivial conversation about the church service, the weather, about the state of the garden, resplendent in the distance beyond the enormous lawn.

Whilst Mrs Langdon and Elaine were attending to the few remaining details regarding the lunch, Charles invited Thomas to join him in inspecting the garden. They stepped down from the French windows onto a large paved rectangle enclosed by a low wall. Seats and a sun canopy occupied part of it, along with several huge urns containing exotic looking plants.

A gravelled footpath led them through the middle of the close-clipped lawn towards its southern edge that was bounded by a beech hedge.

They walked slowly as Charles pointed out his favourite shrubs and trees to Thomas, who expressed a genuine interest but admitted readily to having little knowledge of horticulture. When they reached the boundary hedge, which was only chest high, he was intrigued by the view he found before him. He had briefly forgotten that they were on top of an escarpment. He now saw that they had turned almost full circle since leaving the town. After climbing steeply out of the river valley in which the town lay, the rest of the drive had been on the plateau that overlooked the valley, but trees and a few intervening acres had obscured the point where the land fell away.

He had never seen the town from this perspective. Starting almost from his feet there extended many acres of green corn shimmering on the gentle slope in the stiff breeze.

Beyond that, as the ground began to fall away more sharply, he could see pasturage which soon became the scrubby grassland approaching the railway lines. A smoking goods train moving slowly out of the station picked out the direction of the track for him.

Across the lines the river, from this distance and in good light, was the colour of lead. It coiled itself like a huge serpent around the town, delineating the scar of the gypsy encampment in relation to it. This area Thomas knew like the back of his hand. He could just make out a row of houses, one of which had been his home. Their straight narrow line pointed at him like a dagger to his heart. Sunlight winked at him mockingly, reflecting off the windows of some of the gypsy vans that stood on either side of the row. The house that faced him, although too far away to be distinguishable from the others, now sheltered a sick and reclusive woman, his mother, looked after by a loving, caring daughter.

Despite its squalid setting and its constant subjection to the sulphurous grime of the trains, it had once been the best in the row. Its doors and curtained windows were well painted. It was clean inside and the stone flags outside were swept daily and washed clean of the ordure of the marauding curs.

Yet Thomas could now feel only a huge sense of inadequacy because this area had once been his home. Elaine did not yet know of this. She knew of his room in the town, although she had not seen it. But that was somehow less demeaning. Lots of single people lived in rooms. It could be seen as just a temporary existence before one rented a house, or even bought a house, not that he had contemplated doing either of those things.

But where your parents lived, that was your home too. Your origins, how you began in this life often said much about how you might leave it. Thomas did not want Elaine to know more about his family than she did already. He was becoming acutely aware that he had drifted into something that was going to become very awkward at least, certainly embarrassing and perhaps even painful.

His mind was brought back to more immediate matters by Delia Langdon announcing from the French windows that lunch was being served. Charles and Thomas re-entered the house and went to the table.

Delia was already serving slices of beef onto plates and passing them out in a brisk and efficient manner. Tureens of steaming vegetables occupied the centre of the large mahogany table. Thomas sat shyly with his hands by his sides, not eager to help himself before anyone else. Elaine came to his aid, taking his plate and spooning ample portions of vegetables onto it. Soon they were all served and Charles was opening a bottle of claret, murmuring the faintest criticism of Mrs Buck for failing to decant it earlier as he had asked.

Lunch was a more pleasant affair than he had anticipated. There were no long awkward silences, but more importantly, no probing questions. Charles talked about various items of current news and just a little about his business until Delia asked him not to talk shop.

She fixed Thomas with her critical gaze several times and appeared about to frame a question to which he felt he might not have a suitable answer, but each time Elaine, as if sensing his unease, side-tracked her mother and managed to change the subject completely, bubbling along from one thing to the next, seemingly without effort.

He was now becoming slightly alarmed at the thought of spending the rest of the afternoon in close conversation with the Langdons, which they would surely turn into an interrogation. He would have much preferred the sole company of Elaine, but he had to accept the fact that she was part of a family, and that the family were part of a social class far removed from his own. If he was to retain his friendship with Elaine, and perhaps it would be better if he didn't, then somehow he must also relate to her parents. Perhaps it would be better to attenuate the friendship?

Just as his mind was forming an excuse for an early departure Charles Langdon unwittingly created an avenue of respite.

'Glad the weather has brightened up,' he said. 'We had planned an afternoon out in the country. Last night I thought we would have to forget the idea, but one couldn't wish for a better afternoon than this. At least not in May.'

The thought of a drive out seemed a lot less threatening to Thomas than an afternoon spent at the Langdon home. It seemed more like neutral ground, and there would be more diversions he hoped, more to deflect Delia's steely gaze away from him.

'Pity about last night's rain,' continued Charles. 'It would have been dry under foot but for that. You could do with some stouter footwear Thomas.'

He felt even more inadequate, as if he was about to be perceived as an encumbrance to the party.

'Edward has got some heavy walking shoes you could borrow. He forgot to take them back to university with him. Would a size eight fit you by any chance?'

Thomas said it probably would and thanked Charles for the offer. He declined to say that he really needed a half a size larger. If Charles Langdon would so readily proffer the loan of his son's shoes it seemed churlish to quibble about a half size. He just hoped they would be well stretched and a generous fit.

'Good. That's that then. I'll throw them in the car.'

Thomas liked the matter-of-fact manner in which the offer had been made. Brisk, no nonsense, and certainly not intended to make him feel that a favour had been done for him.

'Excuse me now whilst I go and look for them.'

Charles departed from the room leaving Thomas alone with Elaine. He hadn't noticed Delia slip away, but clearly she must have gone out of the room several minutes ago, as when she reappeared she was wearing a casual tweed suit. She then engaged him in light conversation whilst Elaine went off to change.

Both she and her father re-appeared almost simultaneously a few minutes later, Charles now wearing an old but well-made sports jacket and twill trousers, a cravat and a pair of stout brogues. In his hand he held another pair, those belonging to his son. Elaine was dressed in a long, loose-fitting tweed skirt, a cardigan and similarly practical shoes.

The smoothness with which this operation had been carried out amazed him. He had not been left alone for one moment. One person's conversation had been picked up and carried over by another. All three had changed their garments effortlessly, as if they had rehearsed this scene many times before. Obviously they had well-ordered wardrobes and probably left their clothes around for someone else to put away. Within moments, it seemed, they were all outside, crunching across the gravel drive to the car.

The preparation for the drive in the country seemed to Thomas more appropriate for a safari. As a young child he had been on a sort of picnic a couple of times, mounted on a seat fixed to the crossbar of his father's ancient bicycle. Their sustenance then a flask of tea and a few sandwiches in the saddlebag. That seemed frugal indeed compared with what was now being loaded into the car.

Four folding canvas chairs went into the capacious boot, followed by an expensive looking wickerwork hamper large enough to hold the entire contents of his mother's larder. Clearly the hamper had been packed earlier in the day despite the dubious state of the weather at that time. A fine linen tablecloth and matching napkins plus some substantial woollen rugs completed the load. The whole operation took only minutes to complete. Then the expedition set off.

The car purred back down the drive, joined the road and turned away from the town. They travelled through several small villages, all of which Thomas had been through at least once before as a questing schoolboy on his bicycle.

Soon after leaving the last, Brampton Woods came into view, a large, dense plantation of conifers and deciduous trees. Charles turned off the main road heading for the heart of the woodland. This lane was heavily shaded, trees on either side almost meeting overhead. The gloom was punctuated every few hundred yards by bright flashes of sunshine where wagon-ways joined the lane from the west.

Recognising one of these that was much broader than the rest, Charles turned into it. Finding bottom gear he crept along its un-metalled surface for a quarter of a mile before stopping and switching off the engine. Everyone alighted. Charles hauled the heavy hamper from the car, asked Thomas to take one end by the leather grip and made off through the trees for another fifty yards. Elaine and her mother had pulled the rest of the paraphernalia from the boot and were trooping along behind.

He now saw before them an ever-widening field of green corn and realised at once why Charles had chosen this particular place for a picnic. The dark woods behind might have seemed claustrophobic, dispiriting even, and certainly cool so early in the year.

But here the open country in front of them was brilliantly sunny, uplifting, the shimmering sea of green promised a bountiful harvest. The trees on either side of them were alive with bird-song.

Charles proceeded briskly and efficiently to set up camp. A large and heavy rug placed on the thin grass was surrounded on three sides by the folding chairs leaving the outward vista clear. The linen cloth occupied the centre of the rug with cutlery and napkins appropriately spaced. The breeze hackled the edges of the rich cream linen but Delia had anticipated this. She produced an ornately embossed silver cylinder from which she withdrew several bodkins and proceeded to secure the tablecloth to the much heavier burgundy coloured plaid underneath. Clearly outings such as these had been made many times before. The matching napkins were secured by the weight of substantial cutlery.

When these small tasks were completed to Delia's satisfaction, Charles proposed that they all take a stroll. Thomas was mystified. They had just set out a canteen of expensive cutlery, glassware and crockery, not to mention the food in the hamper, which he supposed was of equally high quality, and were about to leave it all unattended in this secluded glade.

Charles must have apprehended the thought behind his bemused expression.

'This part of the wood is private,' he explained. 'It belongs to a very good friend of mine, Henry Draycott. He farms the land you see out in front of you and hundreds of acres round and about. Used to shoot over this land with him. Still join him occasionally when he has a get-together, although my sight is not what it used to be. He's got farms in Africa as well as this one. In fact, he's over there at the moment. Might see his son around though. He sometimes takes a stroll through these woods on a Sunday with the dog. About the only day of the week he gets any time to himself.'

Leaving the unattended picnic now made more sense to Thomas. These people were incredibly secure in themselves. They effectively assisted each other in policing their properties. If the landowner's son should happen upon their belongings in their absence he would at once recognise the distant car and know that all was well in his part of the plantation. Similarly, if Langdon should see anyone else walking in the wood, he would know at once, from their looks, their garments, their bearing, whether or not they were trespassing, and act accordingly. He knew that things would be just as they were when they all returned to base.

They began their walk parallel to the field and followed it for a while around the perimeter of the woods. Then they turned more deeply into the trees, always following the broad pathways known as "rides". Although these were wide enough to permit the four of them to walk abreast, Thomas noticed that Elaine and her mother had slipped away to the rear, leaving him to talk with her father. He felt that she would not have left him so readily with her mother.

Thomas did not feel so uneasy with Charles, although he realised from the line of conversation that he was trying to get the measure of him as it were.

'Elaine tells me you were at college once. Did it not work out for you?'

Thomas wanted to tell the truth without being overly explicit.

'No, it didn't. It was a bit of a disaster really. I made the mistake of going straight from a catholic school to a seminary, without giving it very much thought. Then, in mid-stream, I began to feel that I was swimming against the current as it were. You know, beginning to question the doctrine and unsettling both myself and those around me. The tutors began to lose patience with me and I with them. In the end I opted out, not quite knowing what I wanted to do. Now I couldn't easily get back into academic life even if I wanted to, and I certainly can't afford to re-train for anything else. I appear to have backed myself into a corner I suppose. I don't dislike what I am doing at the moment, but I can't see what the future might hold.'

Thomas' honest self-appraisal completely surprised Charles, who had expected a more defensive answer to his leading question. Never one who would seek to put a man down without sound reason, he gave him the chance to bolster his image.

'But you get by all right, don't you? I mean, you do artwork and that sort of thing, Elaine tells me. You're self-supporting are you not?'

'I am. Well, I get by, just about, if that's what you mean. But I'm not an artist.' Thomas knew that he needed to blur the lines a bit here.

'There's a certain irony to this. I was – briefly – training to teach, and I might have taught art and craft, but I could never have made a proper living at it outside of teaching. I haven't the smallest fraction of the artistic skill or the creative imagination of Elaine. Her pictures make mine seem very inadequate, and I've seen a photograph of some sculpture that she's done which I would give anything to be able to emulate. No. The best that I can do is to make an attractive shop sign with a scene to complement the lettering, or maybe create an attractive window display. But that is not art, nor will it ever earn me more than a pittance. But it's the best that I can do and all I can see myself doing for the foreseeable future.'

'Still, better than some occupations,' mumbled Charles, unable to think of any.

His generous spirit was trying to surmount his growing unease. Whilst he was amazed at this young man's frankness and, in a way, admired it, he could not see why they were entertaining him – admittedly at their daughter's request. He clearly did not fit in with their scheme of things. And he was also, it appeared, something of a misfit even among his own kind.

The stroll continued, with the conversation between them rapidly diminishing. Elaine, in the rear, must have sensed the awkwardness between them, for she hurried her mother to catch them up, and then went ahead to Thomas, leaving her father to drop back and join his wife.

He felt a sense of relief sweep over him. Elaine, in her usual easy manner chatted on about plants, birds and the surroundings generally, and so the four of them slowly wound back to the picnic place they had left an hour ago.

As they walked up the ride towards their chosen spot they were suddenly aware of a raucous commotion in the trees above. A barn owl was flitting from tree to tree, desperately trying to evade attack from a mob of smaller birds. Jays, blackbirds and thrushes scolded him incessantly, flying within inches of his head. The poor bird seemed bewildered, quite unable to cope with this abuse and intimidation, and fluttered around helplessly.

Thomas was surprised to see the owl in the wood, and in broad daylight. He realised that it must have a home further away, over the cornfield, and for some reason had strayed into foreign territory. He scooped handfuls of fir cones from the forest floor and flung them at the mob, but his actions frightened the owl as much as the other birds and all flew further into the wood, their shrill cries unabated.

'There's the cause of the problem,' said Charles, pointing out over the cornfield.

In the distance on the far side of the field was a crumbling red brick barn, its pan-tiled roof overhung by a huge elm. An overgrown blackthorn hedge interspersed with ancient dead trees almost hid it from view. Along the line of the hedge, where presumably lay a cart track to the barn, two small boys could be seen hastening away in the direction of the next village.

'Little villains,' said Charles, 'they disturbed him from his perch in that barn, or the adjacent elm and he flew across to here for safety. Unfortunately for him he was out of his element. An owl in the woods in broad daylight is bound to be set upon. Not to worry. He will probably eventually make his way back to where he belongs, relatively unscathed.'

'I hope so,' said Thomas. 'They're such dignified birds. It was unseemly to subject him to such an ordeal. Especially by the jays. They're such coarse birds despite their fine feathers.'

'Everything in its place,' muttered Charles, more concerned now with opening a large thermos containing the tea, peace and quiet having returned to the woods.

Delia dispensed the delicate salmon and cucumber sandwiches from one metal container set inside a larger one. The space between contained ice. Thomas was again surprised at such attention to luxurious detail. They all settled into the canvas chairs to eat.

He had no appetite and wondered how the others could eat so well after the recent lunch. The conversation dwindled almost to nothing, not that the Langdon's had necessarily run out of things to say or questions to ask. He was glad of the respite.

After they had eaten Elaine produced a sketch pad and, setting her chair slightly apart from the others, began to draw an interestingly gnarled old oak tree set right on the boundary of wood and field. Waist-high rosebay, not yet in flower, surrounded its base. Directly behind it, but at a distance she'd reduced, the red-roofed barn from where the owl had flown gave depth to the scene.

Elaine was quite unselfconscious when Thomas walked across to look over her shoulder. She rightly sensed that he needed to move away from her parents. For a while they were both absorbed in her art, exchanging sentences quietly and naturally, almost as if they were alone in the wood. Charles and Delia seemed glad to leave them to themselves.

Their reverie was disturbed by the barking of a dog. They looked up to see a robust man in his early thirties, clad in remarkably well-tailored tweeds, a shotgun resting comfortably in the crook of his arm, a gundog at his heels.

Thomas knew nothing of guns. He disliked their sudden power. In a moment they could effect the most powerful transformation of all, that of life to death. They refuted compromise unless met by replicas of themselves.

Yet the artistry that had gone into the gun's creation could not escape his eye. The damascene steel of the barrels was in itself a work of art, shimmering like Chinese silk. The barrel ends above the lock were ornately chased, as were the metal plates that married the lock to the stock. Thomas could not quite make out the lettering on the elaborate scroll, then decided from the letters he could discern that the word must be Holland. He presumed, naively, that that was where it had been made. The burnished walnut stock had a compelling beauty of its own. He wondered why such loving care had been invested in a machine designed to kill. He felt almost guilty that such an object should be so aesthetically pleasing to his eye.

The man greeted the party jovially, being particularly courteous to Elaine, who suddenly seemed ill at ease. She looked embarrassed and was clearly trying to avoid his gaze and made great play of throwing the red-gold mass of her hair, teased by the wind, out of her eyes, as if that were the reason she could not meet his look.

'Oh, this is Thomas, Elaine's friend,' said Charles. 'Thomas, this is Gerald Draycott.'

Thomas had rightly surmised that this must be the son of Henry Draycott, upon whose land they were standing.

For a long moment there was complete silence. The wood stilled. No sound of birdsong, or insects. Even the breeze momentarily ceased as if frozen by the piercing stare. Thomas shuddered involuntarily.

Then Gerald spoke, but only his lips moved. His face said nothing. 'How do you do?'

It was the most cold-blooded greeting that he had ever witnessed, let alone received. Gerald then dismissed him by turning his back and launching into conversation with Charles, who seemed delighted to see him.

'How very nice to see you Gerald. Not taking game on a Sunday are you?'

This latter said with a beaming smile and in a warm, jocular voice. Few men could rib Gerald Draycott in that way, but Charles had known him since he was a boy and his friendship with Gerald's father was profound and long- established. Gerald took it in the spirit that was intended.

'No Charles, not at all. Truthfully! I've just seen the vixen I'm after and remembered I'd still got the gun in the shooting-break from yesterday's meet.'

'So, the rufus fox doth run no more, eh, Gerald?'

'Oh yes she does,' answered Gerald. 'She's avoided me once again. I've been after her for two years now without success. She keeps on eluding me. I had a bead on her, but the dog got in the way. He gave chase but she soon lost him. I'll prick her pelt one day though, you see if I don't. She's become a challenge.'

'I'm sure you will Gerald,' said Charles. 'I'm sure you will.'

The dog sniffed Edward's shoes then Thomas' knees, gave a disgruntled 'huff' and turned its attention to the picnic hamper, devouring crumbs of cake and sandwiches.

Charles and Gerald discussed farming, Gerald's father and his African interests, and various other topics. It was obvious that they had not seen each other for a while. Delia Langdon joined in animatedly and intelligently, but clearly lacking her husband's knowledge.

Charles was extremely well informed about current farming techniques, considering that he had made his fortune from retailing. It was in his interests to be knowledgeable as many of his customers were wealthy farmers and it made good business sense to be able to relate to them on their own terms. To know how the vagaries of the weather might affect the value of their harvests or the price of seed or stock was useful, as there might be a need to extend their credit now and then. Charles always believed in knowing your man's current worth. But he also had a genuine interest and his fundamental knowledge had been gained from his late father who had owned a substantial farm over in the next county. And he kept himself acquainted with recent innovations.

As the afternoon began to cool, the rugs and utensils were packed away and carried back to the car. Gerald Draycott lent a hand before bidding farewell. His curt goodbye to Thomas was cuttingly offhand.

Thomas was not sure what his next move should be. He had simply been invited to lunch. He had been given both lunch and tea and now felt that the Langdons senior had seen quite enough of him and he of them. He would be very glad to make his exit from their company.

Charles and Delia were thinking exactly the same thing. As they set off on the return journey through the villages Thomas realised that they were taking a slightly different route, a shorter route that must inevitably bring them nearer to town than to the Langdon residence. He therefore asked to be dropped off at a particular junction that he knew would not be far out of their way and would leave him no more than a mile or so to walk.

'Are you sure?' asked Charles. 'Quite happy to drop you in the centre of town you know.'

'No, that will be fine thank you.' replied Thomas, wishing to be away from them as soon as possible.

The appointed place was soon reached, and he alighted. He thanked them for their hospitality and said how nice it had been to meet them. He knew he was being disingenuous.

Charles muttered something like, 'glad to have had your company, Thomas.' Delia just said, 'goodbye.'

The car glided away with Elaine waving and smiling from the window.

***

Later that evening Delia Langdon brought supper time drinks into the lounge where Charles was glancing at the newspaper. Elaine was still in her studio.

'A strange cove, don't you think?' mused Charles.

'Who? Thomas?' asked Delia. 'I didn't care for him.'

'Can't say I disliked him,' said Charles, 'but he's got nothing going for him. Feckless probably. No pedigree, at least not one he wanted to talk about. Seems unconcerned about his obvious lack of direction. I get the impression he says and does pretty much whatever he wants without regard for the consequences. But he was neither self-effacing nor in any way conceited. Prepared to say that he might have made mistakes but without any inclination to make apologies for doing so.'

'He'll never amount to much,' said Delia. 'I'm still utterly bewildered as to why Elaine brought him home. She's highly perceptive and can assess anyone in a couple of hours. I simply do not know what she is doing with him.'

'I'm not sure she's doing anything with him, or wants to. As to her bringing him home, that's possibly my fault. She's talked about him so much, ever since he moved into Johnny Breasley's shop, that I said I must meet him. I was intrigued to know why she found him so interesting. I also was a bit concerned for John, in case he'd lumbered himself with someone he couldn't easily get rid of if he wanted to. So you can blame me for that, although I did not suggest she should bring him home. I had intended to drop in on John and meet him there, in a casual sort of way.'

'Well, she pre-empted you there. Anyway, it is done and over with now.'

'I hope so Delia. Elaine does behave oddly sometimes. Remember those two boys she brought home from art school? As far as we could tell she was doing nothing in particular with either of them. The fact that there were two of them confirms that. They were pleasant young chaps from good backgrounds; probably with decent futures once they've matured a bit. But afterwards she never mentioned them again. They were just casual friends it seemed. That's how she is. Gets on with most people in an easy-going manner, without ever getting involved. Not a bad trait really.'

'I suppose not,' said Delia. 'She's never disgraced herself – never given us concern for anything really.'

'No,' said Charles. She is a delight. So lovely to have her around us all the time now she's finished at The Slade. I thought today though she might have paid Gerald Draycott a bit more attention. After all, he's taken her out quite a few times.'

'She was supportive of him when he was feeling low over that incident with the poacher,' said Delia.

'I should think so,' replied Charles. 'Any man has a right to defend himself on his own land – or his father's land at least – without it causing so much fuss.'

'Yes. Why she cooled towards him afterwards I don't know. You can see he's still very fond of her. Did you see the way he cut Thomas?'

'Yes,' said Charles. 'I almost felt sorry for the lad. Gerald doesn't hide his feelings, does he? He hasn't got his father's forbearance. Old Henry will tolerate almost anyone. He has the patience of a saint; one of the most compassionate men I've met. Gerald hasn't inherited that side of his father's nature.'

'Perhaps not, but he's going places. The world will prove to be his oyster. You wait and see. Elaine ought to take him more seriously. She'll never meet another like him.'

'I agree entirely my dear,' said Charles.

'I hope she might come into the business eventually,' continued Charles. 'I know her artwork is good. So many discerning people have said so. But it's no way to make a living. It takes a lifetime to become established, and then only if you are lucky.'

'It would be a good thing if she did come fully into the business,' said Delia, 'because Edward won't.'

'Don't you think so?' asked Charles, looking crestfallen.

'You know he won't,' replied Delia.

'I know it was always your hope that he would. And I agree that that would have been an ideal situation. You and he get on so well together. He could have worked with you superbly well and eventually taken over the business when you retire. But he won't. He'll qualify as a G.P. and – I've not told you this before and I know I should have – he'll work abroad.'

'Why do you say that?' asked Charles, dismay written all over his face.

'Because Elaine let slip something to that effect. You know how close they are. Edward has told her that when he qualifies he'll work abroad. He's talked a lot with Gerald Draycott. As you know, Gerald has spent a lot of time on Henry's farms in Kenya and that's fired Edward's imagination with thoughts of living abroad. Not in Africa. Apparently he's uneasy about the impending problems, given the present trouble out there, but I believe Australia appeals. I'm sorry to tell you this Charles. That's why I've held it back. I know you are so fond of him. And so am I. I would be deeply upset if he went to live in Australia – or for that matter, anywhere outside of Britain. But I believe that is something we must contemplate. So it would be nice if Elaine stays around. And even better if she would enter into the business someday. And staying on the subject of our business, let's get back to the purported reason of Elaine's for her introducing Thomas Clancy to us. She is as acutely aware as we are, that since Harry Bentley has become ill and will be off work for months – indeed it's looking doubtful if he'll ever return – we are in a fix over the window displays. Although Elaine is disparaging about Harry's dull and old-fashioned arrangements, Helen can never hope to take over. She is simply not good enough. She's just not creative. She has been an excellent assistant to Harry and can manage some of the smaller inside displays, but she could not cope with a big window on her own. If we found her an assistant it might put the wrong idea in her head regarding her own limited abilities.'

'I know,' said Charles. 'Harry's been excellent. We've had him with us for over twenty years you know. It'll be a bad job for him and his family if he doesn't make a full recovery from this stroke. I've already spoken to Ian Bradshaw, – you know, the new accountant at Hall & Co, - to set up a fund to help Harry out for the next few months. He's looking into it.'

'Yes, well, about a replacement for him. Elaine could do it, but she's told me she wouldn't want to for any length of time. So she's suggested using Clancy on a freelance basis. She admits that he doesn't know the trade, but says he's immensely creative, has a lot of artistic ability. Apparently he can make absolutely anything with his hands.'

'I take it she's already discussed this with Clancy?' said Charles. 'She's not spoken to me about it.'

'She has apparently, and he feels he'd like to try.'

'Then why the devil has she gone about it this way? Inviting him for lunch. I could have just interviewed him at the store and said yes or no. Damn it all, how can you have employees for lunch. It queers the whole working relationship. Harry's been with us for nearly a quarter of a century and I've not seen him once outside of the store. No need to.'

'Well Clancy won't be an employee exactly. He'll work for a few weeks, we'll pay him, and that's it until the next time. I fully agree with you though. There was no need to meet him socially. And he's not at all our type. I think we all felt uneasy today, except for Elaine of course. She's at ease with almost anyone. I suppose she just wanted you to see him in the round. Perhaps to judge if he would fit in, as it were, should we need a permanent replacement for Harry.'

'Damn funny way of going about it if you ask me,' said Charles. 'But I'll say one thing for Clancy. He's honest. He's been unbelievably frank about himself to me today. And I've heard good reports about him from other tradespeople in the town. He also holds on to his opinions, which is something I admire in a man, although I don't share his. Not that I'd describe him as opinionated.'

'How do you mean?' asked Delia, sensing a contradiction.

'Oh, I made the mistake of mentioning Suez. You know, the withdrawal of our troops from the canal zone.'

'What made you mention that?'

'Well, it is highly topical. And also, I presumed from his surname that he's of Irish extraction, although Elaine hadn't said so. I was just, well, interested in his feelings towards us, the English I mean. One cannot be too careful.'

'And what did you find out?'

'That his father was Irish. He's dead now, some sort of accident. Thomas was born over here. I had thought that I'd detected a hint of an Irish accent, but maybe not. His speech is very different from ours.'

'And Suez?'

'Oh, as I'd half-expected. He hadn't a single word to say in favour of the British position. Said we shouldn't have been there in the first place. Too much subjugation of the Arab world by Europeans. He also said, and I didn't know this, that we were in breach of the nineteen thirty-six treaty. According to that we were allowed to station only ten thousand men there and we've exceeded that by a factor of eight. He was quite condemnatory of it all actually, but he was surprisingly well-informed. I couldn't agree with him of course, but I thought it better to make nothing of it under the circumstances.'

'Well I'm not in favour of withdrawing any of our troops,' said Delia. 'With all the unrest in that area we could do with more. We'll lose access to the canal before much longer if we don't have enough soldiers there to protect our interests.'

'And that would affect our links with what little else we've got left in the world,' said Charles.

That remark focussed his mind back on Thomas.

'That seems to be part of Clancy's problem. He fails to appreciate the need to hold on to things, to not let go of what you have. He'll never acquire much of anything with that attitude.'

'He's a wastrel, that's my opinion,' said Delia. 'Good for nothing, or for very little anyway.'

'Oh, I don't know. I wouldn't say that about him. I certainly don't dislike him. He's improvident, without a doubt, but perhaps that's just the improvidence of youth.

'By Jove, though, he's an odd fish. Enigmatic to say the very least. He's a complete misfit in my opinion. He might get us out of this fix we're in but I wouldn't want him around for a moment longer than necessary. But I don't dislike him.'

'You wouldn't dear, you're too kind. But that's what endears you to me.'

'I hope that's not the only thing that attracts you to me,' said Charles, his previously troubled countenance now relaxing into a warm smile.

'You know it's not,' said Delia. 'You know I love you for all sorts of reasons.'

'Yes, I do know,' said Charles, 'and I'm very lucky. And I love you.'

***

Elaine told Thomas that her father would be glad if he'd do a large window display for him as soon as possible, it being early summer and the present display gave no indication of the changing season.

Thomas began work immediately and Helen was assigned to work with him. The night before he started he studied the working space, scrutinizing the number of mannequins that were currently in use and imagining alternatives to some of them.

When he began in the morning he had some clear ideas. His commission was to complete the first of three large menswear windows. Thomas asked Elaine if she had the means of procuring for him some musical instruments and some large colourful posters depicting travel. She had, of course. Several of her friends were musically inclined. Thomas himself had a large print of Renoir's boating party.

Within three days, a day longer than Harry would have taken, men's blazers, flannels, straw boaters and tennis apparel were gaily arranged. A slogan "Swing into Summer", supported by a large poster of a group of jazz musicians, saxophones, trombones and a cello were interposed amongst the mannequins, and cardboard crochets and quavers strung on a tape measure were stretched out on the back-drop.

Charles Langdon was appalled by such an avant-garde display. He asked himself how could he have been so foolish as to entrust his image as a well-respected retailer into the hands of this young man whom he himself had designated a misfit.

Elaine tried to sooth her father's shattered nerves and assured him that he would not go out of business.

'Just you wait and see Daddy,' she consoled him.

A couple of evenings later, when Charles dared to enter the portals of his club after closing the store, he was pleasantly surprised to find compliments regarding his outstanding display being showered upon him by fellow businessmen. He sank into a leather armchair with a large scotch in his hand, a huge smile of relief on his face. Elaine had been right after all.

Within a month all the window displays had been changed, very much for the better, and trade was improving. Delia Langdon had to grudgingly admit that trade was better than at the same time last year. Even household linens were selling better and she had to hurriedly re-order several items.

Thomas had seen a lot of Elaine during the month he'd been working in her father's store, but only for minutes at a time. She would look in on him every now and then, complimenting him on what he was doing, but also making suggestions. These he valued; her artist's eye sometimes saw things differently and he was grateful for her insight. Helen, the display assistant, knew where every prop and mannequin was stored, knew what sizes fitted a mannequin and how to press, pin, tack and pad every item to make it look its best. And she was becoming more creative herself. Thomas was grateful to her and knew that whilst his competence was improving quickly, he could not have managed without her at the outset.

He also noticed, despite his workload, how useful Elaine was to the store.

She had a wonderful way with the staff. She gave subtle compliments rather than praise. Criticism was gentle but direct and honest. She noticed every little thing; stock running too low, or if it was not moving quickly enough. She could rapidly decipher the cause of any problem and quickly rectify it. She would lend a hand in any department, including the financial office, where her skill with figures would soon discover any mistake the cashier had overlooked.

It was obvious that she was liked by everyone. Her light-hearted, yet assertive manner, her recognition of everyone's worth, gave all around her a sense of direction, security and self-pride.

Towards the end of each working day she took the mail to the post office and the cash taken that day to the bank's night vault. And without fail she called in on Johnny Breasley, puffing on his pipe as he swept the dusty floor of his rope shop.

John was known to most of the shopkeepers as 'Breezy', a lazy corruption of his name, but one that well reflected his brisk, no-nonsense personality. Elaine never used this nickname, or even 'Johnny'. It was always John. She treated him with the greatest of respect. She liked him immensely.

She would sit for a few minutes on a stool, or even on the floor of his shop window if there was space, and ask him how things were. She knew he was alone. A loner, but never lonely. But that could change at any time. He was ageing and the encroaching years make one's mortality ever more real, and one can suddenly feel, overnight almost, bereft and then frail. Elaine cared about things like this.

She would then return to the store, watch her father lock the doors, and walk with him to the car. Then home, unless he was first calling at his club, in which case she would drive and return for him later.

It soon became obvious to Thomas, and Breasley had been aware of this for a long time, that Elaine was not in her true element. She was an artist and was being stifled in her creative talents. The nearest she got to exercising those in the store was when she involved herself in display work, or in choosing new lines for her father to purchase.

The colour and texture of fabrics, whether clothing or furnishings, appealed to her. Glassware and porcelain, cutlery, even luggage, were chosen by her for their aesthetic appeal as well as for their functionality. Any little time she had for herself, it seemed to Thomas, must be spent on sketching or completing drawings. She needed to be able to do more of what she clearly excelled at, he thought.

She had shown him several landscapes she had roughed out, almost asking him for his opinion before she went any further. He questioned himself on this. Why would she require his opinions? She was the true artist. His ability and knowledge of the subject was mediocre; he was limited in what he could produce himself.

Other staff members noticed what Thomas failed to see – that Elaine was trying to find ways of spending a few moments with him whenever there was half an excuse to do so. She also treated him as an equal and never directed him but made only suggestions. She clearly valued his opinions as much as he did hers.

An easy-going spontaneity developed between them. Whereas once he would have carefully framed a question or statement, he now, without realising it, tended to combine both in off-the-cuff observations, followed by 'don't you think?' or 'would you agree?'

Elaine addressed him in the same way. Each was developing an easy confidence in how they related to the other.

Charles Langdon was acutely aware of this too, and slightly uneasy about it. He had little reason to speak to Thomas – he was doing what he was paying him for well enough, indeed, very well. But, that aside, his daughter seemed to be giving him an unnecessary amount of attention. Charles quite liked Thomas, but he'd have liked him a lot more if he was in business or had a profession, or, at the very least, a sense of direction towards a worthwhile goal.

Delia Langdon did not like Thomas. She too was well aware of the over-familiar way she thought he related to her daughter, and, much more to the point, the way Elaine related to him. But she found it difficult to tell a very mature and assertive young woman how she should conduct herself. Especially as without her both she and Charles would have a lot more work to do and she knew without a doubt that she herself lacked that special quality that made Elaine able to float effortlessly through the day with a great deal accomplished at the end of it.

However, for both Charles and Delia, things took a turn for the better. Harry Bentley began to make a good recovery from his illness and after several months absence he returned to the store. He would never regain his old vigour, but Helen had developed new skills. Through working with Thomas she had found new ways of creating displays and was now much more sure of herself. The tired Harry was glad to let her take more of a lead, and, to a certain degree, became something of an assistant to her. With no reason to employ him any longer Charles, and particularly Delia Langdon, were somewhat relieved.

At the conclusion of Thomas' work for him Charles paid him a little more than had been agreed at the outset. Charles was more than satisfied with what he had done for him and felt sure that the increase in sales derived from the much more modern displays.

From Thomas' point of view he had gained valuable experience and some knowledge as to how a large store functioned which he felt, should it become necessary, he could put to good use in the future. Now, back to his odd-jobbing way of earning a living, he found that more people than before were prepared to put work his way. It seemed that working for the most reputable store in town had brought him slightly better fortune.

Elaine missed not having Thomas around. His diffidence, which initially she found annoying, having mistaken it for aloofness, she now knew to be born of a genuine feeling of uncertainty. He was by no means unsociable, just not inclined to advance any opinion that might be ill-formed. He needed to think about things first. She found that he would discuss a subject in depth, providing it was, from the outset, truly a discussion rather than an overbearing statement of supposed fact.

This is what she liked about him. She had known several men like this at art school and had enjoyed the intelligent discourse that generally ensued when they met socially. Since then she had had too much of the company of people who were too sure of themselves to question the basis of their assumptions. Assertiveness was a good thing, she felt, but dogma was deplorable. And most of her parents' associates – and, not surprisingly – their offspring, were dogmatic to say the least. Elaine needed people like Thomas. She needed to get away from the world of profit and loss as soon as possible. Only then would she meet people who thought differently, who looked at the world through different eyes. But for now things would have to remain as they were.

8

Thomas was now working on an ad hoc basis as before, sometimes just a day at a time, sometimes two or three together. Occasionally for a full week. Often, when he had time on his hands, he would sit in the rope shop chatting to Johnny Breasley. John was a man who expressed his opinions firmly, but none of them were oppressive and many of them were well thought out and based on a long life of varied experiences throughout the world. And he could, sometimes, be persuaded to alter a point of view entirely if a more intelligent one was put to him. He was by no means dogmatic or unthinking.

Thomas had at first thought John to be a fixture of the town, as much as the fountain in the market place. An ancient photograph in the shop showed Breasley's father standing outside the shop many years before. He looked very much as John looked now. The same wavy white hair, clipped moustache; the same rolled up shirt-sleeves and sinewy arms. He had assumed that John had worked with his father since leaving school until his father had retired and then inherited the business. Not quite so, he found.

His first job had been with his father and from him he had learned the trade of rope making. But then he had enlisted in the army in the first war and had survived combat in France, before returning home to resume his old job.

After a couple of years, in his own words, he 'got itchy feet' and wanted to travel. His father had a brother with a boat yard in Grimsby, and he found John a job as a trawler hand. After an arduous four years on the trawlers he had switched to the big freighters and travelled the world for many more.

'What made you come back here?' asked Thomas, somewhat amazed that a man so travelled would settle for what seemed by comparison a fairly mundane way of living.

'Don't really know,' replied Breasley. 'I was on a ship two days out from Montevideo, when we broke down. We were drifting for two more days before the engine was fixed. There was little to do except read. I'd never been much of a reader before I worked on long distance shipping. But often there was little to do on a long voyage. I was reading Conrad. Now there's a man who can tell a tale. I can't quite remember how he put it, but something along the lines of, for the sailor, his ship is his home and the sea his country. And I reflected on that, all the while we were drifting. I thought not much of a home, not much of a country. And Conrad's right you know. At least I thought he was at the time. Still do to some extent. I mean, how many seamen really see what they are looking at? Not that you're in port long enough to see much. But what I mean is you're not seeing things through the eyes of the native, are you? You're seeing foreign things through English eyes, or Dutch or German or whatever other eyes. It's a rootless, nomadic existence.'

'So you returned home?' asked Thomas.

'Well, not immediately, but fairly soon after that. I knew Dad could use a bit of help in the rope business. He was very busy then. Not like it is now, you know. There was a big demand for rope then. Farmers and hauliers needed rope for lashing things down on lorries and farm wagons. We didn't think then that trade would ever slacken off to what it is now.'

'So how did you take to life in a quiet town like this after years at sea?' asked Thomas.

'It wasn't as easy to settle down as I'd expected. You see, I'd no pals. Most of the lads I'd grown up with were no longer around. Those that were still in the town had wives and families. So I had to start making new friends.'

'You never married?'

'No. I knew I wanted to travel, so it wouldn't have been a good idea to get involved with anyone. And I was always straight with any woman I met in a port, or anywhere. I always said right off, "I'm a seaman and I won't be coming back." You should always be straight with people. Many of the sailors weren't. They'd make all sorts of promises to the girls they met, with no intention of keeping them. The girls probably knew the score. But it's still not the right thing to do. You should never give people false hope.'

Thomas absorbed this last statement and reflected deeply. Wittingly or unwittingly, he'd always done this. Particularly to his parents. He should never have tried to conceal his doubts; should never have lent an atom of encouragement to their unrealistic hopes. When asked by Paul Hudson prior to leaving the seminary, 'What will you do for a moral compass?' he had replied, 'I'll endeavour not to hurt anyone.'

He had not foreseen just how difficult this might be. Johnny Breasley was right. Be honest with everyone. By all means do what you want to do. But be straight about it. Make your intentions clear. And don't involve yourself emotionally with others.

Breasley was speaking again and he was jerked out of his reverie.

'And then of course, when I'd been back in the shop for eight or nine years, and becoming well settled into the town again, the next war broke out and there I was, back at sea, back into the fray. I wasn't home again until it ended. I can tell you I was glad to be back. I'd seen everything I wanted to see and an awful lot I never even want to think about. I'll end my days here, and be glad to. Although I don't do much business I can manage. I like what I do.'

Thomas now felt that he knew Johnny Breasley. He'd underestimated him. Here was a man who had seen and done things about which he knew nothing.

From then on they were the closest of friends; equals, with no regard for difference in age or experience. Whenever he finished a task earlier in the day than he expected to, instead of going up to his room he would call in on John if his shop was still open.

Breasley often stayed open late, not in anticipation of trade, the town was dead after five o'clock, but because he liked being in his shop. He'd lived above it for several years in the storeroom that Thomas now rented, and in some ways it was still his home. When trade was slack, which it often was, John made hammocks from one type of rope he stocked. The hammocks sold better than the rope. Although he bought rope to sell, rather than making it, as his father had, he still retained those skills and would often splice eyes into ropes or adapt them in some way to suit a particular customer.

Sometimes at the end of a quiet day, Thomas would enter the shop to find John half sitting, half lying in one of the hammocks, swaying gently with one foot trailing on the dusty floor. He puffed his pipe almost incessantly whatever he was doing. Thomas feared he must one day set the whole place alight.

He built an image in his mind of a benign and wise old spider swaying in his web of ropes, for everywhere, walls, floor and ceiling they hung in profusion or stood in huge serpentine coils. John's other main stock-in-trade, hessian sacks, stood in bales and provided him with a soft seat when he needed one.

Thomas noticed that Elaine's regular visits at the end of each afternoon began a little earlier than he felt they had done when he was working at her father's store. Because of this he was inclined to get back to the shop a little earlier than before whenever he could complete a task soon enough. Then a friendly three-way conversation would ensue, about absolutely anything, the state of trade, the government, what was happening in the world at large. Johnny was very knowledgeable about the world.

To facilitate this discourse, Elaine had changed her routine slightly. She would now just pop her head around the door, and ask, 'Any post John?' and proceed quickly to the post office. Then back to the shop to chat. She knew that her father would seldom leave his store on time; in fact he was often up to an hour late in doing so, leaving her plenty of time for conversation.

Thomas enjoyed these late afternoon conversations and wished he could find a way to use them to arrange to see Elaine later, but he had neither the skills nor the confidence to do this. Elaine was four years older than he, immensely more confident and, financially, belonged to another race. How could he ask a rich and beautiful woman if he could take her out? And if he did, where would he take her? So he merely continued to dream about the possibility of doing so.

Breasley had summed things up in his mind for weeks before he said, 'She's got a soft spot for you, you know. And I fancy you find her attractive.'

'Who wouldn't?' asked Thomas.

'Exactly. Who in this world wouldn't? Any red-blooded man in his right mind would be attracted to her, and I've known several, some of them married, that have said as much. But as far as I know she isn't seeing anyone.'

Thomas did not reply. He did not wish this conversation about someone whom he secretly adored to degenerate into a base discussion about Elaine's attributes and what it might take in a man for her to be attracted to him.

But Breasley was not a man given to base calculations. He too thought Elaine was a truly beautiful person, in her charming, compassionate nature as well as her stunning good looks. John simply concluded the conversation by saying, 'You ought to say something to her.'

Thomas pondered this suggestion without forming any idea as to how he might proceed.

The situation was resolved the following afternoon by Elaine herself. In front of Breasley, without hesitation or self-consciousness, she said to Thomas, 'Would you like to come with me to the theatre? I was going tomorrow night with the same friend that you met. But she can't make it now, so there's a ticket going begging if you'd like to. I can borrow Daddy's car. He rarely uses it in the evening.'

Johnny held his breath. This was the moment any man would give his most treasured possession for. What would Thomas make of this opportunity?

Thomas breathed deeply, wondering how he could sound casually grateful. He was hardly sure if he had heard her correctly. He controlled his voice carefully, trying hard not to let it tremble as he said, 'Yes. I'd love to. Thank you.'

He realised immediately that Elaine had not named the play. Had he been too quick to accept, or would it have been churlish to have asked the question? He was momentarily flustered.

Elaine knew she hadn't said what they might be going to see. Her ploy was deliberate. She had her own question answered completely. Yes. He would come with her and because he would like to be with her. Not just to see a particular event. That was all she needed to know. She sensed his embarrassment and quickly ended it by telling him the title of the play. He knew it well but had not seen it performed by a professional company.

'That's good,' said Elaine. 'Fine. I'll pick you up here at quarter to seven. Right?'

'Yes. Fine. Thanks very much.'

And with that Elaine was gone. This was the briefest call Thomas could remember her making to the shop. He stood entranced, looking out of the window trying to avoid John's gaze for a moment whilst he found something to say. John spoke first.

'Lucky man! What did I tell you? She likes your company.'

'Oh, I don't know. She had a spare ticket. And she could have gone on her own.'

'She could. And she could have easily gone with a score of other men. And she's plenty of female friends too. Come on, Tom, use your head. She's popular. Everyone likes her. But she likes you.'

Thomas was absolutely elated. John was right. Thomas knew he was, but he found it hard to believe. Half the upper-class men and women in the town would have been glad to have joined her at the theatre, but she'd asked him. For the first time in months he was truly happy. And very nervous.

Thomas took his leave. As he left the shop, John, with merriment in his warm, kind voice, uttered the words, 'Sleep well.'

He knew as well as Breasley did that sleep would not come easily tonight. He walked round to the back of the shop and began to climb the rusty iron staircase. Pausing on the landing he looked around him and wondered at the strangeness of his life, before ducking inside the low door of his austere cell. He'd better make sure that his shoes were polished and that he had a clean shirt for tomorrow night. Pressing his only suit and re-sewing a loose button on the cuff might reduce his pulse-rate a little.

***

Elaine collected Thomas at the appointed time. She pulled out of the almost empty market square and headed for the city. She drove faster than her father did, not excessively so, but smoothly and with great confidence.

The play, they agreed, was well cast and superbly performed, with an interesting set. Returning home Elaine drove more slowly, as if she was not in a hurry for the night to end. When she dropped him off the town was quiet. The last few drinkers were standing around outside the now closed taverns and were gradually dispersing.

Elaine pulled in to the edge of the square and switched off the engine.

'I've enjoyed your company tonight Tom, thanks.'

'My thanks to you. It's been lovely. I've enjoyed your company very much.'

Then silence. The seconds passed.

'Then perhaps we'll do it again,' said Elaine.

'Go to the theatre?'

'Not necessarily, but we could go out somewhere. You're supposed to ask me. Or don't you want to?'

'I'd love to. I can't think of anything I'd rather do.'

'Well, there you are then. Think of somewhere you'd like to take me.'

'I will.'

'You don't sound altogether enthusiastic.'

'I'm sorry Elaine. I'm just a little overwhelmed. I always enjoy your company. I'm sorry that I see you so briefly now. Now that I'm not doing any work at your store, I mean.'

'Well what's overwhelming about that?'

'No, that's not it. I've not been out with girls much. I don't know quite why you want *me* to take you out. You must have lots of male friends.'

'Look Tom, I'm not a girl, I'm a woman. You are a man. Men and women do go out together. They usually do it because they enjoy each other's company. Yes, there are men who would like to be my friends. But, in point of fact, they are acquaintances and I wish them to remain acquaintances. I enjoy your company. I feel I know you quite well, especially since you worked at our store. I don't really know why I call it *our* store. I don't really want to be part of it. I know that you haven't got much money and I don't want to embarrass you by paying for everything. But we could see each other without spending a fortune. That is, if you really wanted to. If you don't, then I've just made a complete fool of myself in making this speech.'

'I'm sorry Elaine. That is a huge compliment you have just paid me and it's making me feel wonderful inside and I'm sorry for appearing so reticent. I really would love to spend time with you. Yes, I'm short of money and at present I can't seem to rectify that situation. But I know you don't judge people according to how much money they have. It is a real problem and I must get over that. Much more importantly, it's been obvious from the start that your mother dislikes me, and your father, whilst he's been generous to me, would hardly want me for a friend. So if you and I were to be seen out together in a small town like this it would be of some concern for your parents and that might rebound on you. I don't wish to bring you any problems. I've caused enough of those already.'

'Not to me you haven't.'

'No. Not to you. But to others, and in a significant way. And I'm still trying to come to terms with the consequences of that. I feel quite elated that you would like to see more of me. I never expected that.'

'Perhaps you should expect more Tom. You're well educated, personable, considerate. People like you. I know several who have said they do. But I'm beginning to wonder if you like yourself. Do you?'

Silence. Thomas thought long and hard. No one had ever asked him that question. He'd always been told what to do, what to think. The only times he'd been asked for answers were when his interrogators wanted to check that he'd grasped whatever he'd been told to do. He wasn't sure what his self was, or even if he had a self. This moment's reflection told him that he'd reason in abundance to dislike whatever his 'self' might be. 'I don't know, Elaine,' he finally replied. 'But that you can find something in me to like means more to me than I could ever explain. Thank you.'

'Better not become too introspective Tom. Leave it at that. It was rude of me to make that remark. I'll wait for you to come up with somewhere to take me.' Elaine started the engine and he got out of the car.

'I'll probably see you at John's tomorrow afternoon. Goodnight.'

***

Thomas' head was swimming. He had never experienced such a deep sense of pure pleasure, of elation, euphoria. Elaine encompassed all that was desirable in the human form. She had stunning good looks and a commanding presence. But, more than those attributes, she had a deep warmth for humanity and a zest for life. She was extremely alluring, but "Thou shalt not covet" was etched into his being.

He longed for a deeper friendship with Elaine, and now, she had made it clear that the possibility of this existed. Such fortune was beyond his wildest dreams. Yet he was no longer dreaming, it was becoming real.

Thomas tried to think logically, to mentally construct a friendship that might roughly fit the evidence he had and move it forward in time a little and see whether it would hold. Elaine was educated, had, in his considered opinion, an outstanding artistic talent, and was from a 'well-heeled' background. Educationally he was perhaps not so far behind her he thought, and intellectually he was possibly her equal. In terms of artistic merit he knew only enough about art to recognise just how good she was, and how great she might become.

But in the skills of life he knew that he trailed miserably in her wake. She was respectful but never diffident; confident but never brash; direct without being inconsiderate; assertive but without the faintest wish to be overbearing. Her only weakness as far as he could see was that she was a caged bird.

The cage was extensive, with gossamer-thin bars that he felt would not hold her for much longer. But she was caged nevertheless. Perhaps the bars were to some extent at least, of her own fashioning, insofar as she had yielded to a sense of obligation. Her parents had willingly supported her at art school, in fact they would have encouraged her in anything she might have wanted to do. Money was no object to them. They wanted her to realize fully any and all potential she had in her, to be happy and successful in any career she chose.

Their son also they had similarly encouraged. Edward had chosen medicine. But his father, in an uncharacteristically foolish, short sighted way, had hoped that the business he had so successfully developed would stay in the family when he retired. It was an outstanding example of thrift and hard work, of dogged determination, risk-taking and of belief in oneself. The sort of belief that can overcome seemingly insurmountable obstacles and leave the rewards for posterity.

But Charles Langdon had only the two offspring. He still hoped, but very faintly now, that Edward would do well as a doctor but would eventually, for some never considered reason, tire of that and at the eleventh hour take over the business. Both his wife and his daughter knew this would never happen but because of their deep love for him they had been gentle in their dissuasive observations.

Elaine, on leaving The Slade, had returned home to help out at a time when good staff were hard to find. Her parents had then come to depend on her. Now, and she had told Thomas this, she found it hard to leave.

But leave she would. He felt this must happen. And what then? Probably, very probably, she would return to London and merge into what to him seemed a mysterious world of bohemian artists and dealers in their products.

She would no doubt wish to continue living well. He doubted the image of the starving artist alone in a garret, feverishly producing work that might in a century's time be valuable would ever fit Elaine. Much of the material life she had now she would wish to keep, but with more time and freedom to explore her talents to the full.

So where could he fit in with this? If she became emotionally attached to him she would want him to be with her. But how would he earn his living? He could not hold his own in the company of artists. There was little doubt in his mind that, with his level of education, he could find a reasonable job – but not a good one. He had no professional qualifications. So would Elaine tire of him? Could he cope with that? Even if she did not tire of him, might he become an encumbrance to her? He hated to see a bird caged and one so beautiful as this should be encouraged to fly. Its song should be heard everywhere. He had no wish to imprison a rare jewel in a base setting.

Thomas was afraid to enter more deeply into what at present was barely a relationship at all. He reflected that they had not even touched hands together. Was it perhaps better to keep it like this until the inevitable migration occurred? And yet, and yet... what did he really want? What were his own needs, his own selfish desires?

He knew above all else he wanted to hold this bird in his hands. Not to tame it, nor to keep it, but for a brief moment in time to hold a living jewel. Nothing in his world so far had come close to creating the longing he had for Elaine's company.

He also knew, or thought he knew, that he could not hold her company for long. He felt that it would be a brief interlude that would encompass the most sublime confluence of feelings which would probably not be repeated again in his lifetime. Might it be better never to experience this rhapsody and continue through life in a staid, soberly way? Or to touch the magic and live forever on the exquisite memory of having done so?

Elaine was a strong person. It was he who was weak. If it didn't work out it would not be she who would be damaged in the long run, but only himself. And he was damaged already. Things might not be any worse.

There was now a change in Elaine. She had always been vigorous, energetic, but her vitality was now even more apparent.

She bought herself a lively little sports car so as not to be dependent upon the loan of her father's vehicle. She often let herself into the store early in the morning, before opening time, to carry out bookkeeping tasks or stock replacement ordering or any job she could do alone. This was done to allow her to finish a little earlier in the afternoon, although she still called in on John Breasley at some time during each day. Without putting it into words she was making it clear to her parents that she had no intentions of working in the store much longer. She even went so far as to suggest to her father that as he was getting older he should consider employing a manager.

Elaine made the most of the long summer evenings by driving out to sketch landscapes taking Thomas with her whenever he was free. Mostly, he made sure he was. He endeavoured to finish any work as early in the day as possible in order to accompany her. Elaine had a high quality camera with which she photographed birds and animals, particularly herds of cattle, to combine detail with her pencil sketches and these she turned into fine paintings when she returned home.

Elaine had had her own studio ever since returning from art school. It had been a garage adjacent to a stable where, as a child, she had kept her pony. These had been combined into one building. A large window had been put in at either end, as well as a skylight, to enable her to paint throughout the day. There was also a stove to heat the place through the winter. This, next to her parent's house, gave her a feeling of having her own space.

Elaine increasingly enjoyed Thomas' company and his knowledge of the countryside and the birds and animals within it. They were becoming closer now. A hand to assist in the crossing of a plank bridge over a stream had broken the inhibition of touch. In a sudden downpour, whilst sheltering beneath a bridge she'd jumped into his arms at the sound of a heavy roll of thunder.

The hot, humid summer had led, of necessity to the wearing of the lightest of clothing and Elaine was not afraid of revealing her figure. She was not easily embarrassed. She had, on several occasions, shown Thomas work she had produced at The Slade. This had included many portraits and several nudes, both male and female. He marvelled at the frank way in which she pointed out the flaws and immaturities of these pieces.

On one of these summer evening walks with the camera, a sudden thunderstorm had driven them to seek shelter in the same barn where, on the afternoon of the picnic with Elaine's parents, they had witnessed the hapless owl escaping the trespassing schoolboys.

By the time they reached the barn the rain had almost ceased and the early evening sun was already breaking through the clouds, but by then they were saturated.

The barn was shadowy at one end, light entering it at that point only through the absent pan-tiles. At the other end light poured through the one unglazed window. Elaine's silk blouse stuck to her like a second skin. She could have concealed her form by standing in the shadows but instead she chose to stand near the window looking out into the strongly slanting western sun at a magnificent rainbow.

To Thomas, who stood a few feet behind her, her back appeared naked. Then, slowly, she turned sideways and her breasts were revealed through the wet silk. He was amazed by her relaxed composure. He knew that she must be aware of how she looked to him. Her beauty was magnificent. He trembled with excitement mixed with apprehension. He could find no words. He simply stood and revelled in the vision before him. He was truly at a loss as to what he should do.

Elaine now stepped past him, then faced him, caught now in the light from the window as well as that shafting down through the openings in the roof. She knew just how much she was revealing to him.

In a totally calm, soft voice she said, 'I should take off this blouse, it's drenched. But you could hardly lend me your shirt, it's just as wet.'

Thomas remained wordless. He'd just heard Elaine say that she would have been prepared to exchange clothes with him but there would be no point in doing so. What was he supposed to say?

She waited. Then, 'I'll just unbutton it. It's too clinging.'
Her brassiere was now exposed, although this was no more revealing that the hitherto clinging silk. He now saw that her thin cotton skirt was stuck to her thighs.

Before he could stop himself, almost as if to say, 'but you can't take everything off,' he said in a voice that was difficult to control, so shallow was his breathing, 'Your skirt's wet too.'
'Shall I take that off as well?'

Elaine had now placed the onus directly upon him. She had established beyond reasonable doubt that she was prepared to undress and was awaiting his approval to do so. Like a chess player, she was forcing a move.

He could see only one outcome if he responded as he thought she wished him to. The nearest he could come to equivocation was, 'Perhaps you should.'

Slowly but deliberately, without fumbling, with her eyes firmly fixed on his, Elaine unhooked the fastener on the waistband and her skirt fell around her ankles. Thomas knew it had dropped, heard it rustle the straw around their feet. His eyes never left Elaine's. He neither moved nor spoke. Still wearing her shoes and stockings she stepped out of it. Another step and she was face to face with him.
'You are so beautiful.' he murmured, as if in a dream, then placed his hands upon the tops of her arms, an instinctive compromise, neither a full embrace nor a rebuff. He did not want to encourage her into an act she might regret. Nor into a commitment that either of them might find painful.

Elaine pushed herself inside his arms and kissed him. Thomas, now dismissing all sense of caution, responded fully. He knew he had not coerced her into anything.

Four years older than himself, well educated, worldly wise, Elaine was making the running. He was glad she was, but he knew nothing and was still afraid of making a fool of himself, of leaving her wanting. If she thought so much of him, he did not want to disillusion her.

Elaine pressed her whole body against his. He was surprised at the strength of her arms as she hugged him to her. She pulled his soaking shirt from his trousers and rubbed his chest, kissing him all the time. Her hands left him only for the moment it took her to unhook her brassiere and fling it aside.

He was now fondling her breasts with an intensity that was almost painful. Elaine's hands were unbuttoning his trousers, pulling him free of his underwear.

'Come over here.' she commanded, leading him past a rusting old tractor to a corner of the barn where a few straw bales lay. By now she had somehow discarded her underwear. Only her shoes, stockings and suspenders remained.

She sat, then lay on the bales, pulling him down on top of her. This was totally new territory for him. He had never been intimate, or even close to intimacy with a woman before. He knew the procedure in theory but the practice of it all had been a world away.

Elaine squeezed him with her legs and he entered her immediately and thrust powerfully. She winced then gasped and cried out, trying hard not to.

Then she pushed against him again with a strength that amazed him, the heels of her shoes pressed deep into the bales, arching her hips into him with a violent rapidity, writhing in ecstasy. After only moments Thomas gasped and pulled away from her, groping belatedly for the new white handkerchief he knew he had in a pocket.

'It would have been alright, darling.' whispered Elaine. He did not know what she meant and wondered if he had failed her and what particular circumstances made it all right.

Afterwards he found blood on his handkerchief that he reconciled with Elaine's gasp of pain. He wondered now why someone so worldly wise, so experienced in life's varied avenues, someone with so many opportunities open to her, could have waited so long for the likes of him.

9

The summer was long, the heat lasting well into September. It provided ample opportunity for Thomas and Elaine to drive out into the country. Langdon's store, like all others in the town, was obliged to close for an afternoon during the week, another opportunity for them to be together.

Elaine sketched, then afterwards they made love. That was sometimes the first thing they did. Then Elaine sketched. Then they made love again.

They made love everywhere. In the little car. In the fields and woods. Often in the old barn, which they had made more comfortable with some blankets and cushions. They could not get enough of each other. Their loving was fiercely addictive.

After their first glorious outburst of passion they had spoken of the possibility of pregnancy. Elaine had explained that the first time was safe because her biological calendar had favoured them. But they could not always take risks.

Although she had never, until now, needed contraception, she knew that some of her art school friends used such devices and told Thomas he must obtain these. He knew of the existence of such things. His former faith condemned them utterly and condemned those who used them.

He could not bring himself to buy such things in his own town. In such a small community almost every retailer knew almost every other. Elaine's father was the best known of all of them, which made Elaine very well-known also. If Thomas was seen buying such things – to him, an embarrassing enough situation in itself – and if he was also seen out with Elaine, then people would talk. He could not bear the thought of anyone talking about Elaine in a derogatory or over-familiar fashion. Therefore, occasional trips to the city, either on his own by bus, or, more rarely, with Elaine by car, became necessary. Thomas' face was anonymous to the men's hairdressers over there.

This problem resolved, their enjoyment of each other's bodies continued in various idyllic settings. The cold-blooded interruption of love making when the device was required was something they both disliked but it was a price worth paying for peace of mind.

Although Elaine sketched and photographed over a wide area of countryside, the dilapidated old barn attracted her and Thomas back for rapturous lovemaking more and more. One reason for this – perhaps the main reason – was the wonderful memory for both of them of giving their bodies to each other for the first time. But also for its tranquil spaciousness and shelter from the summer showers. The corner where the straw bales lay remained dry even in the wettest weather and lying there during a hot, humid summer downpour, and watching the steam rising from the vegetation beneath the open window as the sun reasserted its power was a sensual experience for both of them.

They had become used to the clatter of wings as they entered the barn and birds flew out. Once, a fox shot out of the window frame as they entered through the door. They often heard mice in the rafters and more than once saw bright timid eyes peering down at them. They liked this sharing with animals. It made them feel at one with nature.

They would sometimes be naked for an hour or two at a time, sometimes walking around, even outside in broad daylight, such was their certainty that they would be undisturbed. On warm moonlit nights they would make love on the dewy grass, then lie on their backs gazing at the flittering bats silhouetted against the moon. The isolated setting of the barn, so far from the road, surrounded by fields, trees and high hedges, and accessible only by a rutted track now overgrown made it their secret Eden, their private love nest.

Unfortunately, Elaine's red sports car was conspicuous. Although she parked it a mile away from the barn, where the cart track met the bend of a little used country lane, it would have seemed likely to anyone who knew of the barn's existence that the absent occupants of the car might have headed in that direction. Especially as it was the only walkable track in the vicinity.

Gerald Draycott thought this might be so. When walking his dogs around his father's vast acreage, usually with a gun under his arm, he had seen the little M.G sportster in several places. More recently he had seen it at the end of the cart track more than once.

His curiosity aroused, he had walked up to the barn. Not that it mattered to him; the place was virtually derelict. There was only a worthless broken-down tractor in it and a rusty harrow as far as he could remember, and they had been owned by a previous tenant farmer. He hadn't been into the place for a couple of years. But still he walked up to it. Just out of curiosity.

The door opened surprisingly easily. A half-empty tin of tractor grease stood on the floor just inside. Beside it was a short length of thick hemp rope, the centre of which was impregnated with grease. He looked at the massive ancient hinges. They were greasy. Lathered with grease. It was obvious that the rope had been used to apply lubrication to them. Otherwise, after all this time, they would have been seized by rust.

Gerald's eyes, now accustomed to the gloom, took in the rest of the space. The sun was catching the window frame. In its beam he saw a couple of pencils, recently sharpened, resting on the ledge. Then, lying on the tractor seat, a drawing book.

It confirmed his suspicions. Only a week ago someone had mentioned to him in passing that Elaine Langdon now had a red M.G sports car. She might have asked him for the use of the barn, he thought. Still, it hardly mattered. Artists are like that. They exist in the moment. Don't always see things as the rest of us do. Surprising though, that she'd taken the trouble to grease the door hinges so thoroughly.

It was only as he turned to leave that his eye caught sight of the bales. Shafts of sunlight were just beginning to reach them. There was something on them. He couldn't remember what had been there before. He walked over. Blankets. Checked horse blankets. Partly covered by a cleanish sheet. And cushions. And what was this on that cushion? A handkerchief. A large one. A man's handkerchief.

Everything suddenly made sense. Two pictures, clear as photographs, entered his head in a split second. One, a tea party in his father's woods, early in the spring. The other, a lover's tryst. A scene of the utmost, delirious pleasure. The bitch. The dirty, fornicating bitch. Gerald did not have to guess who the dog might be.

Calling his spaniels, Gerald walked down the track towards his shooting brake. Seething with furious rage, suffused with hatred, he wanted to destroy someone. All right; so they had disagreed. Fallen out, if you like. Yes, they had had a serious argument, a row. That was the trouble with women these days. Too bloody sure of themselves.

The war was the cause of that, Gerald supposed. They had had to stand in for the men and the country was grateful to them for doing so. But now they were reluctant to relinquish the foothold they had gained. But surely it did not have to lead to this? Surely she would have come round to seeing things his way given time. And he had given her plenty of time. Well, he would resolve this situation once and for all. From now on he would pass this way more often. A man had a legal right to keep trespassers off his land.

***

Only two days later the red M.G. stood again at the junction of the cart track and the lane. Gerald Draycott was looking out for it. He had been out shooting magpies. He disliked magpies intensely. He believed they took too many eggs and chicks from the nests of his game birds. He didn't much care for any of the crow family, all of them too bold, too much above themselves like some people, raucous and rascally. But magpies he particularly disliked.

As usual he had been shooting them with a .22 rifle. It was good target practice. It was far too easy to take careless aim with a twelve-bore and blow them to bits, sometimes two together, wasting an expensive cartridge each time. Much more difficult to hit them with a bullet from a small-bore rifle. That required careful sighting and a very steady hand. A bit risky if you missed. A rifle bullet, even a .22, carried a long way, so you needed to consider what or who might be in the next half mile or so immediately behind your target.

But Gerald didn't miss very often. He prided himself on his marksmanship. But did it really matter? All of this was his father's land; his one day. If someone got in the way, well, that was their lookout, wasn't it?

Another reason he often preferred to use the .22 when out on his own was that the light crack of the rifle made much less noise than the cannon-like boom of a twelve-bore shotgun that sent flocks of squawking birds high up into the sky and alerted any poacher for miles around. Gerald was by nature a stealthy man.

He walked alongside the high hedge that bordered the track and would soon pass close to one end of the barn, the end where the glassless window was. He would then need to be the other side of the hedge.

When he was within a hundred yards of the barn he began to look for a weak spot in the hedge. He soon found one. Where a couple of large elderberry bushes had, for some reason, died off, there was space to squeeze through without being ripped by the thorns. He was now walking almost soundlessly through long grass, hidden by the hedge that was more than head high.

He could see the eaves of the barn so knew exactly where he was in relation to its window. To his immense satisfaction there was a tall hawthorn growing in the hedge exactly at the spot where he faced the window. It shielded him from the light, making him almost invisible to anyone looking out of the barn. He carefully pushed a little of the hedge aside, wary of the thorns. He could see the window-frame clearly but the interior seemed only a black hole.

Gerald stared hard into it, waiting for his eyes to adjust to the gloom. Then, a movement; the back of a light-coloured shirt just inside the aperture. A man's head. But the dark head was ringed around by feathery reddish-gold. Then, suddenly, he understood. A redheaded woman had her lips locked onto those of a man. They were fastened together in a deep, lingering embrace. They parted, then closed again, nuzzling each other gently.

Gerald slowly eased himself away from the hedge without taking his eyes from the scene before him. He gradually lifted the rifle up to his shoulder. His intense fury was getting the better of him and his hands were shaking. He pushed his shoulder into the trunk of the hawthorn. The shakiness diminished. He started to control his breathing. They were still kissing. There was no need to rush. He sighted the rifle onto the back of the man's head.

One light crack. That would be the only sound. Not much more than the noise of a branch breaking. There was no one else within a mile, he was sure. It would not be heard. One small, neat hole drilled cleanly into the back of the skull. Not even a lot of blood. The bullet would plug much of the wound it made. The man would fall without a sound.

Elaine would be too stunned for a minute to guess what had happened. Then she would fall to her knees to attempt to revive him. He would slip away.

Then his vindictive nature moved up a notch. The man would feel no pain. He would know nothing. He would not know why, or who. He ought to suffer. Suffer for the theft of something Gerald thought he should own.

He sighted the rifle a couple of inches lower, onto the man's neck. That would be better. That shot would paralyse him, but he might live. Then he'd know what it was to lose something you desired; to lose everything except your very existence. To be trapped within an existence. To exist with no more than your thoughts, your memories, your emotions.

His finger tightened on the trigger. But wait! Whilst a bullet could bury itself in a skull and remain there, it might well pass clean through the man's neck. Straight into Elaine's face. She deserved it, the bitch, but Gerald wanted her for himself.

He re-sighted; back now to the skull. For a brief moment he almost checked the wind direction. Force of habit. He was used to shooting stags in the Scottish Highlands. There, using a high velocity gun, you might kill a stag half a mile away. You had to allow for a side wind pushing the shot off target. Try to gauge its strength and direction and aim accordingly.

But now, at this close range, twenty feet or so, a gale would not deflect the shot. He couldn't miss. Gerald smiled sardonically to himself at his obsessive caution. Just force of habit. He was a calculating man. His finger again tightened on the trigger.

Then: the sound of a tractor some considerable distance away. He knew whose tractor it would be. It would be on the lane at the end of the track. His shooting brake was parked there. Next to the red car. That was a problem.

And then something else came to mind. Early that morning, as he drove through Brampton Village on his way to massacre magpies, Gerald had stopped at the letterbox outside the post office to post some mail.

The post office had not yet opened, but the postmistress had seen him. She had waved from her window. Brampton was a couple of miles away, but too close for comfort. And then there was the incident with the poacher not so long ago. Not at all his fault, it had been decided. Nevertheless, it might add to the risk. Better not to take the risk. Not today at least. Revenge would have to wait.

10

By spending so much time with Elaine, watching her draw, noticing how she composed a photograph to take back to her little studio and create a stunningly good picture from it, Thomas could see clearly just how much artistic potential she had. She discussed every detail of a sketch with him and was highly critical of her work if she had not quite achieved the effect she had hoped for. She would spend an age seeking to know why, re-working a picture endlessly, until she was almost satisfied. Almost, but never fully satisfied; she always asked more of herself.

It was a good thing, he thought, that her parents had recognised her precocious talent when she was very young and had done everything they could to develop it. They had paid a tutor, a retired art teacher, to spend a lot of time with her and were glad to support her when she was accepted by The Slade School of Art. Of course, at that time there was never an expectation that she might be needed in the business. That is what they had a son for.

Despite Edward's obvious aptitude for biology and chemistry during his school years, and his stated intention at the tender age of twelve to become a doctor, Charles had never seriously considered that Edward would not, at some point in his life, take on the business.

Because commerce meant so much to him and because it had provided so well for all of them, it seemed obvious that Edward would eventually step into his father's shoes. It was the one flaw in Charles' rationally objective attitude to life, an ostrich-like insistence to himself, a belief that the business would go on, generation to generation, until it became part of the town's history.

It had seemed equally obvious to Elaine that she would never be expected to have a hand in it, as she had no real interest in retailing or in any form or commerce.

However, when Edward's course in life was firmly set, she was dismayed to find herself becoming increasingly involved. She would be eternally grateful for her parent's support of her in her artistic endeavours and also for the freedom they had allowed her in so many ways.

She often brought home art student friends to stay over the weekend. Their sometimes radical discourses on socio-political matters – usually at odds with her parents pro-establishment outlook – caused them to raise their eyebrows, but Charles and Delia stifled their own opinions somewhat and never objected to the company she kept.

By now they were in no position to object to what she was doing. At twenty-six years of age she could not be talked down to, and in any case she was as good as any three other employees in the store. They depended on her. She could lend a hand in any department; good reason not to quarrel with her.

But they knew she was seeing Thomas even though she never mentioned his name to them again. They could not see why she found him so interesting. Decent and honest he might be but, in their eyes, purposeless. As Delia had more than once remarked to Charles, 'Too many like him and we'd have lost the war. The man is utterly without direction.'

They knew of his relationship with their daughter only by default. The fact that Elaine was out of the house a great deal and never said she was with anyone else led them to think he must be keeping her company. Once or twice Charles had been asked by business associates, 'Who was that good-looking young man I saw your daughter with, careering around the countryside in the red M.G?' Charles had tried to make light of such questions but was troubled by them.

Thomas and Elaine were hardly ever seen in town together. They met frequently in Breasley's shop, but that did not provoke discussion. Every trader nearby knew that she called in on Johnny practically every day, whether Thomas was there or not. She had been doing so for several years, by now it was routine.

Elaine was far too confident a person to care about guarding the relationship from others. She was not secretive about it in any way. She also felt strongly that it was no-one else's business. But there was little that was obvious and that might fuel the lurid imaginations of the curious. When she picked up Thomas in her car it was at the end of the working day and it was dark by the time she returned him. If they went to the theatre or a cinema it was always in the city, a twenty mile drive away.

Johnny Breasley knew about this of course, and he loved them for it. He had always been fond of Elaine and had taken to Thomas very soon after he had moved into his upstairs room. He now liked him immensely, almost like a son, and sympathised with his plight.

He never questioned him but always listened carefully whenever he needed to speak about it. It was obvious to John that Elaine was in love with Thomas, and equally obvious that Thomas loved her so much that he was denying it to himself. Breasley probably understood the reasons for this better than he did himself.

Thomas had, in his mind, placed Elaine so high up on a pedestal of virtue that he did not want to do anything that might bring her crashing down. But also, he could not believe enough in himself, in any virtue of his own, that might permit him to stand on that pedestal with her. Nor could he see a way of offering her any permanence in a relationship, if indeed, that was what she wanted.

He knew that she would not stay much longer in her parents' business, nor indeed, in the town.

Her artwork was outstandingly good now, contributing more and more to his own sense of inadequacy. There was a distinctive edge to her paintings that had not been there before.

Her landscapes had infinite distance with out-of-focus objects towards the horizon, leaving one wondering just what they were. They invited the imagination of the viewer to speculate, to look for more than was figuratively described. Or else they had dark spaces within woodland that held a brooding menace.

Her portraits were acutely accurate yet also captured inner personal depths. She had asked him to sit for her a few times while she sketched him quickly and he was amazed at the finished pictures she had painted from these. They seemed to get inside his mind.

She also showed him a nude she had reworked. He had seen the original sketch. He had thought it good, but not memorable. Now, complete, it took his breath away. It was defiantly erotic, the eyes holding unrelentingly the gaze of the viewer. And they were Elaine's eyes. She had worked her own features into what had been the face of a Slade model. This defiance was becoming part of her demeanour. She was making change happen.

She had now given herself a whole day off mid-week instead of the half-day she had previously taken, in order to paint. She had also re-established contacts in London, now sending pictures to a dealer she knew from her days there as a student.

Finally the day came that Thomas knew was inevitable. In late autumn Elaine asked him to move with her to London. Her plan was to rent a flat there, to paint and to sell her work through the dealer she was already using. She had stayed in contact with many of her artist friends and believed she would establish herself in the art world in time.

Elaine made it clear that she needed Thomas to come with her. As he had no work of interest to him here, nor even a steady income, just a precarious hand-to-mouth existence, she saw no reason why he wouldn't join her. They would be together all the time.

He asked her how her parents would manage the store without her help. 'They could easily employ a good manager for a lot less than I am taking out of the business,' was her reply. 'I've suggested this before, but Daddy wouldn't consider it. So I've got to make him do it. He's doing far too much himself. This life is choking me. They know it is, and they don't like it either. They want me to be happy, to do what I need to do, but they've allowed circumstances to control them.'

'What will it do to them – your leaving? As parents I mean, not just as business people?'

'I'll still see them. Just as I did when I was at art school. London's not so far away. They'd have no fear of losing contact with me. We are a close family. Feelings don't change.'

'I know you're close,' said Thomas. 'You're right, the business would carry on much the same no doubt, and of course you would see them. Often. In fact these past few months you can hardly have seen as much of them as I am sure you would have liked, apart from when you are at the store. That's my fault I suppose. I take you away from them.'

'It's more likely their fault,' said Elaine. 'I should have talked to them about you, about us, but I didn't. Because I know that they – Mother in particular, not so much Daddy – found you, well, not on their wavelength shall we say. That's not your fault. They're just a bit blinkered. And it's not just a class thing, although I know you think it is. It is partly that, but also the fact that you have not been able to find your way. To have a goal. I understand that, understand why, but they don't. They expect a man to have a clear direction in life. And although you tried not to make it obvious on that one occasion when you lunched with us, they could hardly have failed to notice that you were a bit "anti" the upper classes.' Elaine smiled as she said this. She had not said it reprovingly.

'I'm a bit of an outsider, I know. I've been thinking about this – this conversation we're having now. I've seen it coming. I'm sure we both have. From the very first time I saw you I was fascinated by you, as I have already told you. I might have dreamed of something great happening between us – which it has. But that was before I realised you had any interest in me. If I could have looked ahead I'd have thought about it twice – at least. I never wanted to weaken you, to become your Achilles' heel so to speak.'

'You've done the exact opposite of that Tom. You've helped me to find myself. I was doing very little artwork. I was becoming ever more ensnared in the business. Admittedly I was leading a more overt social life then, but not one I really liked. Dining out with the likes of Gerald Draycott, going to the theatre with Ralph Phillips?'

'Who's he?'

'Oh, another of Daddy's business friends' offspring who had designs on me. And there were others. They bored me. All of them. Life can be incredibly boring in a town like this. One can feel like a prize heifer that's wearing the red rosette and is now on display for the delectation of all the young bulls. It's sickening really.'

'But realistically, Elaine, I have become your Achilles' heel. We can't go on forever like this. Meeting, if not exactly in secret, at least very discreetly. I'd never have fitted in with your parents. As much by my choice as theirs. I feel as they feel – that we have no common ground.'

'But you and I have common ground, don't we, Tom?' Thomas detected a hint of doubt in her question.

'Tom, we love to be with each other. Don't we?' Elaine seemed almost frightened of what the answer might be.

'Very much so, of course we do. I suppose what I am asking is where do we go from here?'

'To London. Please come to London with me Tom. Why not? What is the difficulty? We can be ourselves there. And in a strange way, given time, I think my parents might grow to accept that you and I are together there. But that wouldn't matter. So long as we were together we'd be fine. They wouldn't try to put obstacles in our way. They're not like that.'

'How would I fit in?'

'Well, for a start you would have a far better chance of finding employment that interests you. Something creative and challenging. I know you've always managed to support yourself against the odds, in this God-forsaken place, but you've had little to satisfy your artistic instincts. You'd easily find work in the capital. I know I can find us a place to live. I've got contacts there. I've already asked a friend to look around at accommodation. I'm expecting to hear something from him any day now. Tom, you've got nothing to keep you here.'

'That's very true. Not if you leave.'

'I'm not talking about me leaving. I'm talking about us leaving. Tom, you're starting to worry me. I thought you'd be full of enthusiasm for a new start together in a place where people can be themselves. A place where one isn't troubled by tittle-tattle and petty prejudices as one is in a small town like this.'

'Do you think you'll sell well enough to survive?'

'My agent thinks so. And Daddy will give me a small allowance. Enough to pay my rent.'

'It would be better if you could manage without depending on him, wouldn't it?' said Thomas. He wished he'd got the courage to say, 'You shouldn't have to depend on your parents.'

Then he reflected on his mother's last words to him, about all they had sacrificed for him. How hard they had tried to make something of him. Something good, something worthwhile. And he'd thrown all their efforts back into their faces. And maybe, just maybe, he'd brought about his father's death through his self-indulgent ways. No, he had no right to suggest to others what they should or should not do, how they ought to live. Certainly no right to preach to Elaine who was, in all respects, a much better person than himself.

'Yes, of course it would Tom. I'm sure I won't need their help, but they would actually feel happier if they were putting enough to sustain me into my bank account. They wouldn't worry about me so much then. It wouldn't be for long. I'll soon show them I can be solvent on my own. Tom, you will come with me, won't you? I need you to. I want you with me. Always. We'd be fine in London. We've nothing here except each other. And that's wonderful. But we could have that and more. Much more. We could have a sense of freedom, freedom to be ourselves. You might start doing something more creative than dressing shop windows or making shop-fittings or painting signs. You're good at it I know, but you have a lot of talent you're not using. In London you'd meet artistic people who I'm sure you would find stimulating. You're wasting your time in this town.'

'Perhaps I've wasted myself. I've had some opportunities. They just weren't the ones I wanted. I doubted their substance.'

'What do you want Tom?'

'I don't know. That's the trouble.'

'Maybe in London you would know. You'd find yourself; find whatever it is you need to put you at ease with yourself.'

'You are all I need. As well as, of course, a decent, regular income.'

'So, there's no problem then? We go to London? You'd have me wherever we live. I don't want that to end. As for an income, you've a much better chance in London than you'll ever have here.'

Thomas remained silent.

'Tom, you are starting to frighten me. I thought you'd come with me anywhere. I've never known such pleasure as I have had since I met you. I don't want it to end. I thought you felt like that too. If you won't come then I won't go.'

Johnny Breasley's words were ringing in his ears. "Don't make promises you can't keep." "Always be straight." "Don't create false hope in others."

He had, he now realised, made promises, even if he had not used words to do so. He had allowed Elaine to love him. They had shared each other's bodies and each had given the other reason to believe that this sharing would continue. That was promise enough wasn't it?

Elaine was saying that she was going to keep her promise. She would go to London only if he came with her. If he would not then she would stay here with him. Even here, in the town she said was choking her. Being with him counted for much more than anything else. He had trapped her with honeyed kisses as surely as the gypsies trapped, with their sticky concoction of crushed mistletoe, the tiny feet of the warbling song-birds. Either way, Elaine was now caged. It wouldn't matter if she stayed here or went to London. Or anywhere. She was attached to him. That should have been wonderful, and for her, right now, perhaps it was. But for how long?

For Thomas also the attachment was wonderful, yet too heavy an obligation to carry. He wasn't good enough, he thought, even though she had told him he was all that she desired. He now felt that he had deceived her, he'd encouraged her by false pretences of some sort. He thought that he'd been honest and that she had recognised his limitations and simply made allowances for them.

But now he could see that she really did regard him as an equal, even though he was not. Perhaps love did not make such comparisons. Did not rank differences, did not list failings, kept no score of merits or de-merits.

Perhaps love simply desired reciprocation. He wondered did he know, had he ever known what love was? Would he ever grasp its essence? Was he in love with Elaine or was she just some almost unattainable prize that he had lusted after and had now soiled? Had she dropped in his esteem because she considered him to be her equal?

It was now becoming clear to him that this mature, immensely capable, self-willed woman was beginning to be afraid of losing him. It was the first time Thomas had seen anything less than total confidence in her. Might this fear now weaken her in other ways? He did not know.

He now realised that he was responsible for this course of another's life and the sense of responsibility was tearing him apart. 'Go with her,' said his logical mind; to the ends of the earth should she wish.

What could they lose if it didn't work out? They could start out over again. It was obvious, perfectly logical. Yet he was afraid. He did not know how the strength of Elaine's love could overcome life's setbacks. And if he had not the means to defend them in times of hardship, what then? He asked himself again if he really did love her?

He could not love himself, he thought, so how could he love another? He ought to have wanted for her what she was saying she wanted for herself, for both of them, but he couldn't see that.

A huge cloud of guilt and inner turmoil obscured his view. Yet again his self-indulgence had led him into a situation that he felt he could not control. He wanted Elaine to be free. Free of her entrapment within her father's business. Free to be an artist and live how she pleased. Free of her love for him. Yes, her love for him, that was the cage he had made for her.

He felt that he should not have let her love him. If only he'd recognised the futility of it all from the beginning and ended it there. But he had not. Again, as always, he'd done what he wanted to do at the time, without wider consideration. He had indulged himself in all the pleasures she'd signalled to him. Should he go on doing so or end it now?

This tumult of emotions, doubts, fears, hopes overwhelmed him. It was like being beneath a waterfall, where, for one moment a breath of air supported hope of life, and the next he was being battered against the rocks, gulping water when he needed oxygen. Hope and hopelessness exchanging places every second.

What if he did set Elaine free by tearing himself away from her? What then? He knew she would survive. What about the pain of loss he would feel? Surely he deserved pain. He'd lived with it before. It was what you had to live with if you did something wrong. It was right that you should have to live with it. One should not get off scot-free, having committed a misdemeanour. One should pay for one's mistakes.

Thomas recognised now that his life so far could be measured only in mistakes. There was not a single achievement that could be taken into the reckoning. Whatever decision he made now might be another mistake. Perhaps the greatest mistake of all.

Right now, he knew one thing only: he had to talk to Johnny Breasley.

The following morning he entered the rope shop. John was surprised. He rarely saw Thomas before the middle of the afternoon, more usually at the end of the day.

Apart from its owner, the shop was empty of people, as it often was these days. Rope and sacks were not in great demand among most of the shopping public. Johnny received only a handful of customers, sometimes only one or two in the course of a day. Farmers and hauliers mostly. They usually gave him a sizable order.

'Just making a drink Tom. Want a cup of tea?'

'Please, John. I'd love one.' Thomas, like Elaine, always respectfully called him John. "Breezy" or "Johnny" were names used by others, not by them.

'What brings you in so early Tom?'

'I need to talk to you John. I've a lot on my mind. Are you busy right now?'

'Look around,' said John, indicating with hand and eyes the empty space. 'This is about as busy as it gets these days. What's on your mind?'

Thomas outlined the bare bones of the conversation he'd had with Elaine, the possibility of their going to live in London. John listened in silence, sipping his tea. When he'd finished speaking John remained silent. He took a few more sips from his cup.

After half a minute or so he said, 'You sound as if you're asking me what you should do. Am I right?'

'Yes, I suppose so. I'm a bit bewildered at the moment. I can't seem to think straight.'

'I'm not inclined to tell a man what he ought or ought not to do. Anyway, I've nothing to go on. It's you that knows the situation – both of you that is. A decision like this is always hard to make if you're looking for the rights and wrongs of it. You'll never know the outcome unless you make the move. What seems right today can seem wrong tomorrow. I can tell you only two things with absolute certainty. First, if you do go I'll miss you both a great deal. I like the pair of you immensely. Secondly, whatever you choose to do, I hope it turns out well for you. I would hate to see either of you hurt.'

Thomas pondered the ensuing silence. Was that all? Did John have no more to say than that?

Then, 'Most men of your age would be gone already. They'd have jumped at the chance. But I know you are not like most men. That's one of the reasons why I like you. No doubt that's why Elaine likes you. Now let me see if I've got this right. It seems to me that both of you want the same thing but only one of you believes in it. Believes it'll work I mean?'

'Yes. Yes, John. You're right.'

'Do you believe in anything, Tom?'

There was a long silence.

'Fundamentally, no, I don't suppose I do. I believe what my senses tell me but I don't believe I understand. I've no real convictions I suppose. There's not much in the world that makes sense to me.'

'I know what you mean. When the last war started I thought it doesn't seem so long since I was fighting in the first one. It didn't seem to make much sense to me. Life's like that, it seems. We make a decision, run with it a while, then make another one. Who's to say whether a decision is right or wrong until after its consequences make themselves known?' Another pause. 'Tell me Tom, do you think you're not good enough for Elaine?'

'No. I'm not. I know that for sure.' He had answered instantly.

'I'd say most men aren't,' said John. 'I know I'm biased, I've known her for so long and I've never found a fault in her. But if all men thought as little of themselves as you do, Elaine would never have much chance of a deep friendship, would she? It's refreshing though, to find a young man with so much caution in his make up.'

Thomas waited. John was at least talking to him, more than it seemed he would at the outset.

'Do you trust Elaine's judgement?' he asked quite suddenly.

'Yes, yes I do. She's a clear thinker. Very logical.'

'She's very sensible,' said John. 'Probably the most level-headed woman I've ever met,' he continued. 'So, it seems to me that there are two possibilities. Either she thinks that you are every bit as good as she is - you are all she wants in a man. Or else you're the best she thinks she can get. Which is it?'

'I think she could get any man she wanted.

'I'm absolutely convinced she could,' said John, smiling broadly. 'So, there's your answer. Now tell me something else. This sensible, logical, clear-thinking woman – we're both agreed on that it seems – must surely feel she knows you well and understands you. But how well do you know yourself?'

'It's hard to say, John. I've learned so much about myself in the last couple of years that I might be inclined to say that I do know myself. But in reality, what I've learned only tells me how little I knew myself before. It makes me doubt if there was much "self". Perhaps I was too much the creation of others, too much given to doing and saying what other people wanted me to do and say but always wondering whether or not they were right. If you believe completely that the beliefs of others are exactly right then you can go along with them and they become right for you too. But I didn't, I tended to go along with them, but uncertainly. That doubt was always the problem.'

'Well, that's progress of some sort,' said John. 'You might have left it a bit late, but at least you're trying to come to terms with yourself now. In that respect you are most unlike Elaine. I'm sure she's always known who she is, what she stands for, and I'd have said that about her ten years ago at least.'

John drew on his pipe in silence for a minute. Then he said, 'I suppose if you ever married Elaine and had children it might bring you closer to the rest of the family. I believe children can draw a family closer together. Although I'd be the last to profess any first-hand experience of course.'

Tom reflected on this for a moment and inwardly disagreed. His father's siblings and their offspring were scattered over the globe, with hardly any contact between them. Thomas was sure that their families, like his own, ended each day with the communal recitation of several decades of the rosary. The harsh economic realities of a rapidly changing world made familial togetherness a difficult thing to attain. The leaflets stacked on a rickety table in the church porch saying "The family that prays together stays together" were a lie deserving only sardonic laughter. It certainly did not square with his experience of "family".

John was exploring possibilities and Thomas was grateful for everything he said. He needed to listen and to reflect, to try to clear his own mind, organise his thoughts.

John spoke again. 'I'm not going to suggest what you should do. I've no right to do so. I cannot put myself into your shoes. From what you've said it seems to me that you've been told what to do for most of your life. I'm not going to add to what others have done to you. Whatever decision you reach could affect the rest of your life. I hope that what you decide is the best for both of you.'

They drank more tea, then Thomas thanked John for listening to his problems and climbed the steps to his cell. He needed to be on his own for a while now to think a bit more. He needed to get to the heart of the problem.

He ran possible outcomes through his mind. If they went to the capital, Elaine would be free of the ties of business, although, at least for a time, she would need a little of her father's money. But how would he fit in with her new lifestyle? Would she have to support him with her father's allowance until he could find work? Would he be an encumbrance to her? Realistically his job prospects would be much better and he should soon be able to support himself, but his commitment to whatever job he found might, of itself, impair their relationship. If they stayed here in Banebridge, everything would conspire to strain it. Here he would never fit in with Elaine's family and friends. He would always be the outsider he knew he was. How would she feel about that? It would be as if she had a married lover who had to be passed off as a casual acquaintance and seen only in secret.

But then, he wondered, would she do that? No. She would not. She was too strong a person. She would introduce him as her man; let them think what they liked. That might cost her; she could be shunned. And did he wish to know her family and friends? They were upper-class snobs as far as he could tell. So to go with her to London made better sense. There they would both meet interesting people with wide ranging interests, arty people in the main, hopefully not class ridden.

Yet he was still overwhelmed by doubts and fears. He started to question his obligations to Elaine. He had made no verbal promises to her. She had made the running, as it were, with no idea as to how he might respond. So she ought not to be surprised if he did not fall in with her expectations. He had felt at the start of their relationship that she was more than capable of getting on with life without him. Maybe she would have to.

But hadn't Elaine said that if he wouldn't go with her to London then she would not go either? It was then clear to him. If he did not move with her then he would be tying her down, choking her in this place, denying her her potential for artistic freedom and happiness. He would be stifling the instincts he had re-awakened in her.

He would go. Go with her. They would start something new together. As Johnny Breasley had said, you cannot predict the outcome of a decision until you have made it.

The very next day Thomas was pushed into making an unexpected decision. A woman not known to him had left him a note with John Breasley. It was about his sister but had not been written by her. Apparently Mary had suffered a serious hand injury at the brewery where she worked. She had somehow thrust her hand into a crate of broken bottles in an ill-lit storeroom. She's cut the guiders in her hand and cannot move her fingers. She's in the hospital, the note said.

Thomas surmised that some tendons must have been severely damaged. He guessed that permanent disability was being hinted at. That would no doubt jeopardise Mary's employment, not just at the brewery but almost anywhere else. As Mary looked after their mother, with whom she still lived, the problem was substantial to say the least.

Thomas relayed the little information he had to Breasley, knowing that he would tell Elaine that evening, and set off for the hospital. He knew that if the accident had been exaggerated and the injury was not so bad, then Mary could be back at home. But he did not relish facing the hostility of his mother in a household that now would be gloomier than ever. In any case, the note seemed to understate rather than magnify the situation.

He found Mary with her wrist and hand heavily bandaged and splinted, her arm in a sling. She was still badly shaken and tearful, fearing that her working days might be over. As she had no movement in her fingers her appearance and her ability to look after herself and their mother would be severely compromised. She was awaiting the visit of a surgeon to pronounce as to what degree of restoration might be possible.

Thomas kissed her and held her gently. 'Don't cry Mary, it mightn't be as bad as you think.'

'I think it is bad Tom. I can't feel the ends of my fingers. I don't know how we'll manage.'

'We'll sort something out. I'll go and see mother when I leave you. I'll help out as best I can.'

'No, don't go there Tom. She'll not see you. She's becoming more bitter, more superstitious than she ever was. She'll find some way of blaming you. She'll say you bring bad luck on us. She's unreasonable. It will be a horrible scene if you go there.'

'But how will she manage on her own?'

'Oh, she'll be all right for a while. Betty, my friend who brought the note to you, has agreed to shop for her. She can cook and otherwise look after herself. If she wants to. I'll be home, probably tomorrow, so I can push her to do things. It's just that she won't go out of the house, except to the church of course.'

'How about money?'

'Dad left her a little bit you know. He'd managed to put a bit by. We didn't know at the time.'

'OK. So now tell me how this happened?'

'My friend Betty began working at the brewery only this week. In the bottling plant, like myself. I persuaded her to leave her job at the factory. The wages were worse there. She saw a crate of broken bottles in a place where someone might have fallen over them, so she put them in an empty storeroom whilst she went to ask a supervisor how she should dispose of them.'

'That sounds reasonable. So what happened?'

'The storeroom had only one small light in it. All the other bulbs had failed over time. Because it was not used officially, the management had never replaced them.'

'So what were you doing in it?'

'It's adjacent to the ladies toilet. Several of us used it unofficially. One or two left their bikes there out of the rain. I left my bag there. Several of us did. And our coats. We had no proper cloakroom.'

'You've still not told me what happened.'

'The whistle had gone for break-time. I had some cigarettes in my bag. I went in to get them. I didn't even bother switching on the lights because the only bulb was the other end of the room. I somehow shoved my hand into the rack where the bottles were, instead of the one next to it. I screamed with the pain and people rushed in, but it was so gloomy in there that no-one could see what I had done until they got me outside. There was blood gushing everywhere and I passed out. They wrapped towels around my hand and somehow got me into one of the manager's cars and he drove me round to the hospital.'

'That's terrible luck.' said Thomas.

'That's not the worst of it. Betty has been round to see me. They've sacked her. For putting the bottles there. She's feeling terrible for causing me such an injury and I feel awful for getting her to leave the job at the factory. But she left them there for only a minute. No one could have foreseen that happening.'

'I suppose she'll find another job. I'm only concerned about you.'

'I don't suppose I'll find another job in a hurry. I don't know how long it will take this to heal. Or if it will. They've told me not to expect too much.'

'For how long will they pay your wages?'

'I don't know. It's only the salaried staff who get sick pay. Although the manager who brought me here said, "Don't worry about anything. We'll see you all right." I don't know what he meant by that. I wasn't in a fit state to think.'

It was clear to Thomas that Mary and their mother would need financial support and he immediately assumed that responsibility. Such provision might, in some small way, atone for his enforced estrangement from his mother. He knew that she would never forgive him but she might grudgingly accept his presence in her house once again. It might at least make him feel better about himself, and Mary would be glad of any help she could get.

He realised that he must quickly find a regular mode of employment. He had barely supported himself up to now. He could not go on like this. He must now support three people.

He began by combing the job vacancy columns in the city newspapers knowing full well that his hometown offered little chance of decent, secure employment.

He found that one of the big department stores needed an assistant window dresser. The pay was abysmal especially when one accounted for the daily cost of travelling there. But it would be regular money and if he could find cheap accommodation nearby it might prove worthwhile.

But such a move he did not know how to discuss with Elaine. He felt sick at the thought. She might, as a temporary measure, understand his need to take a city job to support his remaining family for a while, but living there would be an insurmountable problem.

Thomas applied for the job, boldly giving Charles Langdon's store as a point of reference. Most unusually for a store in a market town, Langdon's had an outstanding reputation for quality and service that reached far beyond its geographic boundaries. That reputation extended also to its staff. He felt that Charles Langdon would give him a good reference, albeit based on only a few weeks work. In any case, he might be pleased to ease him out of his daughter's purview.

And so it proved. Within weeks he was travelling to the city to work at a job that was not unpleasant or particularly difficult. The display manager gave him all the guidance and support he needed and he fitted in with the other staff reasonably well. He was given little scope for his own ideas but the fact that he had plenty of them, and was a willing worker, marked him out for a salary increase and possibly promotion.

The relationship with Elaine deteriorated rapidly. Not only was the travelling to and fro taking much time out of the day, but frequent visits to his sister, whose recovery was glacially slow, meant that Thomas could find little time to spend with Elaine.

She continued with her plans for moving to London, but inwardly doubted if he would join her.

It was Thomas who decided the issue. A work colleague told him that he was vacating a flat on the edge of the city, within walking distance of the store if you got up early. The rent was cheap. He took up the tenancy and Elaine knew it was over.

Her tremendous sorrow expressed itself first in torrents of tears and in pleading with him to change his mind about the flat. She reiterated an earlier offer she had made to provide money to support the mother and sister she had never met and about whom she had developed a poor opinion.

Then her anguish turned to anger and bitterness. She accused him of being too weak to know his own mind, of being feckless, without direction, all the things his mother had accused him of in the past.

Elaine also said she could not see now why she had ever thought that he had creative talent, as any artist would seek to use his skill more creatively than just dressing windows. Her last words were, "I hate you Tom!" And afterwards she hated herself.

Thomas was startled by her vehemence, shaken to the core by the magnitude of the pain he had caused and the wrath it had aroused. He moved to the city as quickly as he could, still trying to deceive himself that he had done only what was necessary to help Mary and their mother, and to maintain the more grievous deceit that Elaine would be better off without him.

Elaine tried to maintain her anger, to hide from herself her desperate sorrow. Until she met Thomas life had been so good and she had always thought that it could only get better.

The few years she had spent at the family store were not what she had intended, but the experience had done her no harm. Her involvement had helped her parents, and she felt she owed them that for all they had done for her. It had also provided her with an extremely good lifestyle, albeit limited in its scope. She had become well known and well liked within the community of business people. Although this had taken her out of the art world for a while, that might not have been such a bad thing in terms of overall self-development. Just a hiatus really.

But now her whole world was askew. A girl friend had once described to her a car crash: one moment driving along serenely, then a tyre burst, the twist of the wheel out of her grasp, the lurch off the road, earth and sky bewilderingly interchangeable, tree-trunks looming up, no control. Then impact, concussion and, slowly, returning consciousness with a terrible sensation of excruciating pain.

But within days *that* pain was diminishing, bone was healing, bruises subsiding. Life quickly returning to normal. For Elaine it seemed as if nothing could ever again be normal or without pain. She had never known such emptiness, so little point in anything, even in living. Her world was still spinning like the wheels of the overturned car, but it would not come to rest. As if in a nightmare, she could not regain control, could not grasp the wheel or find the brake. It seemed an ordeal without any possible end.

For a while a deep depression set in. Every move she made was an effort. Every word she spoke was forced, deliberate. Like a person who has witnessed a catastrophe she had to plod laboriously through each day and try to link herself to that reality rather than relinquish everything to the chaotic turmoil of her mind.

The day-to-day running of the store, living by calendar and diary, helped her in some ways. Boring routine was useful up to a point; it might keep her going until she could find a way to move forward. But a continued mundane existence would only be destructive in the longer term, especially for someone with an artist's sensibilities. .

She knew she must get out, move away. Continue with her plan to go back to London, alone now, and re-engage with the people she knew there. Only a creative vibrant environment might bring her out of this weird stupor that enshrouded her. She had to get Thomas out of her mind forever, somehow cauterise the wound and let it callous over, so that part of her would be indifferent to pain again.

She was not sure what supreme effort of will that would take, but involvement with artists, people like herself, might help.

Although, when she reflected upon it, she found she was no longer sure what her real self was. The last year had changed her. Thomas had changed her. Before meeting him she would never have believed that she could have been shattered into fragments by a short-lived love affair. Just what had happened, she asked herself.

She began to look back on their early meetings. A young man had rented a room above John Breasley's shop, a place she visited briefly at the end of each working day. He was often in the shop when she called, chatting to Breasley. They had conversed warmly, as a threesome, she had not for one moment seen him as an intruder. He was good-looking, well spoken. He talked intelligently in a circumspect, unassuming sort of way. He seemed refined, quite well educated. He had once, to their surprise, interpreted some Latin for them, quoted in a newspaper she and John were reading. He was artistically inclined, although diffident about his abilities. She had later found out that his father had drowned in the river and recalled that the newspapers had conjured up some mystery surrounding the event. It was said that the family lived amongst gypsies, and had no fear of them. She had noted for herself that he would not join in with, and even strongly refuted, some of the more egregious criticisms of the travelling community.

Then, one night she had gone with a girl friend to a theatre in the city twenty miles away. There she had seen Thomas. They had spoken briefly when she realized he was intending to catch a train home, so she had offered him a lift in her father's car.

On the way back they had discussed the play, Rattigan's "The Winslow Boy." He had seemed to know it well, having seen it more than once. He had seemed strangely moved, troubled even, by the essence of the plot, the desperate need to clear one's name at any cost when falsely accused

He said that it was a lucky man who had the means of refuting a falsehood, by which she thought he meant the financial means. Which was the case of the father of the accused Winslow Boy, although it almost bankrupted him. She had bridled at that, being defensive of modest wealth, honestly gained by effort and thrift. She had stated that to him. Bluntly, forcibly.

'Per ardua ad astra' you mean?' Thomas had asked her, jokingly, but with a slight edge, she thought.

'Yes. I think that is quite possible.' she replied.

How ironic that remark now seemed to her. She had reached the stars with Tom, effortlessly it seemed. And now all the stars had fallen from her sky.

But he had not meant what she had thought. He had meant that you were lucky if the evidence existed by which you could prove your case. If there was no evidence then one must suffer indefinitely under the weight of an unfounded slur. She did not understand him and he had apologised for being abstruse. He said it was difficult to put into words just then, but that he would explain it to her another time perhaps.

When they became close Thomas did tell Elaine of his mother's accusation, adding that whilst there existed no evidence to support it there was none to contradict it either.

Elaine had been horrified: 'How dreadfully hurtful,' she said, wondering at the cruelty of such a mother.

She felt that there was something in his upbringing that led him to assume guilt too readily. It was not so much a case of admitting you were wrong when you knew you were, it was more to do with never knowing if you were right. Never having the confidence to say, "I believe…"

Elaine reflected on how she had carried him along on her own confidence. Taking him into her parent's house when she hardly knew him, under the guise of finding him work at her father's store when, deep down, she wanted some kind of attachment, however slender, to this non-committal, intriguing man.

They had gone out together, but not at his request; she had made the suggestion. And they had made love for the first time because her erotic provocation would have tempted a bishop.

So perhaps she had brought about their downfall, put an abrupt end to this sublime episode that she had hoped would last forever. But equally, perhaps not. She had certainly done things in a hurry, but, left to himself, it was difficult to guess what Tom might or might not have done.

Elaine felt no trace of guilt, just an enormous sense of empty, aching loss, a depth of profound sorrow she could never before have envisaged.

The only loss Elaine had ever known before was during her childhood when the family dog had died. That had been painful, but it was an old dog and her parents had told her that it was better for it. It was now at rest and free from pain.

Her own pain then had subsided quickly. She felt that *this* pain could never subside. How could it? Her whole being was consumed by it. She must go on for the rest of her life carrying the weight of emptiness. Her world had changed forever.

11

Elaine approached John Breasley's shop. It was early afternoon, a time deliberately chosen because she knew there would be no possibility of meeting Thomas. She had fully composed herself and had rehearsed in her mind what she was going to say. She opened the shop door.

'Hello John. I've called to say cheerio. I'm off to London tomorrow. First train in the morning.' She said this with a mentally practiced gaiety.

'So it's not goodbye.' said John, trying to force a smile, hearing his voice threatening to betray his emotions.

'No, of course not. I'm sure it won't be long before I'll be dropping in again.'

'I can't tell you how much I'll be looking forward to that,' said John, his voice close to breaking now.

The old man knew that he was about to lose the close company of two young people who were very dear to him, two people who were very much in love, yet one of them would not believe what his heart told him. It was as if a family was about to tear itself apart for some inexplicable reason.

'And Tom, when will he join you?'

Elaine had not prepared herself for this. 'I – I don't know John. I don't know.'

She had told herself that she wasn't going to cry. Now her shoulders shook and her trembling hands sought a handkerchief. Her chin had fallen to her chest.

John put his hands around the tops of her arms, feeling her whole body quivering. It was only then that he realised that in all the years he had known her this was the first time he had touched her. Her perfume reached his nostrils; her luxuriant mass of red-gold hair was in his face. Even when drowning in her sorrow she was beautiful. How could Tom allow himself to lose such a treasure? Why would he hurt someone so? Yet John instantly knew why. He knew Tom's fears; his doubts had always been visible, tangible almost. He knew that Tom was not his own man; perhaps he never would be. He'd been too much moulded by others and had never found himself.

'It'll be all right Elaine, you'll be fine.' John knew that he was lying, as much to himself as to Elaine, just trying desperately to make a wish come true.

Elaine turned on her heel and rushed to the door. 'I'll write to you John,' she sobbed.

John stood motionless, silent, tears streaming down his cheeks. A sudden gust of wind slammed the door behind her.

***

Elaine established herself in London. Her parents knew she must. Money was willingly provided to ease the transition. She re-established contacts, helped enormously by the agent who was already organising the sale of her work.

She began to work anew, hesitantly at first, then with increasing vigour as she found success with a very different style.

Her mode of living changed dramatically. She needed to live differently in every way from how she had lived in the past year. It was as if she could get Tom out of her mind only by expunging every aspect of how she had spent that time. She had to break every habit, every convention she had established. She discarded long held beliefs, changed her mode of dress, her hairstyle, everything short of changing her name. It was a descent almost into nihilism, in the hope that eventually she might be re-born.

Time seemed not to matter; the existence of all that was encompassed within it was all that counted. Elaine would work in her studio for days on end, existing on only bread, cheese and fruit and endless jugs of coffee, as she painted continuously. Unwashed and dishevelled, she slept on her studio couch only when too exhausted to continue.

She sold her work infrequently but for significant prices, as her reputation was growing rapidly. She no longer needed her father's help to pay her way. In the main she lived frugally, the rent of her studio and austere living quarters being her main expense.

When not working she went to all-night parties, mixing with millionaires and paupers, debauchees and addicts; with artists who were household names and many who would forever be nameless.

The need to extirpate memories of Thomas and all the events of the past year, led to her total immersion in her art and the art of others around her.

She was seldom satisfied with what she created and re-worked pictures incessantly. When a picture was as good as she could make it, and she could agree with herself that it was finished, she slept for a day and a night. Then partied wildly for several more before burying herself in something new.

But her frenetic life still revolved around a huge void. Before she knew Thomas she could easily have lived alone. Now she could not. When not lost in her work she needed the company of others. The gaping wound that the separation had inflicted would not heal. She began to believe that it never would.

Elaine had always thought that one should shape one's life, not simply submit to destiny. If a chosen avenue did not lead to the hoped-for destination, then try another. "Endeavour to control circumstances, don't let them control you" had been her mantra.

She now found this to be impossible. An avenue she had entered with confidence, which at first had led to delirious pleasure, had turned into a high-walled cul-de-sac. But, worse than that, a portcullis had dropped down behind her.

It was not possible to go back. She could not start again. Such helplessness terrified her. How long could life go on like this?

A deep depression set in that worsened day by day. A sense of impending doom prevailed. Still she painted, bleak, gloomy works that informed opinion said were the best she had ever done. The form of her work had now changed entirely, becoming more abstract, only semi-figurative. It was moodily haunting, often horrific. She seemed to be painting only feelings, expressing graphically the pain that tortured her.

Yet she worked on, relentlessly, as if on a treadmill, alternately painting and sleeping, now rarely seeing friends. The signs of malnutrition etched themselves into her face and body. She could not recognise them. Her unframed canvasses stacked up on tables and on the floor, gathering dust. She knew she must end this pain It had to be done. She could not go on like this.

12

Thomas settled into his new found work quickly and more easily than he had expected to. The fluid hustle and bustle of city life suited him. He was practically anonymous. Apart from his immediate work colleagues no one even knew his name, yet he no longer felt like an outsider.

As he walked each morning to the store, he saw himself as part of a national workforce flowing along the arteries of streets and alleyways to a place of industry. A place where he produced something to be exchanged for the products of another's labour. An atom of an anonymous interdependency, barely acknowledged, at least not consciously, by any of the actors, yet which imparted a sense of belonging, a feeling of being part of a greater whole. A part of something that mattered to everyone.

No one asked about him. No one was interested in what he did or what he thought. Where he went when away from work was his own business. He liked this. He did not have to account for himself. So long as he worked reliably and achieved the desired result, then he was a satisfactory person. He wondered why it had taken so long, been so difficult to become such a being.

Having a regular job with achievable goals, where, after initially establishing himself no one enquired of him any further was a relief. He recalled that when he had worked for himself, and all that amounted to really, was odd-jobbing, despite the creative effort he put into it, he always had to expose himself. He had somehow to sell himself to every new paymaster, giving examples of what he had done and for whom. In a small-town situation that meant people would talk behind his back, fitting together all the bits they thought they knew and then embellishing them. Thomas felt freer now. In grey suited nine to five-thirty anonymity, he was almost his own man.

The morning walk from his flat to the city centre was a long one, so he had to rise early. Only in the worst of winter weather did he take a trolleybus. He therefore had little time to think about anything other than the day in front of him before setting off to shape it.

At first he tried different routes to the store for the sake of variety and to get to know the city intimately but he soon settled for a particular way, a deliberate choice of regularity over variety. He felt somehow that conformity, some sort of habitual behaviour, might benefit him in some way he was not yet sure of.

He started to recognise some of the faces that came towards him each day. He began to wonder, to speculate, about the lives behind the faces. Why might they have the same regularity of purpose as he had, when the purpose itself was no doubt very different?

Eye contact, at first averted, was then held momentarily, progressing to a nod, then a smile. Eventually to a tentative, "Good morning."

This was perhaps how you came to respect the individuality of others, their intrinsic worth. What mattered surely, was the value of their varied existences without having, or needing to have, any idea of their backgrounds, their beliefs, their *raison d'etre*.

This ceaseless flow of humanity around itself, not so much interacting, but simply acknowledging the validity of the other's existence, entered into Thomas' being with all the warm mellowness of a glass of good wine.

After a while a feeling of habituation settled upon him. Simply seeing the same bus numbers going by at the same time each morning, or recognising the same dogs being walked each day, began to make him feel that he belonged to that part of the city, but equally, that it did not own him.

It was a shared existence. The anonymity meant there were no echelons, no levels or stations of rank about which judgements could be made. Each person had a purpose about which the others knew nothing. They could guess if they liked, but the abstract *other* remained just that.

The job was undemanding insofar as, being merely an assistant, Thomas had no decisions to make. The only challenge, albeit a fairly stiff one, was to empty and re-dress a big window as quickly as possible. An empty window lost the store money. Therefore there was pressure on the display staff to work quickly. It was often necessary to work late or through lunch breaks to meet deadlines.

This suited him, it gave him little time to think. Better not to indulge in the dubious luxury of introspection, not to dwell too long on anything unconnected with work.

Even the relationships between himself and the staff within his orbit were necessarily brief and superficial, but superficiality had much to commend it. It side-lined thought, neutralised commitment. It precluded the need for discussion, obviated statements about what one felt about the world. Civil interaction and focussed communication were all that were required, along with the ability and willingness to follow instructions. Friendship was unlikely to evolve within this setting. All this, for Thomas, was reassuring. The only friendship he now wished to hang on to was that with John Breasley.

There was no scope for individual creativity at this level. He would have liked more of an artistic challenge. But right now that was not important. All displays were arranged according to photographs taken in a studio and disseminated to the firm's branches, where they were adhered to as closely as possible by the display managers.

Thomas knew that his job lacked substance, was, in reality, mere frippery. It even had an element of deceit about it, insofar as he colluded with others in making objects appear more attractive and desirable than perhaps they really were.

He deemed this deceit to be venial, of no greater magnitude than the stratagem of the car salesmen polishing the vehicles on their forecourts to make them look a little newer than they actually were. Certainly nothing like the huge deceits practiced by certain organisations of which he himself had once upon a time come close to being part of. And utterly insignificant if compared with the deceit he had been guilty of perpetrating against Elaine.

He had in the past used "window dressing" as a pejorative term for something that was merely a veneer, an outward suggestion of quality for something that in reality lacked substance, and now he was doing just that to earn his daily bread.

Overall though, the work suited him. It caused him no anguish or consternation, no inward turmoil. He could do no harm, he thought, through this mode of employment. It made him a meagre living and enabled him to contribute a small amount of money to his sister, by which donation he also helped their mother.

***

Whenever Thomas visited his sister he tried also to call in on John Breasley. John was always delighted to see him; it seemed almost as if that was all he now lived for.

Although they talked at length it now seemed odd to sit in the shop alone with John, knowing that Elaine would not be joining them.

In better days one of them would drop in and before long the other would turn up, then they would talk together as a family; there was mutual warmth, easy jocularity. Now, there was a profound sense of loss, of incompleteness.

The shop seemed as lifeless as a funeral parlour. Customers were few, so the stock hardly changed. Cobwebs hung in profusion amongst the ropes. The floor was never swept these days and John would sway in his hammock, scratching with the toe of his shoe surprisingly recognisable outlines of continents in the fibrous dust.

Thomas was pleased to find that several of the many shopkeepers who had known "Breezy" over the years would drop in for a few minutes each day to chat to him. He was also glad to learn that Charles Langdon visited him at least once a week, but was amazed to hear that Langdon also enquired about himself.

'About me!' he had exclaimed, the first time John mentioned it to him. 'Why on earth would he ask about me?'

'I don't know why, but he has, and on more than one occasion. And his interest seemed to be with the best of intentions as far as I could tell.'

'Well, I'm astounded,' Thomas had replied. 'I didn't think he liked me.'

'I don't think he ever disliked you. Probably didn't think you were good enough for his daughter.'

That was the only time John had ever referred to Elaine since she had left the town.

'What did you tell him – about me, I mean?'

'What could I tell him? I said you seemed to be all right. And that you were working in a business much like his own. He mused on that for a long time.'

As John never spoke about Elaine, Thomas felt certain that there was nothing to tell. He'd always thought John knew nothing of Elaine's whereabouts, other than her being in London. He knew him to be too honest, too open, to conceal a fact from him, even if it was a painful one. It was unlikely that Charles Langdon would discuss his daughter's activities with anyone outside the family.

***

There was a time when, because of work commitments, Thomas couldn't visit either his sister or John, for several weeks. He wrote letters to both, but only Mary replied.

When next in Banebridge he went straight to the rope shop. The door was locked. The place, always poorly lighted, was now in darkness. Both the door and the window blinds were down. He could just about discern a few envelopes on the floor beneath the letterbox. He entered the grocer's shop next door to make enquiries.

'Didn't you know?' said the man. 'They buried him last week.'

Thomas was badly shaken. He was well aware of Breasley's age, but he hadn't appeared particularly infirm when last they met.

'What happened to him?' he asked.

'Nothing really,' came the reply. 'A couple of weeks ago the newsagent was opening up about five in the morning and he noticed a light was on in Breasley's place and the door blind was up. He tried the door and found it unlocked, so he went in. Breasley was lying in his hammock, one foot trailing in the dust, his pipe on the floor. It was a wonder the whole place hadn't gone up in smoke. The pipe must have gone out

before it fell from his mouth. He was a grand old chap, you know.'
'Yes. Yes, he was,' were the only words Thomas could find.
'You'll see his grave, close to the railings on the west side of the cemetery. It's still fresh. There are lots of flowers.'

***

The rope shop stood empty, shuttered and forlorn, for several weeks. The next time Thomas visited the town its window was brightly lit, displaying gaily- patterned wallpaper and tins of paint. All of his painstakingly crafted sign-writing had been burned off and a man in white overalls was completing a gleaming new façade in bright bold colours. The existence of two generations obliterated. The place of the most sublime pleasure, of the deepest friendship, and also of heartbreak, was now only a memory.

***

After a time, having become well settled into his job and city life, Thomas was promoted. The increase in salary made life marginally more comfortable.

He did not now have to spend the whole of every evening alone in his apartment, having left the store as late as possible to save on electricity. He could now afford to go out occasionally, have a drink in a pub, always remaining aloof from all but the most casual of social contacts. He always made a point of departing quickly on the rare occasions when he saw someone whom he knew from the store.

Another year on and promotion to display manager made life much easier and he settled into store life if not enthusiastically, then at least with some sense of satisfaction.

Window display to a blueprint had ceased and staff were now chosen for their artistic abilities and expected to be startlingly creative. This made his life much more interesting, challenging and more satisfying. He was also much better paid. He was now able to start to buy a decent flat in a better area and to live relatively comfortably. The premature death of his mother and an upturn in his sister's fortunes released him from his self-imposed financial obligation to them.

A year later and Thomas' creative abilities were becoming noticed and remarked upon by senior staff within the organisation. It was suggested that his duties within the store be taken off him for a couple of weeks and that he should work with the display team at the firm's prestigious branch in Bath. It was hoped he could lift the somewhat dated and uninspiring standard of display that had become established there.

He readily agreed to this temporary move. Living alone, he had no one else's needs to consider. Therefore the thought of a brief change of workplace and a stay in a hotel appealed to him. He had never been to Bath, and, although he knew that he would have little time for himself, he might be able to see some of the city.

The firm would arrange and pay for travel and accommodation. He was to present himself to the branch manager, a Mr Slater, in one week's time.

He spent that week reading about the history of Bath and its environs and noting one or two places that he would particularly like to see if time allowed. He found himself looking forward to the trip.

The company had booked him into a hotel for two weeks commencing on the Sunday night prior to his meeting with Mr Slater the following morning.

Thomas wished to see the store and note its position in the town and to have at least a vague knowledge of the geography of the place before that meeting. Therefore, he travelled to Bath on the Saturday evening and booked into a cheap guesthouse for the night in order to wander around at will on the Sunday.

He spent at least a couple of hours that day studying the store's current – and staid – display and envisaging improvements, as well as noting what the commercial opposition had to offer.

On the appointed morning he entered the store and asked for directions to the manager's office. An administrative assistant from his office was sent for, who apologised for Mr Slater's absence – he was sick – and who instead took him to the assistant manager, Mr Hudson.

Whilst that name seemed to have a familiar ring to him, he thought nothing of it, but on meeting him he was both amazed and delighted to recognise his old friend Paul.

Although now showing a moustache and smartly attired in a charcoal-grey suit, Paul looked not a day older and far less careworn than when Thomas had last seen him.

After the initial moment of pleasurable surprise, Thomas immediately anticipated a perhaps unfriendly reaction, but there was none. Paul was as happy as he that this serendipitous reunion should have occurred.

The assistant left them, closing the office door behind her.

They both started to say, 'What are you doing here?' and both immediately laughed at the empty banality of the question. Then they hugged one another warmly.

'What happened to you Paul? I mean – why did you leave the seminary?'

'Did you not get my letter? I wrote to you almost straight away.'

'No. They chucked me out. They blamed me for your disappearance. Was I the cause of it?'

'Yes, in a way. But, in a good way. Don't worry about it. You did me a lot of good. Look Tom, we've a lot to talk about, but we can't talk now. We've both got work to do. I must introduce you to the three display assistants. They've not had a manager for six months. They've been struggling through on their own. They'll be pleased to see you. They're good though. You'll get on all right with them. I'll have a quick working lunch with you in our restaurant. Fill you in a bit. Then you must come home with me tonight. Meet Annette and our baby.'

'Gosh, you've moved on a bit.' said Thomas.

The working lunch was just that. Little time was available to chat about personal affairs. However, Thomas met the display assistants and they planned the work for the next week. How to blend seasonal themes and current trends and link those with the demands of the local area was the subject of discussion in the absence of managerial guidance. Sorely needed display equipment was listed and left for Mr Slater's consideration when he returned to work.

The day, which he enjoyed, passed quickly – too quickly in fact. Thomas had hoped to accomplish a lot more than he did. There was time though to catch up. He was prepared to work into the evenings if Paul could arrange that for him.

When the store closed Paul led Thomas to a newish Morris Minor parked in a nearby street. They drove to a village not far away and pulled up outside a small neat house that fronted directly onto the street. Annette met them at the door, a baby girl in her arms. Paul had telephoned during the day to say he had met an old friend and was bringing him home for a meal.

Thomas found Annette quite charming. He thought she showed traces of Asian origins and later in the evening that was confirmed to be so. The child, placid, but very alert, he found enchanting.

He could see that Annette was a good twelve or more years younger than Paul, but it was obvious that age did not concern them. They were very close.

When the meal was finished, and the remains cleared away, Annette took the child to bed. Thomas and Paul sat down to talk.

'So what happened? Why did you leave so suddenly? I couldn't believe you could have left, I thought something dreadful had happened to you, but they said they had a letter from you.'

'I felt terrible about that last meeting, Tom. I was berating you for losing your faith, telling you how to overcome your doubts, denying that you had any foundation for them. I can hardly believe now that I was so overbearing, so dictatorial. I was just talking you down. As soon as we parted that night I realised that it was myself I was talking to, not you. I had doubts too – for a long time – but they were different from yours.'

'How do you mean?'

'Well, I wasn't losing my faith, as you were. At least I wasn't until then. After that I was not so sure. I'd always had a few niggling doubts about doctrinal issues. I don't think that's uncommon. But it wasn't that. It was doubts about myself, about my ability to be a priest. I remember, very clearly, saying to you that night that priests had to be strong to support their parishioners who might be faltering. And I knew that I wasn't strong.'

'You seemed very strong to me. I think I was in awe of you.'

'No. I was simply regurgitating all that had been stuffed into me throughout my life. I was there for all the wrong reasons you see.'

'I don't see. To me you seemed to have all the makings of a priest.'

'I was there to hide Tom. To get away from the world. To bury myself in a deep burrow, away from reality. I'd seen too much reality. I couldn't take any more.'

'The war you mean?'

'Yes. That, and its aftermath. I'd seen first-hand what people could do to one another and I include myself in that. I know I killed people. That's hard to live with. The seminary was good to me Tom. It provided a safe haven. I needed that. I had no trouble getting in. After all, I was from a good catholic background. I'd been to an outstanding catholic boarding school.'

'I didn't know that,' said Thomas. 'I really don't know much about you at all.'

'I suppose I didn't give much away. I wasn't what you would call a well-integrated person.'

'I don't know. I was glad of your support in the early days.'

'Despite the private schooling, I was not a good academic. There again, the seminary was kind to me. The priests made allowances for my limitations and kept helping me through.'

'So what made you leave so abruptly?'

'Remember I had been there for two years before you started Tom. I was becoming ever closer to being ordained. That was beginning to frighten me. I knew that soon I would be back out into the real world and having to involve myself in other people's problems. Spiritual problems, as well as the difficulties of everyday life. It was the everyday problems that most troubled me. People trying to cope with poverty, having children they could not afford to feed and the church telling them to practice celibacy when sometimes the love they wanted to show for each other was almost all they had to keep them going. It wasn't right, Tom.

'And there was something else. Before I joined the army I was engaged. I was looking forward to the day when we might be able to marry. We wanted a child Tom.'

There was a long pause, as if Paul had lost the thread of what he was saying. He seemed deep in thought.

Then: 'She left me Tom. Whilst I was away. She wrote to me. It was the end. I don't blame her. I didn't blame her then. That's just how it was. Everything seemed pointless. Afterwards, I didn't want children. Or a relationship. I couldn't see the point of anything. The whole history of humanity seemed to be inextricably bound up in famine, pestilence and war. Particularly war. And that's probably the most frequent cause of the other two. It seemed wrong to even want to have children, to create a life when there was no way of knowing if you could give it any security, even meet its most basic needs in such a deranged world. I suppose I was also afraid of another relationship going wrong. After some time in the seminary I began to regain some hope, perhaps even a little faith in human nature. Probably because I was seeing only a very limited amount of it. Looking back, it was a strange existence there. As I began to feel better about the world I once again wished for a family. The nearer I became to being ordained the more I feared losing that opportunity.'

Thomas interrupted urgently, hopefully. 'So I wasn't the sole cause of your leaving then?'

'No. But the discussion that night was the coup de grace. When you started talking about an omnipotent, omniscient God, my mind was immediately back in the war. Back to the wholesale slaughter of men, women and children. Particularly children. How could they ever deserve that? The wanton destruction of everything that defines civilisation appalled me. And they tell us that God works in mysterious ways. Although I was arguing with you that night I was aware that what I was saying was utter drivel. Those were empty words. I knew it. Afterwards, I felt that I had exposed myself as an idiot.'

'I'm sorry.' was all Thomas could weakly reply.

'Don't say that Tom. Look at what I have now. A wife. A child. A home. I've never been happier. And I've found you again. Life continues to improve.'

'That's good, that's great. I'm glad it's turned out well for you. Tell me, what did you do immediately after leaving the seminary? How did you survive?'

'I went back to London. Some friends put me up for a while. I found work on a building site. It half-killed me, it was so hard. I felt hunted. Looking back it all seems so foolish. I thought I would be pursued, like a criminal, so I didn't look for permanent work, through which I might be traced. On the site no one asked questions.

I didn't think I would last the first week out, but it became easier as my fitness improved, so I did that job for about four months in all. Then a friend found me a job in retailing. I had some business background so I took to it easily. It led eventually to what I am doing now. To finish the speech I've just been making Tom, let me say this: the Church is right to say that all evils in the world are man-made and nothing to do with God. Of course they are. But the Church won't accept that whatever is good in humankind also has nothing to do with any deity. God has a hand in everything or a hand in nothing. If the Church admitted that it would be out of business.'

'You've really shrugged off the yoke haven't you?' said Thomas.

'I think so,' Paul replied. 'But it wasn't easy.'

'You sound as if you've become a godless heathen like me Paul.' continued Thomas, with a broad smile.

'I suppose I have, although Annette and myself look for some way of acknowledging that there is much we don't understand and possibly never will. We think that there are ways of being that are good, and others that are bad, although such absolutes are hard to define and are of course subjective.'

'Yes, they usually are. Few absolutes stand the test of time.'

'We both incline towards Buddhism,' continued Paul, 'although neither of us would call ourselves Buddhist. We just try to stay awake to the transience of existence, the need for –the fact of – mutual interdependence. We look for some form of guidance that is non-theistic. We are no longer worshipful of gods or deities.'

'I think that just about sums me up too,' said Thomas.

13

Rose had died. Her miserable existence had not extended many years beyond her husband's death. She might have made her daughter's existence miserable too, had Mary not been so forgiving of her mother's difficult, demanding ways.

Rose's overriding priority each day was to visit the church, a routine begun soon after Pat's death.

At first, Mary had willingly accompanied her, but as time went by she did not wish to be there at all. Even Sundays and Holy Days had become a chore. But still she joined her mother on at least a couple of days each week.

The church was often bereft of worshippers, other than themselves, for much of the day. It was cold, mostly, and Mary hated sitting or kneeling there in the silent gloom, watching the guttering flame of the tiny oil-lamp beneath the Sacred Heart of Jesus.

Mary's occasional refusal to accompany her mother usually attracted barbed comments or even a vicious diatribe; Rose could never see any reason why her daughter should not be at her side.

Mary did not respond to the invective. She judged it understandable. Her mother's life had been a sad one. She had lost so much. It was easy for Mary to forgive her angry rants.

So it was with considerable sorrow that Mary remembered the last time she had refused her mother's wish, the last time that Rose herself had set foot in the church.

She had been in poorer health than usual for several days. Mary's advice to her, to see a doctor, or at least stay in bed, had been ignored. Rose was clearly intent on carrying on as usual.

'I'm going across to the church, Mary. Will you be coming with me?'

'You were there this morning, Mam.' she had replied.

'I need to go. Will you come?'

'I was with you yesterday, Mother. And the day before. I can't find the time to go today.'

'What have you to do?' asked Rose.

'I need to go across to the town. I'll have to make two journeys. With only one good hand I can't carry much each time.'

'Do you need that much?' asked Rose.

'We need things, Mother. It's not just me.'

'Well, there's some coppers in my purse. See if one of the kids next door will go with you to carry a bag.'

'They're starting to ask for more than coppers, Mother. We cannot afford to keep giving money away.'

'Suit yourself.' replied Rose.

Shawled and hatted, she set off for the church. Eyes downcast, she skirted the town by the back-streets and alleyways, avoiding the glance of anyone who might recognise her.

With any luck one of the three priests might be in the church. Occasionally, one of them would join her in prayer. That always made her feel better.

Mary made the two visits to the town, having decided not to ask for help from the neighbour's children. It was late in the afternoon when she returned home for the second time. She was surprised to find the house still empty

Her mother should have been back from the church by now. She put the kettle on the embers and waited.

An hour later a parishioner called to say that her mother had been discovered in a collapsed state in one of the pews when the lights were being switched on for the evening benediction.

The prognosis was not good. Rose had an advanced cancer of the womb. She died within weeks.

Mary stood up well to the bereavement. She had loved her mother dearly despite her trying ways, and she missed her presence around the house. But she took it in her stride, as she did all of life's iniquities. She felt that Rose had been released from an inner turmoil that for years she had struggled to bear.

Thomas did not take his mother's death so well. He had always hoped for the reconciliation that now could never be. He'd also hoped for exoneration, the lifting of the blame with which she had damned him.

Or, if not that, then at least some explanation of why she was so certain that he had been the cause of his father's death. But, above all, he sorrowed most for the hurt he had caused her.

Now their mother was dead Thomas saw more of his sister. There was no longer the awkwardness of conducting a conversation feeling that they were being listened to by a lonely recluse, steeped in bitterness and sorrow, from the other side of a closed door. Their meetings had, of necessity, been shortened because, although they never said it, Thomas' brief appearances were effectively trapping Rose in her grief.

Now, every couple of weeks he caught a bus or train to visit Mary and they talked easily, openly, over pots of tea, well into the evening. His next visit was almost due and Mary was very much looking forward to it.

She had much to tell him.

Thomas arrived to find Mary in good spirits. The trade union had finally pushed the brewery into admitting it was the cause of her accident and had won compensation for her without going to court. She told him the sum that was to be awarded to her and he was pleasantly surprised at the amount. Given that her hand and wrist were badly scared, and that articulation would always be limited, he did not think she had been over-compensated, but he was nonetheless surprised, as the brewery had seemed likely to contest the case for ever.

'Now listen, Tom,' said the delighted Mary. 'You've helped me out for a long time. I want to pay you back when I get this money. I know you've struggled a lot.'

'Now you listen, Mary,' said a laughing Thomas. 'I don't want a penny from you. Yes, I have struggled, but I'm not struggling now. Since my promotion I've earned enough to live as well as I want to. I'm buying a decent flat, I dress well, I eat well, and I can afford to go out occasionally. What more do I want? And I've heard that I'm in line for a pay rise.'

'It seems unfair that you are having to buy a flat whilst I am living in this house. You have as much entitlement to it as I do.'

'Do you not want to continue living here?' asked Thomas 'I thought you liked being here. Speaking for myself, I wouldn't want to come back. The bad memories outweigh the good. But I've always assumed that you like it here. And if you don't, you could sell up and move away. It wouldn't sell for a big price, it's in the wrong place, but it would give you a start somewhere else. I certainly don't want anything from it. Do what you want with the house and the money that's coming to you. You deserve it. You've suffered enough, looking after mother through her final years.'

'I think we've both suffered Tom, but you a lot more than me. Mother's accusation was cruel and unjustified, and I know how much you were hurt by it, and by the gulf it created between you both.'

'I still hope it was unjustified. I'll never be sure. I didn't believe that my leaving the seminary caused Dad so much anguish, but I can't deny that not qualifying as a teacher wounded him badly. I know that he struggled with that. Then my leaving the faith altogether was another blow to him although I have always felt even that didn't hit him as hard as my failing the teaching exams. Whether or not all those things combined were enough – you know, to – to do it, I cannot say. I know that he was cut up about it though. Dad loved education, but never had the chance to get much of it for himself. You never know; we'll never know. I have to admit it. She could have been right. That's a cross I'll have to carry. Such is life. Tell me what are your plans now you're coming into the money?'

'I'm glad you're prepared to let me stay in this house and, as I've said, I'd like you to have some money in lieu of it, but I know you won't take it. I've a business idea in mind and I could run it from here.'

'I wouldn't think you could run much of a business from here. It's hardly what you would call a "good address". What have you in mind?'

'There's plenty of parking space Tom, where the two old cottages used to stand. If I owned a big car and a telephone I could run a taxi service. Although we are cut off from the town by the river we're close to the bridge. We're only a few hundred yards away from the town centre, and less from the train station, so it would be easy to respond to a 'phone call. And most people order a taxi by 'phone unless they are arriving at the station. It's easy to go down there and meet the trains.'

'Just one thing Mary; you cannot drive.'

'No Tom, and unless this hand gets a lot better I probably never will. I've been speaking in a casual sort of way with Mick Dempsey. Now he's got a child he doesn't want to be away on long-distance lorry driving for much longer. It keeps him away from the family. And the local work doesn't pay well, not that anyone around here is looking for a driver, according to what he tells me.'

'How would you pay him?'

'We'd take out the capital costs, the running costs and split what's left over.'

'Would Mick take a chance like that?'

'I think he would. He's sick of the distance work. We've had a couple of chats about this, just, you know, mulling it over as a possibility. He's keen.'

Thomas laughed to himself, then said, 'You'd need a big car if Mick is going to be driving for you. He's a giant of a man.'

'That's what you need, for humping the luggage. He could carry a suitcase like I'd carry a handbag. And he has such a lovely nature. So patient, always smiling. He can put anyone at their ease in a minute. He'll talk to anyone, any class of person. Before he went on the lorries he trained as a motor mechanic, so that makes him doubly useful.'

'And if it doesn't work out?'

'I'll have a car to sell and then a job to look for, although I wouldn't leave the brewery immediately. Not for a few weeks at least. I'd wait to see if any insurmountable problems might arise. But I wouldn't want to carry on with the job I'm doing for the rest of my life. Mick knows it might not work out. He accepts that possibility. He'd always find another job. He says he'd like to try this idea because it's the nearest thing to being self-employed. That's what attracts me to it too. I think we could make a go of it, him in the car and me in the office. If my hand improved enough for me to pass a driving test we could get another car. If there was enough trade, that is.'

'That would be the big question. Do you think there would be enough trade? There's one firm in town already, and he's been in the business for years. Would this town stand another?'

'The town has grown considerably in the last few years Tom, and people are becoming slightly more affluent. I think there is more than enough trade for us. If I don't try it surely it won't be long before someone else does. I've been hanging around the stations Tom, watching what happens when a train comes in. Nearly every time there are people left waiting for a car. Hackett shouts to them to wait and he'll come back for them, and if they have heavy luggage that is what they have to do. If they've no luggage they walk. I think it's worth the chance, Tom. You have to take chances, or else you're left wondering what might have been.'

Thomas winced inwardly as if he had been kicked. 'I have to hand it to you, Mary. You seem to have it all worked out. How long have you been thinking about this?'

'The idea came to my head when the union started pressing my case for compensation. I never thought they would get me anything like the sums they were talking about. In fact, I didn't think I'd get anything at all. But after a while you get to dreaming, "What if I did get that much? What would I do with it?" I never said anything to anyone until a couple of weeks ago when I happened to have a long chat with Mick and found he was looking out for something new. By then it was looking likely that the brewery might be giving ground. I took a chance and mentioned it to him. He loved the idea. With you telling me to stay in the house it now seems possible. I think I might risk it. That is if the council will licence another taxi firm in the town.'

'I think it will work Mary. You are right. The town is growing. I've seen new businesses. There's more money around. The best of luck to both of you.'

Thomas caught the bus back to the city with a sense of happiness that things were improving for Mary. She was game. A severe injury had not daunted her. She was always optimistic, and optimism could take you a long way. As most of the world is always ready to put you down there's no point in doing that to yourself. Why not take a chance? Mary had always taken chances. The past had never gripped her as it had held on to him. Life is short. Within it there is much to lose, much to gain. No point in throwing chances away. Why had he, he wondered?

14

It was approaching eleven p.m. and Mary was ready for her bed. It had been a busy day, although the phone had not rung for forty minutes. The last train in from London had been and gone. Only one passenger had alighted, whom Mick had taken to a local address. Mary had then sent him home early so that he could spend half an hour with his wife before retiring. Their young child would have been long abed, but Mick might see him for a few minutes in the morning before returning to work. She had told him that if a call for a local run came in she'd do it herself and any out of town journeys she would decline.

Mary had known from the moment she awoke that morning from an unsettled sleep that she would have to struggle through the day. It was the anniversary of her father's death. She had paid for a mass to be said for him, as she had for all the previous anniversaries, although by now she no longer believed. It was just her way of honouring his memory.

She was just about to turn off the office light when the 'phone rang. She ignored it for a minute, but it persisted. She eventually picked up the receiver. It was her friend Francesca Mackie, with some urgency in her voice.

'Hello Mary, sorry to trouble you at this time of night, but we need a car for Buckie Scanlon. You know it was his cousin Martin's funeral today?'

Mary knew; she'd been at the service.

'Yes I know. Where is Buckie now?'

'He's over here at the Railway Hotel. All of Martin's family are here. They're over from Roscommon, they're staying overnight. They've all had plenty to drink, especially Buckie, and he's not fit to find his way home.'

'Can he not stay at "The Railway" with them?'

'No, the place is bursting at the seams. Martin's family has taken every room in the place. Besides, you know how morose Buckie can be, well, he's very depressed tonight. He was close to Martin, they were like brothers. He needs taking home, although I'm not sure if he's fit to be left on his own. You know about Maureen I suppose?'

'I do. I'll come and get him. I'll be about ten minutes. He won't be sick in the car will he?'

'No. He's thrown up twice already. They've had him on orange juice for the past hour. He's starting to pull round now, but he oughtn't to be on the streets on his own.'

'Right; I'll see you soon.'

Mary put on her coat and switched off the light. Locking the door behind her, she walked over to the cars.

The automatic was parked behind the manual. Mick had walked home. She took the manual; there wouldn't be a lot of gear changing to do at this time of night, she hoped. She backed the big Ford out of the yard and onto the dirt road. She always had difficulty finding reverse because of the damaged hand. There was no need to hurry; the streets were almost empty of traffic. And the longer she took the more sober Eamon would be. Mary never liked using his nickname, "Buckie".

Martin's death had occurred more than two weeks ago. The funeral had been delayed by the inquest. He had fallen from the tower of a power station that was under construction a few miles away. Minor accidents were happening all the time on these big sites and fatalities were not as uncommon as they should have been. But this one had been particularly horrifying.

Martin was a gregarious young man; fit, strong, handsome. Full of fun and banter. He was liked by all who worked with him. On the day it happened it had been raining and everywhere was slippery underfoot. Martin was pushing a heavy wheelbarrow up an incline on the inside of the tower, trying to manoeuvre it onto the scaffold where a tradesman was waiting for its contents. The wheel had dropped in between two scaffold planks, stopping it abruptly, one of the metal handles gouging Martin in the groin. As the barrow fell into the depths of the tower Martin had toppled over it towards the outside. He'd grabbed for a scaffold bar, but his wet hand failed to grip the slippery steel. A workman next to him had made a grab for his jacket collar but his hand had merely brushed Martin's neck. The man had thrown himself on the scaffold floor, clapping his hands over his ears to silence the long, drawn-out scream, screwing up his eyes to try to shut out the dreadful image. He did not, at least, hear the dull crump, like a hundredweight sack of potatoes exploding on the ground two hundred feet below.

Silence fell around, no man could move. All faced inwardly, no one could bear to look over the side of the tower. The man worst affected was the one who had momentarily touched Martin's neck. He had touched warm living flesh, which, in a couple of seconds, was dead. He was never to return to the station; he could not work at height any more. He would recount the tale so many times that people would turn away from him when they saw him coming. It was as if he were trying to purge himself of the guilt he felt for failing to grasp Martin's collar.

The silence on the scaffold was eventually broken. 'Who was it?' someone asked.

'Martin.' someone answered.

'Oh, Christ! Not Martin.' came the choked reply.

Men stood motionless in the grey rain, staring down into the well of the tower, tracing the skeleton of the scaffold down to the ground. Minds sought evidence of solidity, substance, reassurance. At this height distant nature seemed frighteningly intangible, ephemeral.

The name 'Martin' could be heard being passed like a prayer, an invocation, along and down the levels in a stage whisper, a desperate plea for a horrifying fact only moments old to be repudiated. The babble and clangour diminished. The laying down of tools was the last sound to be heard before the whole tower fell silent.

Then one of the older men made a move, away quickly down the ramps to ask if a priest might be telephoned. One never knew, even if vital signs could not be detected. If a man could hear his confessor and wished to repent then the last rites might save a soul.

This prompted movement in others, releasing them from their stasis. Signs of comradeship were necessary when speech was absent. Cigarettes were pulled from pockets and handed around wordlessly. No one wanted to speak, voices might break. It was good that the drizzling rain still glistened on men's cheeks.

Although Buckie was not near the scene of the accident – in fact he was working on another power station that day – the description of events inevitably reached him. The suddenness of the fall re-awakened a recurring horror of his own and his emotions disintegrated. It was no wonder that in the dismal atmosphere of a wake such a melancholic man would be sunk in despair.

***

When Mary reached the Railway Hotel the funeral party had Buckie on his feet and at the main door. He walked to the car more steadily than she expected and they got him into a seat without much difficulty. He even offered a few words of apology to Mary for getting her out so late.

Mary knew him well and liked him a lot, so she did not mind the little trouble he was putting her to. She kept him talking while she drove, partly to keep him awake, largely to try to divert his mind from his cousin's death. She was in a melancholic mood herself and could do without both of them being maudlin. She drove slowly so as not to make him sick and opened a window slightly to give him air. Despite her best efforts Buckie's thoughts turned in on himself.

'I suppose you know Maureen's left me again?' he asked her.

'Yes, I heard,' replied Mary. 'How are you managing?'

'Well, this time it's for good, and I don't blame her. I wish her well. I think she'll be better off without me.'

'How do you know it's for good this time?' asked Mary.

'Oh I do,' said Buckie. 'She's found someone else, a chap from London, and that's where they've gone. She'd had enough of my drinking.'

Everyone knew the form that Buckie's drinking took. A few said he was an alcoholic, but most knew that he wasn't. He only drank now and then, probably every couple of months, but then he hit the bottle hard. This dragged him into the depths of despair and for two or three days he could hardly move. Then, with some supreme effort of will, he fought off the terrors that held him, went back to work and began to live again. He was never nasty to Maureen; it was just that for a few days every so often neither she nor anyone else could make contact with him. He was away in some place of his own.

'Perhaps it is for the best.' said Mary, pulling up outside the little house Buckie rented just beyond the town boundary.

'Do you love her?'

'Not really, but we got on well together most of the time.'

'How much did she love you?'

'About the same.'

'What made you get married?'

'We had to. Or at least we thought we did. We thought she was pregnant.'

'But she wasn't?'

'No. It was a false alarm. We found out later that she was unable to conceive. Perhaps for the best really, as things turned out.'

'You never know,' said Mary, 'but perhaps it was.'

Mary switched off the engine. 'I'm having a bad day myself,' she said. 'It's the anniversary of my father's death.'

'I know,' said Buckie, absent-mindedly. He was lost in his own thoughts.

This remark failed to register with Mary. A moment's silence, then:

'That evil bastard Henty.' said Buckie, staring straight ahead of himself as if gazing into the past.

The name Henty brought Mary out of her reverie. 'Eamon, what are you talking about?'

Buckie was now like a man in the confessional who had finally managed to pluck up the courage to admit to the priest some dreadful mortal sin. Then there's no going back. It might be the saving of your immortal soul but the temporal consequences could be hellish.

'It was Henty who pushed him in the lock.'

Mary was angry now. Eamon was rambling. He couldn't help it she felt, but he was trespassing on private grief, about something of which he knew nothing.

'He didn't drown in the lock,' snapped Mary. 'They found him nearly two miles down-river of the town.'

'I know,' said Eamon, 'but Henty pushed him in the lock.'

Mary struggled to contain her mounting anger. 'How would you know?' she demanded.

'I was there.'

'You were not. You were not there. You were not even in England then.'

'I wish to Christ I wasn't. But the truth of it is – I was.'

Eamon's head was clearing. He knew he'd gone too far to turn back now. He'd opened a vein and the blood would have to gush until the pressure dropped. If it killed him, so be it.

Mary tried to calm herself. She could see that Eamon knew more than she did. She always knew there were unanswered questions about her father's death. She had always wondered if Lud Henty had been in some way involved.

She took several deep breaths, then, putting her hand on Eamon's hand, she said, 'Take your time Eamon. Tell me what you've got to tell me.'

Eamon pulled himself together, knowing that his explanation needed to be detailed and accurate. He didn't know, couldn't think of where this awful confession might lead, but he had to make it, come what may. He struggled to make a start. Befuddled as he was, he knew he had to go back a bit before the death, so that it made some sense.

'I was just after getting into England about two weeks before. I'd hardly got off the boat in Liverpool when I was robbed. Somebody knocked me to the ground and stole one of the two wallets I was carrying. Half my money gone straight away. They'd told me when I'd left home, "be careful Buckie. Over there it's every man for himself, and God for His own," but I didn't expect to find the truth of that so soon. I was only eighteen and full of myself. I thought I could roam the world without coming to harm. I had the address in this town of a man named Hennessey. They said he would give me board and lodgings and provide me with work. Farm work. So I carried on till I got here and sure enough, he gave me some accommodation. Very rough it was, sharing a dirty room with three others in a big lodging house. And he put me to work in the fields. Took us all there in a big old van. At the end of the week I went to him for my pay. He gave me almost nothing. He kept back most of what I should have earned for the board and lodgings. I could not believe that an Irishman would do such a thing to one of his own. But he was a big rough character with several sons of similar disposition so I couldn't argue with him.'

'What's that got to do with the death of my father? Come on Eamon. You're not making any sense.'

'I will Mary. Just give me a minute. The next day I found better lodgings in a small house near the police station. A very nice Englishman kept it and his wife made us a good breakfast. I foolishly thought Hennessey would still employ me, but he wouldn't. I had little money left, so I was getting desperate.'

Mary by now was becoming more than desperate. Her anger was mounting, but she bit her lip and waited.

'Someone told me there was a scrap metal dealer called Lud Henty who had a yard in the town and might give me the odd day's work sorting and breaking up scrap. So I went to him. He said he'd give me a try and pay me by the day as trade was unreliable.

Mary blanched again at the mention of Henty. He'd always been a source of serious concern when she was younger. He was a sinister creature who had haunted her and had shaken her easy- going composure whenever he could.

Eamon continued, 'At the end of the first day he said he'd no money on him but that if I met him in The Angel pub that evening he'd pay me. The Angel used to back onto the river, against the locks. It's no longer there.'

'I knew it,' said Mary. 'It's better gone.'

'When I met him we were the only people there, apart from one man sitting on his own, who just looked at us but said nothing. Henty paid me – not very much, for what I'd done, but better than nothing. I offered to buy him a drink and he said he'd have a glass of lemonade; he didn't touch alcohol. He also bought himself a meat pie. I bought a small bottle of Guinness and we sat down. I wanted to be out of the place as soon as possible so as not to spend the little money I had. For some reason Henty chose to sit at a table immediately behind this other man, despite all the other tables being unoccupied. The place being almost empty the barman was spending most of his time serving the customers in the lounge bar and chatting to them.'

Mary was by now wishing she had not accepted the request to transport Eamon. He was simply rambling, making no sense. She would give him another minute and then tell him to go.

'After only a couple of minutes Henty started talking very obscenely. This embarrassed me greatly and I drank quickly so as to be on my way. There was no one else to hear all this except this one man and Henty was talking loudly as if to offend him."

Mary was starting to panic; she could sense what was coming. She remembered now, she had seen Henty, admittedly at a distance, the day after her father disappeared. There was something odd about his face she had thought, although she had been too racked with worry about her father to concern herself with that. And, instead of coming near to make some obscene remark, some disquieting comment, he had made off away from her into his citadel of a scrap yard. That was unusual.

"He was talking about a woman in particular. She seemed to be a local woman who went with the bargemen, so he said. He was being very coarse. You hadn't heard of her I doubt?'

'I – I think I knew of her once,' said Mary. 'She doesn't exist anymore.'

Eamon was too far out of his wits to ask the obvious question.

Mary's mind was still on Henty. He'd always wanted her sexually and had known she was 'friendly' towards other men. The fact that she despised him and made no attempt to conceal her detestation tormented him. Therefore she had been afraid not only of his physical threat but also of the risk that he might make her nocturnal riverside liaisons more widely known. He had said to her on more than one occasion when he'd seen her waiting by the barges, 'I bet your father doesn't know you come down here at night.'

Obviously he'd decided to carry out his implied threat.

'The other man said nothing,' continued Eamon. 'And of course, the barman heard nothing because he was serving at the other bar. I got up to leave, but first I went into the toilets. Unfortunately Henty came in a moment later. Just as we were about to leave, the other man walked in. He was a tall, well-built chap in very good condition.'

Mary knew now that Eamon wasn't rambling. She could visualise the scene. She knew the threat that was Henty, and she also knew "the other man". She was now hanging on to every word Eamon uttered. She waited for the dénouement, knowing it would tear her apart.

'You've got a dirty mouth,' he said to Henty. 'You are pure evil.'

Henty just grinned and said, "There's not much you can do about it," and without any warning he launched an almighty punch straight at the face of the man. But the man ducked the blow and in the space of a few seconds he'd destroyed Henty. He turned his back and started to walk away, but then changed his mind and backhanded me, sending me sprawling into the urinals.

'Whilst I was picking myself up off the floor he walked calmly into the bar and bought a quarter-bottle of whiskey and went out through the back door on to the waterfront. Henty came round and we left a few minutes later after we'd washed the blood off ourselves. Down by the river I was lost. It was dark. One lock was full, the moonlight glinting off the water. An adjacent lock, half empty, in the shadow of a big warehouse, looked like a pit and I could hardly see to pick my way around it. There were lights here and there. They were reflecting off the water and throwing shadows everywhere. I didn't feel safe at all. There seemed to be several shaky wooden walkways, about the width of a man, over and around the locks. They were all at different levels. Henty walked over them like a cat, but I was afraid of falling in. Suddenly Henty pulled me into the shadow of a wall, motioning me to be quiet. The man from the pub was a few yards away sitting on one of the bollards they tie the barges to. I thought Henty was afraid of getting another belting and would turn us back.'

Eamon's voice was starting to break now. He was catching his breath, beginning to cry.

'The man put the bottle to his lips, drank the last of it and threw it into the lock. He then stood up and stretched himself to full height, hands above his head like a man just after getting out of bed.'

Eamon was sobbing now, big, racking convulsive sobs. Mary was crying too, at the picture of her father – contemplating his death. So her mother had been right – he had committed suicide, but she had been the cause of it.

Eamon was sobbing so much now his body was bouncing off the car seat and making the springs creak. They were holding each other's hands. Then he buried his head in her chest, as if to bury the truth. Finally, he pulled himself together enough to continue.

'Then the man picked up his cap from where it had fallen on the ground, put it on his head and started to walk away, steady as you like.'

Mary heaved a huge sigh of relief.

'Then Henty rushed out of the shadows and with the sole of his boot have him an almighty kick in the ribs and he was in the lock. Gone.'

The horror that Mary now saw before her as if it were actually happening was momentarily tempered with a strange sense of relief. Her father's death was not suicide. She and Eamon clung to each other like lovers, the car shaking with their sobs. But then it hit her – although this had not been a suicide, it was a murder, the cause of which was partly herself. For several minutes she sobbed uncontrollably.

Eamon eventually found his voice. 'He sank like a stone, without a struggle. I couldn't move. I couldn't believe what I had just witnessed. A moment before the man had been so close I could have touched him. Now he was gone. There was a mighty depth of water in that lock. Oily, the diesel floating on the surface catching the moonlight. It just closed over him. Henty looked at me in the face, a look of pure evil. He said, "No man gets the better of me. You remember that, or you'll go the same way". I left him there. I saw an alleyway and ran up it. I didn't know where it went to. Eventually I came onto a road that brought me back into the town. I thought it really is every man for himself and God for his own in this country. I went to my lodgings to try to think what I should do but I couldn't think. If I went to the police how could I prove it wasn't me that pushed him in? If I named Henty but couldn't prove it was him –

what would he have done to me? The following day I went to confession, but I couldn't confess. I just told the priest a few small things that didn't really matter. When I came out of the church I realized that I couldn't ever tell the priest because of the weight it would place on his shoulders. He couldn't go to the police. As you know, the confessor's sins must remain with the priest. They are a secret.'

'But it was not you that sinned Eamon. You had done nothing wrong.'

'I know, but at the time I was confused. As time went by it got worse. I'd go into the confessional intending to make a clean slate of it. Then I'd rack my brain for every venial sin I could think of. Then I stopped going altogether; it was just a mockery. And never going is a sin in itself. Two days after it happened I still had no work. I'd my lodgings to pay for and my money was running out. Then, another lodger told me he was going down to Peterborough where there was some farm work to be had, so I caught the train with him. We found work and I stayed around there three or four years.'

'What brought you back up here, Eamon?'

'I had friends and relatives move in around here. Farm work anywhere was getting harder to find. They wanted men who could drive and handle machinery. I wasn't really cut out for that. They were just after that starting to build the power stations up here and all the Irish lads were beginning to move in. The money was great. So that's why I moved back. I was here a long time before I learned that your father had drowned in the river and it was a long time after that before I realised that he was the man in the pub that night. I don't know how you could ever forgive me Mary, but I just wish you could.'

They both cried. For a long time. Holding each other close. It was Mary who finally spoke.

'Oh Eamon. Poor Eamon! What a burden you've carried with you for so long. It's no wonder you have a few too many drinks now and then.'

They spent the next few minutes quietly, recovering from their emotional ordeal. There was nothing to be done except for Mary to contact her brother as soon as possible to tell him how their father had died.

Both Mary and Eamon knew that Lud Henty was dead. In his usual violent way he had picked a fight with a gypsy at the Appleby Horse Fair. A knife in the ribs had finished him. The police had no chance of getting information from the gypsies, nor did they care to try.

Mary, despite her grief, consoled the distraught but by now fairly sober Eamon. They had, for a long time, been good friends. Now there existed a very close bond.

'Tell me Eamon,' she asked shyly, 'why do most people call you

"Buckie"?'

Eamon almost managed a smile.

'When I was a kid everyone around said I'd the teeth of a buck rabbit, so it stayed with me.'

'I think you've got nice teeth.'

'Well, they're good and strong anyhow. When we were kids we were half-starved. I think I must have had the head of a whippet on me and the teeth might have stuck out a bit.'

'I know how it is. I used to be called the witch with the withered hand.'

'Ah, sure that's cruel Mary. You're lovely.'

'Eamon, I don't think you should be left on your own tonight. I've a big settee. I'll find you some blankets.'

Mary started up the engine and turned the car around.

The next day Mary left a telephone message asking that Thomas should contact her as a matter of urgency.

He telephoned her within an hour asking what was wrong. She told him that they needed to meet. It concerned their father's death. It was about the past, so nothing could be done now, but it would be better if they talked.

He took a train as soon as he finished work. He walked around to the house, his mind travelling over the past, wondering what Mary had to say.

She was slightly agitated as she let him in, he could see that, but she was not overtly distressed.

'It's about the way Dad died.' said Mary. She explained in every detail the dramatic revelation of Eamon Scanlon's witnessing their father's death thirteen years ago, and who was responsible for it.

Thomas was not surprised that it was Lud Henty, but this possibility had never occurred to him, perhaps, he thought, because his father had been more than capable of looking after himself in that respect.

'So, you had no part to play in it at all Tom. Perhaps I did, but not you. Mam's accusations were entirely unfounded.'

'I honestly thought it was possible that she knew something that we didn't,' said Thomas. 'I thought Dad might have said something to her that suggested he'd had enough of life, but that it had dawned on her only after the event.'

'No, she had no grounds for saying what she said. I'm sure Dad was as resolute as ever he was on that day. It was just some sort of demon that got hold of her.'

'It destroyed her in the end.'

'It did Tom. And it nearly finished you as well.'

'I certainly struggled with it for a long time. I wonder what made her like that?'

'It was something far back in her past Tom. We never really knew much about her life before she was married to Dad. She was becoming more morose, more obsessive, more isolated before that happened. Looking back I suppose we should have tried to help her, but I'm not sure how.'

'No. You're right Mary. I don't know what went wrong, or what we should have done.'

'I don't think she ever had much of a life of her own when she was young. I think she tried to live her life through yours, to shape you into what – to her at least – seemed the perfect being.'

'Well, she failed miserably.' said Thomas.

'She should never have tried. It's wrong. You shouldn't do that to someone. No one has the right to dictate how another should live. Every person has a right to be themselves. Guidance is one thing. We all need that from time to time. But trying to push someone in a direction they do not want to go just because you believe they should is unfair.'

'This revelation – this confession if you like of Eamon's – it must have come as an awful shock to you. Out of the blue, so to speak. How did you take it?'

'Well, it was horrible to listen to. Eamon described it so vividly it was as if I was watching it happen. But what was worse was the realisation of what it had done to Eamon. He's carried that around with him for years. It's blighted his life. He had known us for some time before he discovered that Dad had drowned, but even then he didn't at first make the connection between what he had witnessed and Dad's death, because of the distance between the lock and the place where they found him. After he had pieced it together the guilt was worse for him than it had ever been before. Every time he saw one of us he knew he ought to tell us exactly what had happened, but he couldn't bring himself to do that. Until last night that is. If he had known that you were carrying a load of guilt around with you following Mam's accusation then I am sure he would have said something. But he didn't. No one knew except you and I.'

'I suppose Eamon knows that Henty is no longer around?'

'Oh, yes, he knows. It soon became common knowledge. He heard what happened to him all right. I doubt if he would have come back here if he had thought Henty was still alive.'

'I'm sure Eamon will be better for getting this off his chest, Mary. Horrible though it is, in a way I feel better for knowing.'

'I think the three of us will be better for knowing the truth. It takes the mystery out of it. Eamon's such a lovely man. He might get his life back now.'

PART THREE
15

Thomas sat in the window seat of a small café at the edge of the market place. It had been almost full when he entered so the exposed position had been his only choice. It was less busy now, nearing the end of the afternoon's trade. He had almost finished his tea, so no point now in moving to one of the empty tables.

He used this place occasionally when he was visiting. It was next door to old Breasley's rope shop, where, in the room above, he had spent the most unsettling year of his life.

Perhaps it was the close proximity to a place of old memories, good and bad, that drew him to this particular café, he wondered. He'd not considered that before. The rope shop was now a hairdressing salon.

Thomas had taken a bus from the city to visit his sister. He usually came on a Sunday when she was seldom working, but he'd other commitments for the next two weekends. He had taken this week off work as annual leave, thinking he might catch Mary between jobs without inconveniencing her. Hence the snack so that she would not feel she should prepare food for him.

A radio somewhere at the rear of the café was broadcasting a discussion about the forthcoming election and the possibility of a woman becoming Prime Minister. Thomas reflected that it must be almost a quarter of a century since he had left the rope shop and also departed from the town. The talk on the radio then had been of Suez, although he had other things on his mind at the time.

The poignancy of those other things now held his thoughts and briefly interrupted the feelings of dismay at the possibility of an intensification of unbridled capitalism. If the election went the way the pundits were predicting it would.

He gazed out over the cobbled square, the comments on the radio cutting in and out of his feelings about the past causing little jets of anger to intersect with pangs of guilt and sadness.

A sleek Mercedes sports car was cruising slowly around the emptying square, fat tyres squeezing the cobbles, the driver was no doubt looking for somewhere to stop. It oozed wealth, power, control. Thomas imagined that its owner would doubtless welcome the impending change of government.

The car pulled in. The door opened on the passenger side and a woman stepped out. Thomas could not see her face, her back being towards him. She was bending into the car, saying something to the driver. He looked at his empty cup, wondering if he should have another drink.

The car pulled away. The woman began to walk across the market place in the direction of the café. She carried a small suitcase made of rich leather. Her long strides were confident, high-heeled shoes striking the round cobbles with remarkable certainty. Her legs were long and shapely. She was expensively dressed in a boldly checked coat and wore a big, wide-brimmed hat at a jaunty angle. A mass of thick red hair billowed out from beneath it. Although not young, she was outstandingly attractive.

She was nearing the café now, but moving at an angle that suggested she was probably making for the hairdresser's next door. She was now only a few strides away.

Thomas was still engrossed in the broadcast and was losing patience with what was being said. He stood up to leave.

Perhaps the slight movement caused the woman to turn her head in his direction. She stopped dead, holding his gaze.

He stopped breathing. His heart leapt, then the feeling of elation froze. Excitement and trepidation combined instantly into something like an emotion he'd once had seconds after receiving a severe electric shock: a weird mixture of being both fortunate and unfortunate at the same time. Of being very nearly dead yet so ecstatically alive, that knife-edge balance between those states, when lambent hope vies with morbid resignation. It was a very long time since such a tumult of emotions had coursed through his whole being. Yes, it was Elaine. Surely, it must be her. What was she doing here? She lived in London, did she not? But there could be no doubt. She was here now.

They looked into each other's eyes for long seconds, mouths half-opened, scarcely breathing. The intensity of their startled gaze might have shattered the glass that divided them. Recognition had been established, too late to deny it now. What to do next? The past is a dangerous place to visit. Ought they to take such a risk?

It was Elaine who made the first move, vainly trying to pull, then pushing open the door of the café with a shaking hand. Inside, in a tremulous voice, all she could say was, 'Hello Tom.' Then, after looking around, 'Are you alone?'

'Yes. Yes, I am. Will you join me? Do you have time?' Thomas did not know why he had asked that question. He did know that his voice was trembling, so he wordlessly indicated a table away from the window.

Elaine nodded silently. She sat down, but with some little hesitation, very unsure of herself. 'I'll have a coffee if I may, please.'

He ordered it and another tea for himself.

'Will your friend be joining us?'

'Sorry?' said Elaine, looking puzzled.

'In the car. The man in the car. I saw you get out.'

'Oh. No, no. That was Edward. He's not coming back today.'

'Do you mean your brother Edward?'

'Yes.'

'I thought he lived abroad. Australia.'

'He does. He's been over here for six months. He's going back in ten days' time. We've been selling our parent's house, after re-establishing them in a smaller one. Edward has made something of a holiday of it.'

Elaine was glad of something factual to talk about. Something to enable them to skirt around the past without causing awkward silences. Thomas could not help but reflect on the unusual choice of car for a holiday runabout. 'Your parents are – are well, are they?' He'd almost said, 'Are still alive, then?' but had stopped himself just in time.

'Yes, reasonably so. They manage well enough; still get around; that sort of thing. Good for their age if you know what I mean. We've got them into a nice bungalow on the edge of town. It's in a quiet, leafy area, no longer in the country, but with country views.'

The tea and coffee arrived. They were both glad of the interruption as the waitress placed the cups and asked if anything else was required. They were hesitant, unsure as to how they should proceed. It was as if they had each been given a key to a long unopened safe that might hold the promise of eternal happiness or, more likely perhaps, bitter disappointment. Who should open it? Should it be opened? They each sensed the other's trepidation, the dread of the alternative possibilities.

Elaine continued with the thread of the conversation she'd started, but the tremble of her fingers betrayed her feelings as the spoon jangled against her saucer. She let go of it quickly. She continued with the factual, trying to remain calm.

'They ought to have given up the old place years ago. It was far too big for them. Edward has been living in it since he's been over here.'

'What's he doing now – for a living I mean?' asked Thomas.

'He's still in medicine. He has a large private practice near Melbourne. This is the first time for years that he has been to England. That's why he decided to make a long vacation of it. He's been visiting a few friends around Britain. He stayed with me in London for a week, but otherwise I've seen little of him.'

'Ah, so you do still live in London?'

'Yes, but only until next week. I'm moving back. I've bought a house here.'

Thomas noticed "I" not "we".

Elaine continued, 'I came up by train on Monday and stayed with my parents for a couple of nights. I needed to sort a few things out prior to the move. You know, furnishings, signing documents at the solicitors. I've used a local firm – the one Daddy's always used. I'm catching a train back to London in a couple of hours.

'So you didn't stay with Edward at your parent's old house then?' asked Thomas.

'No. It's practically empty now. Most of the furniture has been sold, apart from a few smaller pieces they've taken with them to the bungalow. Edward's still there. There's a bed and a few other bits, so he can manage. They will be gone soon. The new owners take possession next week. Edward will spend the last few days in London before flying back to Australia.'

'But you'll be back up here by then?'

'Yes. I know it's a bit odd. But he and I are not that close now.'

Thomas was still curious about the Mercedes. 'He'll hardly be putting the car on the plane. Is it on loan?'

'Oh no, that's not the way Edward does things. He bought it when he came in and the dealer has a customer waiting for it when he leaves.'

Thomas was astounded at such profligacy. It showed on his face. 'Very nice,' were the only words he could find.

Elaine could still read his feelings. 'I know what you are thinking, Tom. That's part of the reason why we are not so close now. Edward is extremely rich and hasn't got a lot of time for those who aren't.'

She realised immediately that Thomas would register this last sentence. He knew she was – or at least had been – well off.

'That probably sounds like hypocrisy to you. You know that I have never been short of money. I've been fortunate, in that way, at least. But I've never been disparaging of those who are not so lucky. I've been close to many very nice, very decent people who are struggling to survive. And it bothers me.'

He noticed that Elaine was trying to justify what she believed, what she did. She was more contemplative. This was a slightly different Elaine.

She continued, 'Edward doesn't think like that. He has no time for the poor. I don't know why. Although Daddy was rich once – though not in Edward's league by any means – he was always a very compassionate man. He taught us to consider others. Mother came from a poor background, which is probably why she worked so hard to support Daddy in the early days of the business. It's amazing how she kept it running when he was away during the war.'

Thomas remembered that her father had seemed to have a caring side to his nature, even thought he'd initially been wary of Charles and his obvious wealth. He was surprised that Delia Langdon had humble beginnings. She had always seemed harder somehow, more mercenary, almost as if she had moved a rung or two down the social ladder to marry Charles, instead of climbing up.

He was pleased to find Elaine acknowledging levels of inequality and showing some concern over excessive and selfish wealth, although he knew it shouldn't have mattered to him. They were separate beings now.

'I'm surprised to find you are still living here.' said Elaine.

'I don't. I live in Nottingham. I've taken a few days off work and have come over to see my sister. I'm on my way there now. She's not expecting me. I usually visit on a Sunday when she's less busy, but I've something on this weekend.'

'So she's still around. Is she O.K?'

'Fine thanks. She's doing well.'

Thomas thought Elaine might have pursued that with another question about Mary, but she had other things on her mind.

'Look, Tom. I've got an appointment with my solicitor in twenty minutes time, so I must go. Anything else I could postpone. I really would like to spend longer with you. Perhaps you wouldn't want me to though?'

'I would. Of course I would. But how can you if you've got a train to catch?'

'There are later ones I could take. Do you have anyone waiting for you?'

That was the big question Elaine had been wanting to ask, but she didn't know how. Now it was out and she held her breath, waiting for the answer.

'No,' said Thomas. 'I live alone. There's no one waiting for me.'

Elaine breathed again. He sensed it had been a loaded question. He knew now that he wanted them to spend some time together. The past was indeed a dangerous place, but some risks were worth taking.

'Perhaps we could have a meal later.' he suggested.

'That's if you could find time. Or have you too many things to do?'

'Nothing I can't change around, apart from the solicitor, that is. Can you amuse yourself for a while, Tom?'

'Yes. I'll make a flying visit to my sister. She's going to be working anyway. Give me an hour and a half if that's all right with you.'

'Fine. Where shall we eat? Would the Crown Hotel suit you?'

'Yes I don't mind.' said Thomas.

'I'll book a table. Say seven o'clock? That will give us three hours before the last train.'

'Yes, but leave me to do it, to save you time.'

'I'll do it,' said Elaine. 'The manager is a bit of a snob and always tries to give the impression that he's fully booked and just might do you a favour of finding you a table at a time that suits him, rather than you. I've known him since we were young and knew his parents too. They were friends of my parents. So he usually tries to oblige me. I'll leave my suitcase with him rather than lug it round to the solicitors.'

They parted, each with a tingling sense of excitement. Both knew there was a lot of unfinished business. Their parting twenty-odd years ago had been painfully abrupt. They would each feel better for knowing how the other was doing, even if it might prove to be their final meeting. It was better to tie up loose ends. To explain misunderstandings. To say "sorry" even. And there was just the faintest possibility that it might not be the final meeting.

***

Thomas walked quickly to the taxi office. His sister smiled warmly at him and raised her hand as he entered. She was on the telephone taking a booking. They were pleased, as usual, to see each other.

'I wasn't expecting you,' said Mary. 'Thought you might call on Sunday.'

'I would have, but I've got to work. We've a big window to change in just two days and they've asked us to work Sunday to get most of it done whilst the store is closed. I've got today off, so I thought I'd drop in on you. I knew you'd be busy but I thought we could chat in between calls. Unless you were out driving.'

'No, Tom. Mick and Eamon are both on the cars today. I'm just taking the calls. Shall I make you a drink?'

'No thanks Mary. I've just had two in a café and I'm out for a meal in a little while.'

'That sounds grand,' said Mary. 'You're looking after yourself. I could have made you something.'

I know you would,' said Thomas, 'but I'm meeting someone.'

'Anyone I know?'

'Well, you do and you don't. I've just had the strangest experience. You'll remember around the time Dad died, I met Elaine Langdon and we went out together for a while and then parted company and she went to London and I took a job in Nottingham?'

'Only too well do I remember. You didn't say much about her but I knew you were in turmoil. Although, much of that, of course, was because of what happened to Dad. But what of it?'

'I bumped into her this afternoon.'

'Where?'

'Here. Here in town. Less than half an hour ago.'

'I thought you said she was in London.'

'She was – is. But she's moving back. Back up here. Next week.'

'How was she? Towards you I mean.'

'Well, all right, I suppose. We were both a bit thrown by it. It was so unexpected. We were pleased to see each other though, so we're going to The Crown.'

'Is she on her own? I mean – does she have any attachments so to speak?'

'I don't know. I don't think so. We spoke for only a few minutes, but it was she who suggested it. Well, I suggested eating somewhere, but only after she said she would like to see me for a bit longer. It would be nice to talk to her for a while. I'd like to know how she's doing. We didn't part on the best of terms.'

'What's bringing her back up here Tom, after all this time?'

'I'm not sure. Her parents are still alive and living somewhere around the town, and her brother intends to remain in Australia, so that might be part of the reason. I suppose she feels she'd like to keep an eye on them. I'll perhaps find out in a short while.'

'I wish I'd met her Tom. She sounded very nice. You seemed to like her a lot. I don't know why you went your separate ways. But that's life I suppose.'

'Nor do I. I could break it down into several reasons that seemed real enough at the time, but looking back from where I am now they would make no sense at all.'

'Things often don't make much sense when you look back. That's why I've always tried to live in the present, with an eye to the future. You can never be sure about the past. Was it real or was it partly imagined? It's a dangerous place, anyway.'

Realising how the last sentence might affect him, Mary tried to soften the blow.

'Sorry, Tom. I didn't mean to disparage anything. I…'

'No. Don't apologise. I agree with you. I could be playing with fire. I've thought about Elaine throughout the years, with considerable guilt and sorrow. I suppose I'm snatching a chance to try to salve my conscience. Anyway, I'll know soon enough.'

There was a reflective silence. Thomas was scouring his mind trying to marshal thoughts about his past into a coherent sentence. He needed to explain to himself more than to Mary why he had not joined Elaine, not started a new life in London, all those years ago.

He was thinking aloud. 'I suppose I was just overwhelmed by her; by the grip she had on life that I did not have. She shaped life, made things happen. I still hadn't made sense of the world. I was forever looking at it, trying to take it all in. I was like a hatching bird chipping its way out of the shell, seeing things for the first time and trying to understand them.

It's a terrible admission for me to make. It still seems hard to believe that I could be that immature, so unsure about everything, at the age of twenty two or so. The hatchling probably cannot make sense of life, but at least it gets on with it. Not like me. I was always holding back. Still partly in the shell.'

'I think it's the way we were,' said Mary, 'something in our upbringing. To some extent I was the same myself. I remember how at school we were always taught that we were somehow better than the kids from all the other schools. We were told not to look down on them, but it was hard not to when you were inculcated in the belief that you were somehow superior. Yet whenever you mixed with those other kids they seemed to have a wider understanding of things, or at least were more questioning than we were. It all added to a sense of perplexity. It sort of shook your confidence. I suppose it was a strange kind of confidence that we had knocked into us. I didn't make much effort to understand, I confess. I just got on with life and took my chances. But then, there was little expected of me, so it was easier for me to do that than it was for you. They placed a heavy burden on your shoulders.'

Mary answered the phone yet again. Then, on concluding the call, noted that over an hour had passed since her brother had arrived.

'What time are you meeting her Tom?'

'In fifteen minutes,' said Thomas, glancing at the office clock. I'd better be on my way. I'll see you again soon. On a Sunday, when you're less busy. Sorry it's been brief today.'

'Bye Tom. Look after yourself. Enjoy your meal.'

Thomas reached the hotel first. The church clock was just starting to chime its hour. He spotted Elaine fifty yards away trying to hurry in her heels, holding on to her hat with one hand. He smiled broadly. She was usually more composed than that, or so his memory told him.

She reached him slightly out of breath, beaming joyfully. She felt a sense of relief to find him there. Uncertainty showed on her face despite the smile. Her mannerisms betrayed her nervousness. Thomas sensed it. He had not seen this side of Elaine before.

They entered the restaurant, which was almost full despite the early hour. Many of the diners looked like representatives of companies, probably taking their first meal of the day before retiring to their rooms to write up the day's business ready for the morning post.

A waiter showed them to a table in an alcove some distance away from the rest of the diners. He apologised for its somewhat isolated situation but said if they would care to order he would move them if another became available before their meal arrived. They assured him that they were more than happy to remain where they were. They wanted only each other's company.

After a glass of wine, the intervening years dropped away. Despite parting in anger, sorrow and despair, and notwithstanding the iniquities of life whilst apart, they talked as freely as if they had always been together. They both knew now that there was no lingering animosity. They were still, at the very least, good friends.

'When I saw you coming across the market square I thought you were making for the hairdresser's salon.' said Thomas.

'I was.' Elaine replied.

'Why? You'd have no time to have your hair done if you were about to catch a train. Besides, it looks fine.'

'I was about to pay them a social call. I know them. But that can wait until after I've moved back up here next week. You see, I own the building and they lease it from me. I like to visit them once or twice a year when I'm up from London. They're good, hardworking people and I don't just want to take rent off them and never see them. I want to know how they're doing. If business is bad they may need a little support. You never know. But mostly it's good. They seem to have a sound business.'

'So you own old Breasley's rope shop. I never knew.'

'My father owned it, but I didn't know he did. It was only when he retired from business and sold the store that I found out. He told me then that he'd owned the shop for several years. It came about because Daddy had known and liked John Breasley for a long, long time. In fact, as a young man, he'd also known John's father, whom he also liked very much. Although the rope business had been in their hands for two generations neither of them could afford to buy the building. They had always rented it. It was owned by a businessman in London. He wanted to put up the rent or sell Breasley the property but John could afford neither. My father heard about this and could not bear to see him lose his business. He knew John would find it difficult to begin again somewhere else. And, at that time, the shop was also his living accommodation – the room that you rented had been John's home. So Daddy made an offer to the London man, which was accepted. From then on John lived there and carried on his business on a modest rent which was never increased.'

'That was remarkably generous of your father. Not many businessmen would have done it.'

'Daddy knew John had been wounded and decorated for bravery in the first war and had some involvement in the next. He knew that he was as straight and dependable as any man could be and he liked him for that.'

'John never told me he'd been honoured for his action in the war, although he did say once that he'd been wounded. That was why he limped, of course.'

'He didn't mention it to me either Tom. That was how he was. Incredibly modest.'

'So when John died,' continued Elaine, 'which was roughly at the time Daddy was selling his business, he gave the deeds of the shop to me. That was the first I knew about it. So, I am quite well off. Daddy said it would be the only security I'd have in my old age. He knew that my wild temperament would make it unlikely that I would plan for my dotage. Because of the rent I get I am not totally dependent on the sale of my work to survive. However, I am selling quite well.'

'I thought you were,' said Thomas. 'I've kept an eye on reports of your achievements over the years. I know you've exhibited at the R.A. and Whitechapel, and I've seen for myself some of your work in the Cork Street Galleries. I've also read reviews in the art magazines.'

'I find that very flattering, that you should have kept me in mind.'

Thomas would have liked to have said just how much Elaine had occupied his mind, Elaine herself, not just her art.

'From the start I knew you were good. You just needed to leave your father's business and go into art full-time.'

'Which is what I did,' said Elaine. 'My parents knew it too. I think they felt guilty about holding on to me. I couldn't leave them to manage the store as they got older, or so I thought. But after meeting you that is exactly what I did do.'

'I suppose I've much to answer for.' said Thomas ruefully.

Ignoring that remark, Elaine continued.

'Edward was from the start a very successful G.P. in Australia and is now extremely so. He was never going to show an interest in Daddy's business, even though he's become a business magnate in the medical world. He owns a company that manufactures medical equipment that sells throughout the world. He always said that the last thing he wanted to be was a shopkeeper. He was at least always open about his intentions. Our parents encouraged him to do what he wanted to do, what he was good at doing. They were good to us both in that way. It was just that Daddy held on too long to some unrealistic hope that one day Edward might change his mind. It became a belief almost. Clouded his judgement and prevented him from seeing other possibilities. It was never going to happen. So I drifted into the business and found it hard to disentangle myself.'

'For how long did your parents remain in business after you went to London?'

'Not very long. Three or four years or so. They employed a general manager as I'd been suggesting they should for a long time, but the store was faltering by then, so eventually they sold out to a big multiple.'

'And they retired on the proceeds?'

'Yes, but not luxurious retirement. The store didn't sell for as much as you might imagine. Although it was once the classiest store in town, by a considerable margin, they had not moved with the times. Quality and service, which is what they traded on, had been pushed aside by fickle throwaway fashion. That was not their style. The manager they'd employed, good though he was, was almost as old as my father. He too could not see the changes that needed to be made. So Daddy's dream ended. That's life I suppose. The world moves on.'

'Some things don't change,' said Thomas, and immediately wondered why he'd said it.

Elaine looked at him quizzically, but didn't reply.

'So what are your plans when you move back here next week?' he asked quickly.

'I've bought quite a nice house overlooking the river. It has a big upstairs room with huge windows at either end. Plenty of light throughout most of the day. I'll be able to work here and sell in London. I've had enough of living there. I've made lots of good supportive friends there and I don't intend to lose touch with them. I'll go back frequently. I want a quieter life now. I also want to keep an eye on my parents. I owe them a great deal and I still love them dearly. Edward won't come back again. We all know that and fully accept it. He inhabits a different world. But he will be financially supportive if that ever becomes necessary. He's said as much and he's always true to his word.'

'You never married I take it?' asked Thomas. 'Sorry, perhaps I shouldn't have asked that question. It's none of my business.'

'Oh, I married. It was an utter disaster.'

'Don't tell me about it if you don't want to. I really shouldn't have asked.'

'It was all your fault Tom,' said Elaine, smiling generously as she spoke. 'You remember Gerald Draycott, the man you met briefly that Sunday when I first took you to meet my parents? You know, the picnic in the woods that afternoon. Well, he had always had his eye on me. I thought I liked him at the time. I'd been out with him a few times. My parents thought he was wonderful and rather hoped we'd get together. I think Daddy's judgement was coloured by his deep friendship with Gerald's father, Henry, who was a really lovely man in every way. Gerald was ex-public school, going places at a considerable pace. He was already wealthy in his own right and stood to inherit his father's significant wealth. They knew Gerald found me attractive and – oh, I don't know –

somehow assumed that I found him compelling. Just because all the women in the county did.'

'You didn't though, did you?' he asked anxiously.

'No, not in that way. He was a friend, or so I thought. I liked him as much as anyone else who was around at the time. Before I met you, that is. He had taken me out to dinner, to the theatre and various other places. I'd also, at his request, visited him at his splendid London town house. It was just off Russell Square, not far from The Slade. I never stayed overnight though. But he did ask me to.'

'I'm sure he did.' said Thomas, wondering why Elaine had made this last point.

'I didn't realise he was that well-off at so young an age. Of course I was given to understand by your father that Henry Draycott was very rich, but I didn't realise that Gerald had so much wealth in his own right at that time. He was only in his early thirties then, wasn't he?'

'Yes, he was. But he had already made a lot of money. In banking. He was extremely good at what he did.'

'So how does all this fit in with your marriage?'

'I married him.'

This revelation struck Thomas like a hammer blow. He was mentally reeling, searching for words, trying desperately to conceal his pain. He had expected Elaine to say that Gerald had unwittingly introduced her to one of his well-heeled friends who had snatched her away, depriving Gerald of his prize.

'Why? Why would you? If he was only a friend?'

Elaine was right. It was his fault. The horror of what he had done was burning into him. He had not only wasted the chance to stay with the woman he loved but he'd driven her into the arms of someone she did not love.

Elaine was speaking again. 'That's the crazy part about it Tom. Why indeed? It was sheer madness, complete and utter stupidity on my part. A psychologist might say it was some subconscious impulse to punish myself, or to punish you for ditching me. It's impossible to explain. I can't explain it to myself, even now. I just did it.'

There were tears on Tom's cheeks. 'Elaine, oh Elaine, what did I do to you?'

Tom was surprised at Elaine's calmness as she continued. 'When you and I parted, Tom, I thought I could lose myself in the London art scene. I produced a huge amount of paintings that, looking back, I now know were good. Several knowledgeable people also thought they were. The trouble was, although I was painting I wasn't exhibiting. I was just piling up work without even trying to sell it. A lot of it was still selling but not through my efforts. My agent kept on moving it but I had no interest in who was buying it. In the end I just gave up. I couldn't keep going. I eventually burned myself out. My mental state was awful. I had to go into a clinic for a time.'

'So that is what I did to you? I almost destroyed you.'

'I don't blame you for that Tom. It's life. We cannot predict the outcomes of our actions every time we do something.'

Breasley's words from long ago leapt into his head. Old Breasley knew. It seemed that he knew everything. What price wisdom?

'Anyway, I married him. I had lost confidence in myself completely. I allowed him to put pressure on me. He persuaded me to put on a big exhibition. He insisted on financing it. I was too ill to take an interest, but he paid a firm to organise everything, transportation, advertising, even the hanging of the pictures, something I would have insisted on supervising myself had I been well enough. I just let him get on with it. He then asked me to marry him. My parents thought it a good thing. They felt it might stabilise me, get me back to some sort of normality. We immediately went to live in Africa where Gerald's father had huge tracts of farmland. He behaved abysmally towards me, almost from the start. He said he knew all about you and I, said it in a bitter sneering way, and said I was a whore to have gone with you. He also claimed that he'd almost killed you once, but never elaborated on that. Just said he wished he had. Do you have any idea what he could have meant?'

'No.' said Thomas, truthfully and with great surprise.

'Anyway,' continued Elaine, 'he was utterly reprehensible to almost everyone, and particularly vile to me. I won't go into the details. He used to treat the black people like an old-style colonialist, regarding them as animals. Then one day he shot one of them. Didn't kill him, but very nearly did. He spent a few weeks in prison but somehow bought himself out of the situation. Paid money to the authorities, I'm sure, and to the man he had injured. By the time he was released I was on a plane for home. Mummy and Daddy were very supportive. I know they felt guilty for encouraging me to marry him in the first place. They said as much. They actually said that they were not very good judges of character and that they had been wrong in the past. They said it in a way that I knew was a reference to you. They did all they could to help me to get over it and back on my own two feet, as it were.'

'Did Gerald just let you go? Did he not try to pursue you?'

'No, he didn't come after me. The shooting and his subsequent arrest made it into the British press. There was a column on the front page of *The Times* and an in-depth article on the inner pages. His father disowned him. Henry Draycott was furious with Gerald, absolutely livid.

'Gerald never loved me. I don't think he even liked me after he somehow found out about you and I. He just wanted to own me, to possess me in some sadistic sort of way. To hurt me, for loving you. But he wouldn't have had the courage to come looking for me after the press exposure and his father censuring him. Although Gerald was very rich and had powerful contacts, Henry was wealthier by far and had considerable influence in many parts of the world. Gerald knew that. He was finished, at least in this part of the world and I should think in many other parts. I never heard from him again.'

There was a long silence. Both of them were looking down at the now empty table, looking at their hands that had now found themselves resting there, finger-tips almost touching. Thomas spoke first.

'So what then? What did you do when you returned to England?'

'I spent some time with my parents and then went back to London and picked up the pieces. I had been in Kenya for only six months or so. The London scene hadn't changed much. I was more circumspect from then on. I was back on a more even keel, you might say. I worked diligently, but not at the old frenetic pace. I don't think my work was ever as good again. I never regained the same raw immediacy. But it was more – more finished. More polished might be better. Some people like that, prefer it even. So I still can sell my work. From then on I have worked steadily and productively. Over time I re-established myself.'

***

By now the restaurant had emptied somewhat. The waiter had taken them at their word and had not offered them an alternative to their alcove. They would not be hurried to leave. They sipped their wine quietly, easy with each other now, the power of their bond having re-established itself. They did not feel the need to continue talking; there was much to reflect upon. It was Elaine who spoke first.

'Enough about me. For now anyway. What about you? What creative enterprises have you immersed yourself in over these past years?'

'Well, compared to you I've done very little. I put that brief but very valuable experience I gained by working for your father to good use. At least it's earned me a living.

'You probably remember that I found a job in a large store as an assistant window dresser? I eventually became display manager. I'm still there. Rather boring, by your standards, but I'm not complaining.'

'Some outlet for your very considerable creative talents I suppose.' said Elaine, not altogether approvingly.

'So you never went in for teaching then? I thought you might have tried again to get back into college. You were more than capable.'

'No. I knew that I couldn't do that. I didn't like telling people what to do, how to behave. I know it doesn't have to be like that, but it generally is.

'I probably told you that I allowed myself to be pushed into college to soften the blow my parents felt when I rejected the priesthood. I supposed it would be the lesser mistake to make if it went wrong. At least it wasn't a commitment for life. It did me some little good, and when I failed the exams it didn't really trouble me too much. As for the creative talent you mentioned, I don't think I ever really had any. Not like you. You're a true artist. I never could have been.'

'Maybe not, although I'm not convinced of that. It's hard to know. I was taught and you were trained. You might say, "what's the difference?" but there is a difference. I was taught to explore things from all angles, to experiment with colour and form; to develop my own ideas and to challenge preconceptions. And from an early age; in that respect I was very lucky. My parents saw that I had some natural ability and paid for me to have private tuition. My school also recognised my talent and pushed me on. Without all that I would never have got into The Slade. I must admit that there the teaching was rigorous and traditional, but only in getting us to grasp what I might call the grammar of art. We were not prevented from finding our own vocabulary.

'Life drawing was *de riguer*. I cannot imagine you did much life drawing wherever you were.'

Thomas laughed. 'No. That would have been quite impossible. Even the literature I wanted to read was dulled by many of the books being proscribed by the Vatican.'

'That's what I mean Tom. You I feel were trained, much the way a soldier is trained. That way you become very good at certain things. One of them is being good at following directions, not at thinking for yourself.

'I gather you eventually kicked over the traces and abandoned the whole cartload, but it seemed to leave you directionless.'

'You're absolutely right. I was lost. Eventually I found my way, but what I lost in between was considerable.'

Elaine did not wish to drive him into deep introspection, or cause him to become maudlin. She was enjoying the evening. She changed the subject.

'Tell me about that dubious sister of yours Tom. What is she doing these days?'

'She's not at all dubious,' said Thomas laughing at Elaine's description, based loosely on what he must have told her long ago. 'She's a decent, hard-working businesswoman. She's married to a lovely man called

Eamon Scanlon, who now works with her. She has a business partner, Mick, another lovely man. Three good friends working together very successfully.'
'What does she do?'
'She has a taxi business.'
'Where? Here in Banebridge?'
'Yes. A thriving business.'
'What does she look like? Is she tall – even taller than me?'
'Yes.'
'And slim, and elegant, with black hair and a very pale complexion?'
'That's her. How could you describe her? I don't remember you ever meeting her.'
'She picked me up from the train station the other day and took me to my parent's bungalow. I noticed that she had a scarred hand and wrist. When we stopped she used both hands to pull on the handbrake. She seemed really nice.'
'She is,' he said. 'She's a lovely person. Very hard-working. And very happy.'
'I remember you telling me about an accident she had at work. That led to your having to support her and your mother. You said at the time that was why you had to take the job in Nottingham. I didn't fully accept that. I knew she had injured herself and that you wanted to help her, but I thought you were just using that as an excuse to get away from me.'

Both of them now wanted to talk freely and openly about the intervening years since their parting. They realised that their feelings towards each other were still strong despite the emotional damage it had caused. Thomas knew that he had to respond honestly to Elaine's suggestion that he had run away from her, without making her think he might be about to do the same again.

'You were right Elaine. It was a poor excuse. Although Mary's injury provided me with a chance to make some recompense to my mother, that was not the real reason I left you. I have always been sorry for using that deceit the way I did. It was a ruinous mistake. I think deception usually is. You offered me so much. You opened up wonderful vistas for both of us. I closed them all down. I fouled life up for both of us I feel.'
'It wasn't entirely your fault, Tom. I know you were struggling to come to terms with many things. The death of your father and its murky circumstances being just one of them. You needed time and I wasn't giving you time. I couldn't help it. You had fired me up in a way that I'd never experienced before. Life itself suddenly became an urgent business. I realised that I'd been drifting in a backwater since I'd returned home from art school. I suddenly sensed where the main current

was and I wanted to ride the rapids. I needed to see the colour, feel the texture, hear the music of life, every atom of it. And with you. I had never known anyone quite like you. I felt that you had so much bottled up within you, so much stifled creativity and emotion. I thought I could pull out the cork as it were and we'd spurt headlong into wonderful new experiences, working together, creating who knows what. If I hadn't been in such a rush – who knows? It might have happened. I was too impetuous. Too headstrong perhaps. Maybe even arrogant. Anyway, for whatever reason, I helped to kill it.'

The word "kill" made Thomas flinch. Was Elaine accepting that between them they had destroyed something forever? Something that had been dazzlingly brilliant, so splendid that its magnificence, in a perfect world, ought to have been eternal?

He knew he had to probe Elaine's mind, and his own, to find if this destruction was so complete, so final. Or was there a possibility of resurrection? If they both felt that they knew no other who could awaken such feelings of profound mutual attraction then surely the jewel they once held had not been shattered.

'I'm not the same person you once knew,' ventured Thomas. 'My whole outlook on life has changed. I'm not so much influenced by the past. I've jettisoned a lot of the cargo I was carrying. We all sustain damage in life's storms, but we can make some repairs. I feel more confident now.'

'What would you say has caused the change Tom?'

'You know my mother blamed me for causing my father's apparent suicide?'

'Yes. How could I forget? It seemed to be slowly destroying you.'

'It was. It shouldn't have been. He was a resolute man who had shrugged off a lot of setbacks in his life. So it seemed unlikely that my apparent disdain for all he'd done for me, all the sacrifices he'd made in order to give me a good education, which I then squandered, should drive him to take his own life. But I had to admit that it was a distinct possibility. I was almost certain that he hadn't fallen into the river accidentally. He knew it too well.

It certainly destroyed my mother. She was dead within a few years of the event. She died of cancer within a few weeks of the diagnosis, but she'd given up long before then. She was a total wreck, utterly neglectful of her physical self. Down to the church every day of the week, sometimes twice a day. Always at confession, yet she'd nothing to confess. And she hated me, I'm sure, until the bitter end. This told on me. It's not easy to live with yourself when you know that it's possible that you just might have caused one person to take his life and as a result of that you have to watch another slowly dying before your very eyes.'

'I'm sorry Tom; I'm missing your point. I understand what it did to you. I saw it for myself at the time. But where are you now?'

'Several years after it happened I found out that it was not suicide, or rather, Mary found out and she contacted me straight away. He'd been knocked into the river.'

'What; deliberately you mean?' said Elaine, with a look of horror on her face.

'Yes. Deliberately.' he said, his voice breaking.

'But that's murder.'

'It was murder. By an evil person we all knew to be evil, although we had never suspected him.'

'Was he brought to justice?'

'No. He was murdered himself a couple of years later. Something he brought on himself. I suppose it was inevitable. He was that sort of man.'

Elaine sat in silence, taking some deep breaths. She was clearly moved by this revelation.

Then she said, 'That's rough justice I suppose.'

'It's not any kind of justice, but it brought some kind of closure to the whole sorry affair. It relieved me of a massive burden. I've been a different man ever since. I never realised just how much it was affecting me until I received the phone call from Mary. I'd been morose for so long it had become part of me. When I was with you I was different, I was in another world. On my own I was miserable, just plodding through life.'

'But I still can't see why you didn't stay with me, come with me to London, push all that guilt out of your mind.'

'That's the trouble with guilt; it keeps on coming back like a ghost from the grave. You think you've buried the thing, then it re-emerges. I thought I would contaminate you with it. That was apart from all the other worries.'

'Which were?'

'Put simply, that I thought I just wasn't good enough for you. The wrong social background. Not enough talent. I was in awe of yours. No realistic prospects of significantly improving my position in life, which has proved to be the case. I'm living quite comfortably, but I'm still only a window dresser. But when I learned the truth about my father's death, terrible though it was, it transformed me. I started to live.

'Mary took it badly at first, but she's fine now. We both are; we're better for knowing the truth.'

They had talked their way through a three-course meal. There was still an hour to go before the last train left for London.

'Let's go into the bar for a last drink,' suggested Thomas.

The bar was half-empty. They could speak freely without the likelihood of being overheard.

'So, Tom. Your past has lost its grip on you. You're at one with yourself. Is that right?'

'Not entirely. I thought I was. But, no, not really. I've shaken off the worst of the past. But I've lost so much of the good. Through my own fault. I've enjoyed tonight though. And this afternoon. After I got over the shock. I couldn't believe it was you. I had it fixed in my head that you were in London. I didn't think your parents would still be alive, so I assumed that you would have no connections with this part of the world after all this time. When I realised it was you I didn't know what to think, what to say. I had a moment of pure delight and then trepidation. I suppose I thought you might hate me. You'd enough reason to.'

'I couldn't do that Tom. Although once I did think I hated you. That feeling didn't last long. It was the sadness, the emptiness that lasted. It never really went away.

'I'm enjoying your company Tom. I feel there is a lot more we could talk about. It's been a strange day, meeting like this I mean. So suddenly. It's thrown me completely. When I first saw you through the café window I didn't know what to do. I couldn't think straight. My stomach churned as if I was on a fairground ride. A real mixture of emotions. I'm all right now. It's been wonderful.

'You've not said that much about yourself. I suppose I've not given you time. Too much talking about me perhaps. Or have you been holding back on me? I'm wondering if you've been playing down your creative talents. I gather that you're enjoying the display work you're doing. You were good at it when you briefly worked at our store, so you must be exceptionally good now.

But I would have thought that you needed more, much more than that, to fulfil your creative instincts. Don't you?'

'I have tried a little something in the way of expressing myself. I've just had a slender anthology of poetry published.'

'I knew it was you,' trilled Elaine, bubbling over with excitement. 'I just knew it. Why have you been holding back on me all night?'

'How did you know?'

'Because a few days ago, at Kings Cross Station I was looking for something light and short to read on the train. I bought it in Smith's. It's short, but certainly not light; it was painful.'

'But you couldn't have known it was mine. I wrote it under a pseudonym.'

'Yes. I realised that. You called the anthology, "Giving Doubt A Voice", right? By Thomas Doughty. I spotted the fairly obvious pun –

effectively, "Doubting Thomas" – which made me think of you. I didn't immediately think that it *was* you who had written it, but just that you came straight into my mind. I think you'd agree that would hardly be surprising, going back to our early days together.   Then I realised the possibility of a second pun-"Doughty", meaning valiant, resolute. I knew that you always had those qualities in you, although they seldom came to the fore. Then I sort of hoped it might be you. I knew for certain it was yours as soon as I opened the first page: The poem about the firecrest.

A living jewel, a gem so rare
I hardly dare to breathe, for fear you'll fly away.'

Thomas interrupted, 'What made you think that I had written that?'
'Don't you remember, just before we parted, we were walking on the edge of some woods. Winter was approaching. A flock of very small birds were in the trees close by. They were mainly goldcrests. You pointed out one amongst them that you said was a firecrest. It had slightly different eye markings from the others. We were both entranced. You said that I was your firecrest because of my red hair. You also said the bird should not have been there. It was too far inland. It was a rare winter visitor you said, that only comes to southern coastal sites. I found that disconcerting.'
'Yes. I do remember that. Very well. I wrote that poem soon after we parted.'

Elaine continued, 'Then, in the next poem, I recognised you again. The one called "Balance". About the eagle and the hare.

"Hunger hanging from a screaming sky,
 the eagle's hunting still,
 though frozen rills that rib
 the drab brown land
 refute the prospect of an easy kill."

'You go on to say, with fairly brutal imagery, that one creature can survive only at the expense of another. That one must die so the other can live. I remembered your views of capitalism, how the fat cats became fatter as the poor mice starved. Do you still feel that?'
'It still troubles me. I find it very harsh. But Capitalism seems to be the only game in town. It's what most people appear to want, even if it does oppress them. I think the forthcoming election will show that.'
Elaine interjected quickly, 'Well, I won't be voting for her.'
Thomas' eyebrows lifted in surprise, which he quickly concealed, and continued.
'And who's to say it does oppress them? I think it does, but I don't want

to give myself the false status of one of the enlightened elite. *That* would be oppressive, wouldn't it? Anyway, I suppose we're all capitalists now.

'I wrote that poem years ago, by the way. Long before I knew you. But your interpretation of it is incorrect, if you don't mind me saying so.'

'No I don't mind. Please explain it to me.'

'It was never intended to be a metaphor for capitalism. It was simply an observation of existence within the state of nature. That's why I called it "Balance". The eagle is as vulnerable as the hare it is hunting, but in a different way. If it doesn't kill it cannot eat. Starvation is always present. It has no choice but to try to kill. It's all part of the randomness of existence. That is quite unlike The Capitalist. He'll never starve, even if those he exploits do starve. He'll simply find others who are vulnerable enough to exploit.'

'I can relate to the randomness of existence.' said Elaine, with feeling.

Each held the others gaze for long seconds as both minds dwelt upon their last remarks, their mutual experiences flooding back into recognition.

Elaine was still intrigued by the fact that this man she had thought she had known so well should have been a poet even before she knew him.

'I never knew you were writing poetry then. You never said.'

'I've written scores of them over the years. Most weren't any good; I've thrown a lot away. But I've dozens left and the publisher is considering another anthology.'

Elaine continued. 'The last poem in the book bothered me the most. It made me cry and I had to sniffle in my handkerchief and feign a cough, as if I had a cold. The other passengers were looking at me.'

'"The Years," you mean?' asked Thomas.

'Yes. "The Years". Recite it to me Tom. I couldn't say the words without crying.'

"The best years: all have gone,
flown by like fleeting birds,
driven into the setting sun
by futile deeds and wasted words". '

She stopped him there.

'Do you really believe that Tom? It seems such an admission of defeat. That everything in the past has been a failure, or not worthwhile. And also dismissive of any time we have left. Do you really mean that?'

'If I had been asked that before today I probably would have said I believed it. Now, I'm by no means so sure.'

'Tom, I've got to ask you this, even if the answer is not the one I want to hear. Could there be a future for us? Are there any good years left? I never got over you, and now I've met you again I know I never will. I always believed that you loved me even when you turned me away. Perhaps I was just being naïve. Perhaps I'm being naïve now. But is there any chance, any chance at all, that we could start again from here?'

Tom's heart leapt. He had felt for the past hour or more that the possibility of re-kindling their love might exist, but he had been desperately trying to push that thought out of his mind. Surely it was just a pipe dream that could never materialise; something that was just too much to hope for. Yet here she was, in front of him, uttering words that seemed surreal. He already knew that she had forgiven him for his heinous deception all those years ago, but how could she ever trust him again? He eventually found words, words that he could hardly believe his lips were forming. His voice seemed distant to him, unreal.

'There's every chance, Elaine. I never stopped loving you. But all those years ago I didn't feel that I was the right person for you. I still think that, at the time, it wouldn't have worked out for us. I hadn't found myself. I was a mess; I didn't know who I was. And I valued you so much I didn't want to cage you. I wanted you, but I didn't want to trap you, and that's what I thought I might be doing. It would have been like caging a wild bird.

'But the past is somewhere else now. Now, I feel sure we could start again. I'd love the chance to.'

'I'm giving you the chance Tom; I'm begging you to take it. I've known a lot of men. I've slept around. I'm neither ashamed nor embarrassed by that. That's life. I've seen a lot of life. Because of that I know more keenly than ever what it is that I most desire from it. You gave me the most I've ever been given. That year we had together has never been matched by anything that has happened since. I know now that nothing else ever will, ever could match it. Except for one thing.'

'Which is?'

'That we start again from where we left off. Is that possible Tom? Please say it is. But not if you don't mean it. Oh, I'm sorry Tom. I'm rushing you again. My hopes are running away with me. I'd give anything to be with you again. I'm terrified that you might walk away, that I might never see you again.'

'I won't walk away Elaine. I want the same as you, for us to stay together. We must; there's nothing in our way. My feelings for you are as strong as ever. Having found you I don't want to lose you again.'

They held hands tightly, saying nothing, simply gazing into each other's eyes. Tears slowly formed there, eventually spilling over. Tears of pure joy.

Then Thomas noticed the clock behind Elaine's head.

'You're just about to miss the last train Elaine. You just might catch it if we could get a taxi straight away.'

'Don't worry about that Tom. When I booked tonight's table I asked if they had a room to spare. Please don't think me presumptuous. It's just that I couldn't leave you until we had talked at length. If I had thought you really did not want to see me again then I'd be on a train now. But I had to know. There's so much I want to know about you. More than twenty years have passed since we parted. There's lots more we must talk about.'

'We could talk for days on end, and I'd love to. I'm pleased you're not catching that train tonight. I suppose you'll return to London in the morning?'

'Yes. Going back tomorrow shortens the time before I see you again. That makes me feel better.'

'I don't know if I could have waved you good-bye from the platform tonight. I think I might, at the last moment, have jumped on the train myself.'

After a short silence Elaine steadied herself for what she had to say.

'Tom, when I reserved the room the only one he had left was a double. With a huge bath and big fluffy towels. Am I being awfully presumptuous now? Would you like to spend the night with me, or is that too soon?'

Thomas smiled broadly, confident happiness enveloping his whole being. This was the old Elaine, the one he had never stopped loving, the one he would love for always.

'I've always thought of hotels as being overnight roosts for migratory birds. I'm thinking we're about to become permanent residents. But even migratory birds must rest a while before they reach their destination.

'Yes of course I will stay with you tonight. This is like a dream come true.'

***

'This has been a strange week Tom; an amazing week. It's a painful business, poking about in your parent's house, delving into the past. You discover things that immediately jolt you back through the years with such clarity that it might have been only yesterday.'

'How do you mean?'

'We were moving an ancient wardrobe out of an unused bedroom. Beneath it was a pair of shoes belonging to Edward. I recognised them immediately. They were the ones Daddy loaned to you that day we all went out to Brampton woods where we had the picnic. Edward never wore them again. They must have lain there ever since. They brought back some very strong emotions.'

'I can well imagine. What have you done with them?'

'They're in my case. Edward threw them out but I retrieved them. They were all I had to remember you by.'

'So you still intend to keep them?'

'We'll see. Right now I feel that I have all I want. All I will ever want.'

'And so have I Elaine. So have I.'

ABOUT THE AUTHOR

Sean Patrick Gaughan was schooled by catholic nuns. Later, as a mature student, he acquired the seeds of an education at Trent Polytechnic, Nottingham, graduating with a B.A. Humanities in 1980.
He lives in Nottinghamshire.

Other Authors With Green Cat Books

Lisa J Rivers –

Why I have So Many Cats

Winding Down

Searching (Coming 2018)

Luna Felis –

Life Well Lived

Gabriel Eziorobo –

Words Of My Mouth

The Brain Behind Freelance Writing

Mike Herring –

Nature Boy

Glyn Roberts & David Smith –

Prince Porrig And The Calamitous Carbuncle

(other Prince Porrig books to follow)

Peach Berry –

A Bag Of Souls

Michelle DuVal -

The Coach

Elijah Barns –

The Witch and Jet Splinters – Part One: A Bustle In The Hedgerow

David Rollins –

Haiku From The Asylum

ARE YOU A WRITER?

We are looking for writers to send in their manuscripts.

If you would like to submit your work, please send a small sample to

books@green-cat.co

GREEN CAT BOOKS

www.green-cat.co/books

Made in the USA
Columbia, SC
24 October 2017